THE MISSING: BOOK 2

SENT

←——— THE MISSING: BOOK 2 ———→

SENT

MARGARET PETERSON
HADDIX

SIMON & SCHUSTER BOOKS FOR YOUNG READERS
NEW YORK LONDON TORONTO SYDNEY

SIMON & SCHUSTER BOOKS FOR YOUNG READERS

An imprint of Simon & Schuster Children's Publishing Division

1230 Avenue of the Americas, New York, New York 10020

This book is a work of fiction. Any references to historical events, real people, or real locales are used fictitiously. Other names, characters, places, and incidents are products of the author's imagination, and any resemblance to actual events or locales or persons, living or dead, is entirely coincidental.

Copyright © 2009 by Margaret Peterson Haddix

All rights reserved, including the right of reproduction in whole or in part in any form.

Simon & Schuster Books for Young Readers is a trademark of Simon & Schuster, Inc.

For information about special discounts for bulk purchases, please contact Simon & Schuster Special Sales at 1-866-506-1949 OR business@simonandschuster.com.

The Simon & Schuster Speakers Bureau can bring authors to your live event. For more information or to book an event, contact the Simon & Schuster Speakers Bureau at 1-866-248-3049 or visit our website at www.simonspeakers.com.

Also available in a Simon & Schuster Books for Young Readers hardcover edition.

Book design by Drew Willis

The text for this book is set in Weiss.

Manufactured in the United States of America • 1011 OFF

First Simon & Schuster Books for Young Readers paperback edition August 2010

4 6 8 10 9 7 5 3

The Library of Congress has cataloged the hardcover edition as follows:

Haddix, Margaret Peterson.

Sent / Margaret Peterson Haddix.

1st ed.

p. cm.

Summary: Jonah, Katherine, Chip, and Alex suddenly find themselves in 1483 at the Tower of London, where they discover that Chip and Alex are Prince Edward V and Richard of Shrewsbury, imprisoned by their uncle, King Richard III, but trying to repair history without knowing what is supposed to happen proves challenging. Author's note includes historical facts about the princes and king.

ISBN 978-1-4169-5422-4 (hc)

[1. Edward V, King of England, 1470–1483—Fiction. 2. Richard, Duke of York, 1472–1483—Fiction. 3. Richard, III, King of England, 1452–1485—Fiction. 4. Space and time—Fiction. 5. Science fiction. 6. Great Britain—History—Richard III, 1483–1485—Fiction.

Series: The missing ; bk. 2

PZ7.H1164 Sen 2009

[Fic] 22

2008011552

ISBN 978-1-4169-5423-1 (pbk)

ISBN 978-1-4169-9644-6 (eBook)

For Todd, Tyler, and Austin

PROLOGUE

Jonah was falling, tumbling over and over, down and down, through nothingness and absence and void.

"Noooo . . . ," JB's voice echoed around him, even though JB himself had vanished. So had the other adults. So had the other kids. So had everyone and everything familiar.

Except Chip and Katherine.

Jonah pressed in closer to his friend and his sister. Both he and Katherine had linked their arms through Chip's at the very last minute, just as Chip was being sent away. Jonah wished he could hold on with his hands—hold on as tightly as possible—but his hands were full. In his left hand Jonah held a Taser. In his right hand he held the Elucidator.

Jonah wasn't even sure what the Elucidator was, but all the grown-ups had acted like it was important. There hadn't exactly been time to ask for a tutorial, not that JB or Gary or Hodge would have explained anyway. What were they going to say? "Now, this button here, if you press it, you'll beat us. You'll win."

Yeah, right.

Still, even without any explanations Jonah had managed to disarm the grown-ups. He'd ended up with all the weapons. He'd foiled Gary and Hodge's greedy baby-smuggling scheme. He'd, well, at least . . . interrupted JB's plan.

Interrupting wasn't the same as winning.

"Jonah, there's been a mistake," JB said. His voice was coming from the Elucidator, loud and clear and deeply troubled. "You and Katherine have no business going into the fifteenth century with Chip and Alex. You're not allowed. You could cause even more damage. And you can't take the Elucidator or the Taser there—"

"You should have thought of that before you zapped Chip," Jonah said. "You should have known that we'd stick together."

It was a miracle of teenage defiance that Jonah's voice could come out sounding so bold and confident. When he'd opened his mouth, it'd been a toss-up what he was going to say. He might have even whimpered, "I want my mommy! I want my daddy! I want to go home!"

He still might. This nothingness was frightening. And—fifteenth century? Had JB really said "fifteenth"? Was that what they were falling toward?

Jonah couldn't think of a single thing that he knew about the fifteenth century. At the moment, he couldn't even remember how the whole century-numbering thing worked. Was the fifteenth century the 1400s or the 1600s?

Jonah probably could have figured that one out, if he'd been able to calm down enough to concentrate. But he was distracted by a hand suddenly clutching his shoulder.

Katherine's hand.

Katherine was a sixth grader, just a year behind Jonah and Chip. Since hitting middle school, she'd become one of those stupid giggly girls who talked about hair and makeup and cheerleading tryouts. But Jonah could remember earlier, younger versions of Katherine, even the cute (though he'd never admit it), sweet (not even on pain of death), adoring little sister who would grab his hand when she was scared and blink up at him and whisper trustingly, "You'll protect me, won't you, Jonah?"

Jonah would never in a million years let Katherine do that now. But her hand on his shoulder made him feel like the protective big brother again. If he was frightened, she must be terrified out of her wits.

"Look, I'll tell you what to do so you and Katherine can come back," JB was saying, his voice strained.

Katherine tightened her grip on Jonah's shoulder, pulling him closer so that, with Chip, they formed a circle. In the near darkness around them he could barely see her face, but her features seemed to be twisted into a distorted expression. Was she crying? She turned her head—no, she was shaking her head, her jaw jutting out stubbornly. She wasn't crying. She was mad. Maybe even too mad to speak.

"No," Jonah told JB, and somehow his voice came out sounding every bit as fierce as Katherine looked. "Tell us what to do so we can all come back." Jonah remembered that it wasn't just the three of them floating through this nothingness. Chip was actually the second kid that JB had tried to zap back into the past. Another boy, Alex, had disappeared first. "Even Alex," Jonah added.

The dimness around them was easing a bit. They seemed to be falling toward light. Now Jonah could see Chip's face clearly, the gratitude in his expression. Jonah felt like he could practically read Chip's mind: Chip was thinking how much worse it would be to tumble through this nothingness alone.

"Jonah," JB protested. "You don't know what you're talking about. Certain things have been set in motion. Chip and Alex have to go to the fifteenth century."

"Then, Katherine and I are going too," Jonah said. He didn't know how it was possible, but he could feel time flowing past him, scrolling backward. He felt like he had only a few more seconds left to convince JB. "What if . . . what if we could fix the fifteenth century? Make everything right again? Then couldn't Alex and Chip come back to the twenty-first century with us?"

Silence.

Jonah had nervous tremors in his stomach. The hand holding the Elucidator was shaking. He wasn't even sure what he was asking for. But he couldn't stop now.

"You have to let us try," Jonah argued. "Let us try to save Alex and Chip and time. Or else . . ." He had to come up with a good threat. Or else what? Oh. "Or else we'll do our best to mess up time even worse than Hodge and Gary did."

The silence from the Elucidator continued. Jonah worried that they'd floated out of range, or that the battery had stopped working, just like a defective cell phone.

Then JB's voice came through again, faint but distinct.

"All right," he said wearily. "I'll let you try."

ONE

It was a rough landing. Lights streamed past Jonah's face, an unbearable glare. Some force that had to be more than just gravity tugged on him, threatening to pull him apart from Chip and Katherine, from the Elucidator and the Taser, from his own self. The image that burned in his mind was of his body being split into individual cells, individual atoms. And then that image broke apart too, and he couldn't think, couldn't see, couldn't hear. He could only feel time passing through him, time flipping back on itself, time pressing down, down, down. . . .

Then it was over. He lay in darkness, gasping for air. Dimly he heard JB's voice say, "Welcome to the fifteenth century. Good luck." But he couldn't quite make sense of the words. It was like hearing something underwater, sounds from another world.

"You're hiding, aren't you? Staying out of sight?" It was JB's voice again, hissing and anxious. "You have to stay out of sight."

"Darkness," Jonah mumbled. "Safe."

His tongue felt too thick to speak with. Or maybe it was too thin—too insubstantial. He didn't feel quite real.

There was movement beside him. Someone sitting up.

"You'd like to keep us in the dark, wouldn't you?" Chip accused. "You didn't tell us anything we'd need to know to survive in the fifteenth century."

Whoa. How could Chip manage to sound so normal at a time like this? And so angry (which was pretty much normal for Chip)? Wasn't his head spinning too? Wasn't his vision slipping in and out of focus? Didn't he feel like he might throw up if he had to do anything more strenuous than breathe?

"You didn't even tell us who we're supposed to be," Chip continued.

Distantly, as if he was trying to retrieve a memory from centuries ago—no, he corrected himself, centuries *ahead*—Jonah puzzled over what Chip meant. *Who we're supposed to be* . . . Oh, yeah. The whole reason they were in this mess was that a group of people from the future had gone through history plucking out endangered children. This would have been very noble and kind, except that they began carrying off famous kids, kids whose disappearances were noticed. JB, who seemed to oppose any tampering with history, was convinced that all of time was on the verge of collapse because of these rescues. He and his cohorts had managed to freeze the effects of the rescues—the "ripples," as they called them—and gone after the missing children. There'd been a battle, and thirty-six kids from history had crash-landed at the very end of the twentieth century.

Chip was one of those kids.

So was Jonah.

For the past thirteen years, though, they'd known nothing about their true identities. They'd been adopted by ordinary American families and grown up in ordinary American suburbs, playing video games and soccer, trading Pokémon cards, shooting hoops in their driveways. They had no way of knowing that their ordinary lives were ordinary only because they were in Damaged Time—time itself, trying to heal, had kept both sides of the battling time travelers out.

But Damaged Time had ended. And JB and his enemies, Gary and Hodge, immediately swooped in, each side eager to finish what they'd started.

And that, boys and girls, is how I came to be lying in the dark in the fifteenth century, Jonah thought, his mind working a little better now. That "boys and girls" line was imitating some-one, someone on TV probably.

Someone who wouldn't be born for another five hun-dred years.

A wave of nausea flowed over Jonah. He wasn't sure if it was because it'd just sunk in that he was hundreds of years out of place, or if it was because his senses were working better now and he'd just realized that the fif-teenth century reeked. A smell of mold and decay and—what was that, rotting meat?—surrounded him. And his nose brought him the first fact he was sure of about the fifteenth century: Whatever else was happening then, no one had modern flush toilets yet.

"Where is that Elucidator?" Chip demanded. He was feeling around on the floor now. "JB, you've got to tell me the truth. Who am I?"

"Well, it's kind of a delicate situation," JB hedged. "We shouldn't be talking at all right now, until you're sure that no one else can hear us. . . ."

His voice trailed off to just a whisper, which Jonah could barely hear. Why was Jonah having so many prob-lems? He'd been holding the Elucidator—he ought to be able to tell Chip where it was. But his hands felt too numb to be sure if he was still clutching anything or not.

Meanwhile, Chip seemed perfectly capable of sliding

his hands all around, groping all along the stones of the floor. He nudged first Jonah, then, apparently, Katherine. Jonah could hear her moaning softly, as if she felt every bit as miserable as Jonah did.

"So help me, JB. If you don't tell me who I am, right now," Chip fumed, "I'll scream so loud that people will hear me in *two* centuries!"

"No, don't," JB begged. "I'll tell you. Just be quiet. You're . . . you're . . ."

"Yes?" Chip said, his voice rising threateningly.

"It's hard to pinpoint the date, exactly, since the three of you took the Elucidator, and that may have thrown some things off, but I think it's probably safe to say, given when you should have landed, that you're . . . um . . ."

"Tell me!"

"I think, right now, you're the king of England."

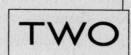

TWO

"The king?" Chip repeated. "The *king*? Of England?"

"Shh," JB shushed him. "Keep your voice down, Chip. I mean, Edward. That's your real name—Edward the Fifth. I think, technically, at that point in history, the title was King of England and France. That wasn't precisely accurate, but—"

"I'm the king!" Chip marveled.

It was far too dark to see Chip's face, not that Jonah's eyes were working very well anyhow. But just from his voice Jonah could tell that Chip was grinning ear to ear.

"All those times my dad told me I was dumb and stupid and worthless and . . . and—I'm really the king of England? And France?" Chip laughed. "That's great!"

Chip's glee reminded Jonah of something. Someone crowing about being king . . . No. About *wanting* to be king. Simba in the *Lion King* movie, singing "I Just Can't Wait to Be King."

Great, Jonah thought. *My mind's working well enough that I can remember Disney movies. Now I'm as smart as the average three-year-old.*

But he couldn't remember everything about *The Lion King*. There was something wrong with Simba singing that song, some twist the little lion cub hadn't grasped . . . something like not understanding that for him to be king, his father had to die.

"Uh, Chip . . . ," Jonah started to say, but he couldn't get the rest of the thought out. Somebody in the movie killed Simba's father, didn't they? And tried to kill Simba, too?

What if it wasn't such a great thing to be king?

Before Jonah could get his brain and mouth to work together to form any sort of warning for Chip, another voice spoke out in the darkness.

"So if he's the king, who am I?"

By squinting, Jonah could just barely make out the shape of another boy, sitting against the stone wall. *Alex*, he realized. The other boy who'd been kidnapped from the fifteenth century. The other kid JB had sent back to the past.

"You're his younger brother. Prince Richard," JB said.

Alex seemed to be considering this.

"One of those 'heir and a spare' deals, huh?" he asked.

"You could say that," JB said, sounding reluctant.

"So what happens to us?" Alex asked. "Happened, I mean—the first time around?"

"I can't tell you that," JB said. "For you it hasn't happened yet."

Katherine moaned again.

"Can you all just . . . stop talking?" she mumbled. "Hurts . . ."

With an effort that seemed practically superhuman, Jonah managed to prop himself up on his arms. They trembled horribly.

"Katherine?" he asked. "Are you all right?"

"No," Katherine groaned. "I think I'm going to die."

"Timesickness," JB diagnosed, his voice slightly smug. "You don't die from it, but like seasickness or airsickness, sometimes you want to."

"Oh . . . my . . . gosh," Katherine moaned. "Is this what it felt like all the time for you guys in the twenty-first century? Being out of place? In the wrong time period?"

Jonah thought about that. He didn't know who he was supposed to be in history—the day he'd found out that he had another identity, there'd been a lot of fighting and screaming and scrambling desperately to get the upper hand. It hadn't exactly been a good time for absorbing life-changing news and thinking through the ramifications and asking good follow-up questions. But if he really did belong in another time, did that mean practically his entire life had been, well . . . *wrong*?

"No," he told Katherine emphatically, just as Chip whispered, "Oh, I see," and Alex murmured, "It all makes sense now."

"What?" Jonah demanded.

"Remember?" Chip said. "I told you. That day on the school bus. I told you my whole life I'd felt out of place, like I didn't belong, like I belonged someplace else. Only, I guess it was some*place* and some*time* else. . . ."

"Do you feel really, really great right now?" Alex asked. "Better than you've ever felt in your entire life?"

"Oh, yeah," Chip said. Even in the darkness Jonah could tell that Chip was nodding vigorously.

"Well, I don't," Katherine muttered. "I feel worse than ever before. This is worse than the time I had strep throat and Mom had to put me in an ice bath to get my temperature down. Worse than the stomach flu. Worse than—"

"Katherine, I can still tell you and Jonah how to come home," JB spoke through the Elucidator, and even across the centuries and through the slightly tinny reception Jonah could hear the craftiness in JB's voice. Reflexively

Jonah clenched his hands, bringing numbed nerves back to life—oh, he was still holding on to the Taser and the Elucidator. The Elucidator just felt different now. Before, Jonah would have said it was smooth and sleek and stylish: a futuristic version of a BlackBerry or Treo or iPhone, maybe. Now he seemed to be holding something rough-hewn and scratchy.

So my sense of touch is still a little off, Jonah thought. *So what?*

"I'm fine," Jonah assured JB. "I don't need to go anywhere. But maybe Katherine—"

"I'm. Staying. Too." It was impressive how, even lying helplessly on the floor, Katherine could make her voice sound so threatening.

"If timesickness is like seasickness, then I bet she'll recover fast," Chip said comfortingly. "No one stays seasick for long once they're on land, right? And we've landed now. . . ." He made a noise that seemed to be half giggle, half snort, and a giddy note entered his voice. "Hey, Katherine, maybe once you're feeling better, you'll decide you like the fifteenth century and want to stay for good. Maybe you'll want to be *queen* of England!"

Wait a minute—that's my sister you're talking about! Jonah wanted to say. But JB spoke first.

"There are actually two kinds of timesickness, and

Katherine is undoubtedly suffering from both of them," he said. "One is just from the act of traveling through time—which probably felt worse to Katherine, since it was her first trip."

Mine, too, Jonah wanted to say. Except it wasn't. He remembered that he and Chip and Alex had traveled through time as infants, before their crash landing. He didn't know exactly how Gary and Hodge had arranged the trip. Maybe Jonah had been all through time as a baby, stopping in one century after another, while the "rescuers" picked up the other kids. Maybe he was like this kid he knew at school who'd circled the globe but didn't remember any of it because he'd done it all before his first birthday.

"The other kind of timesickness comes from being in the wrong time period," JB continued. "It's very technical and difficult to explain, but . . . I think this would be an appropriate way to explain it to twenty-first-century kids. Do you know where your bodies came from?"

"You want to give us the birds-and-the-bees talk?" Katherine screeched. "Now? At a time like this?"

In her indignation she seemed at least temporarily capable of overcoming timesickness. She even lurched up from the floor a little.

"No, no—maybe I'm a little off with my view of your

time period—I meant the *building blocks* of your bodies," JB hastily corrected.

"Are you trying to get at the fact that the stuff we're made of—the carbon atoms and the oxygen atoms and so on—all of it's been hanging around the universe since the big bang?" Alex asked.

"Cleopatra breathed my air," Katherine muttered.

"She's delirious!" Chip said.

"No, she's right," Alex said. "Haven't you heard that thing about how, at any given moment, at least one atom of the air in your lungs was probably once in Cleopatra's lungs? Or George Washington's or Albert Einstein's or Martin Luther King's, or whoever you want to pick from history?"

"So Katherine just has the wrong air in her lungs right now?" Chip asked. Jonah couldn't really see very well, but he thought Chip was crouching beside Katherine now, pounding on her back. "Breathe it out!"

Katherine coughed weakly.

"It's not just the air," JB said. "Every atom that made up her body in the twenty-first century was, shall we say, otherwise occupied in the fifteenth century. The same is true for Jonah, who also doesn't belong there."

"Then, *anyone* traveling through time would be out of place and disruptive in the other time," Alex objected.

"And Chip and I surely have some future atoms in our bodies too, since we were there for thirteen years. What happens? Do the atoms duplicate, so the same atom can be in my body at the same time that it's, I don't know, part of this wall?" He thumped the stone wall beside him. "How could that work? How is time travel even possible?"

JB was silent for a moment.

"Alex, you were severely underrated by history," he said. "And I mean that in the nicest possible way." He cleared his throat. "I can't answer those questions for you in any terms you could understand. Even the best minds of the twenty-first century don't have the right vocabulary to understand time travel, so how could I explain it to kids?"

Jonah wanted to object to that, but he figured Katherine would speak up first. She hated it when people used that "You're just a kid" excuse. And Katherine did seem to be struggling to sit up and talk. But she was coughing again, practically choking.

Chip wasn't pounding on her back anymore.

"Um, Katherine, if you're going to spew, turn the other way, okay?" he said. "Or just go somewhere else. . . . Here. I'll help you."

Chip and Alex both seemed to be trying to lift Katherine. Jonah kind of wished it were light enough that he could see Katherine's face, because he was sure she was shooting really nasty looks at both boys.

And Chip thinks she'd want to be his queen . . . ha! Jonah thought.

Somehow Chip and Alex managed to get her to a standing position.

"Leave me alone," she growled, shaking off their grip. She wobbled toward the door—Jonah could see now, by the thin light that glowed around the edges, that there was a large door leading out of their dark room. He was amazed that Katherine was apparently strong enough to grab the doorknob and yank. The door creaked open a few inches.

Katherine gasped.

"What's wrong?" Chip asked, and there was an edge of fear in his voice. Nobody seemed to be worried anymore about Katherine vomiting. Even Katherine seemed to have forgotten why she'd struggled toward the door.

"I think . . . I think JB must have sent us to the wrong time," Katherine whispered, clinging to the door. Whatever she could see in the next room had her mesmerized.

"What are you talking about?" Alex demanded. "This time *feels* right."

"Yeah," Chip echoed.

Katherine glanced over her shoulder. Even in the dim light

filtering in from the next room her face shone with horror.

"But . . . it looks like . . . both of you . . . the original versions . . . you're already dead," she said.

"How could you know that?" Alex scoffed.

Katherine looked back toward the other room again and gulped. Either Jonah's ears were overamplifying noises now, or her gulp was so loud that it sounded like a gunshot.

"I see your ghosts," she said.

THREE

It turned out that Jonah was capable of scrambling up from the floor—even scrambling up *quickly*. But he wasn't sure that his brain was working properly yet. Wouldn't it make more sense to run away from ghosts, not toward them?

Then Jonah stopped worrying about his brain. Chip and Alex were also rushing to join Katherine by the door. Jonah got there last, so he had to stand on his tiptoes, trying to see. Chip's head was in his way, but if Jonah weaved to either side, the door or the wall blocked his view. He stumbled forward, jostling against Katherine, whose shoulder slammed sideways into the door. The door creaked open wider.

Now Jonah could see.

The room beyond was very dim. As far as Jonah could tell, it was lit only by a single candle. And if these were royal accommodations, fifteenth-century style, the whole interior-decorating industry was still years in the future. There was a plain, colorless rug on the floor, a single bed shoved against the wall.

Two boys sat on the bed.

No, Jonah corrected himself. *Not boys exactly.*

Boys wouldn't have that unearthly glow—these boys gave off nearly as much light as the candle. Boys also wouldn't be see-through. And Jonah was sure that he could make out the exact curve of stone in the wall behind the boys.

But he could also make out their distinct features: their dark blue eyes; their shoulder-length blond curls; their odd dark clothes, a sort of tunic-and-tights arrangement that Jonah associated with Shakespearean plays. The boys sat with their heads together, whispering intently. But Jonah couldn't hear what they were saying. It was like watching a silent movie. And, like actors in a movie, they took no notice of their audience—the four kids staring at them from across the room.

"Hello?" Alex said experimentally. Neither boy budged. "Hello?" Alex said louder.

Still nothing.

"Maybe it's the time travel," Alex said. "Maybe that's just how people from this time period look to us, because we're coming from the future. And maybe they can't see or hear us at all—maybe that's how time protects itself from all those paradoxes."

"But *we* saw JB and Gary and Hodge when they came to our time," Katherine objected. "They looked normal."

"Oh, yeah," Alex said, shrugging. He stared at the eerie figures on the bed and added stubbornly, "But those aren't ghosts. There's no such thing as ghosts."

They sure looked like ghosts to Jonah.

But he could understand how Alex—and Chip—would be freaked out after what Katherine had said. Jonah gave her a little shove on the back.

"You were wrong, Katherine," he said. "Those aren't Chip's and Alex's ghosts. They're just . . . ghosts of some other boys. Or something," he finished weakly.

"They're girls!" Chip insisted, his voice cracking. "Don't you see those curls?"

"Girls would be wearing dresses," Katherine said scornfully. "And are you guys blind? Don't look at the clothes and the curls. Look at the faces. That's Chip and Alex!"

Jonah squinted, concentrating. Block out the girly hairstyle and the weird clothes. . . . For a moment he thought he saw the resemblance. Then it was gone.

"They're younger than us," Alex said. "Like, nine and eleven, maybe? Or ten and twelve?"

"Remember, the people who kidnapped you messed around with your ages," Katherine said. "They made you babies again. So you wouldn't have to be the same age as your, uh, ghosts."

She said the last word apologetically.

Suddenly Jonah felt someone grabbing his left hand, prying his fingers off the Taser, jerking it from his grasp. By the time this registered and Jonah turned his head, Chip was aiming the Taser at the ghostly boys on the bed. He squeezed the trigger.

"That's not me!" Chip said. "It's not!"

The barbs shot out but fell harmlessly through the ghostly Chip, onto the bed. The ghostly Chip and Alex just kept whispering soundlessly, their expressions solemn and intent.

"What just happened?" JB demanded, his tense voice coming from the Elucidator Jonah still clutched in his right hand. "What was that?"

Alex snickered.

"Chip just tried to Taser his own, uh, ghost," he mumbled. "It wasn't very effective."

The next thing Jonah knew, the Taser had vanished. Even the barbs on the bed disappeared. Chip stared at his empty hand, a dumbfounded expression on his face.

"Hey!" he exclaimed. "How'd you do that?"

"You do not use future technology in the past," JB said, and Jonah could tell that he was speaking through gritted teeth. "One of the first rules of time travel."

"But *you* just did," Alex said. "Making things disappear—I don't think they could do that in the 1400s."

"I had to," JB said, still sounding as though his jaw was clenched. "Chip just proved that the four of you can't be trusted with a Taser in the fifteenth century."

Chip was flexing his hand, as if he still couldn't believe that the Taser was gone.

"Wait a minute," Jonah said. "If you can just zap things out of time, why didn't you do that to Katherine and me?"

Katherine, Chip, and Alex all turned to glare at Jonah. Oops. It probably wasn't too brilliant to point out how easily JB could just do whatever he wanted to them.

"It wasn't safe to do that while you were traveling through time," JB said. "And then you convinced me . . . I did promise to let you try to help Chip and Alex."

JB's voice was soothing now, like he wanted to calm them all down. Jonah couldn't decide how he felt about JB. It was nice to know that JB wouldn't break his promises. But he hadn't exactly given them much information. And how could Jonah trust JB's motives in sending the stolen kids back in time, when it was pretty clear that history hadn't been kind to any of them?

"So who are those boys?" Katherine asked. "Are they Chip's and Alex's ghosts from the past?"

For a moment Jonah wasn't sure that JB was going to answer. Then he said, "They're tracers. They show you exactly what would have happened if no one had interfered in their time."

Jonah watched the ghostly boys on the bed. Together they were standing up—no, now they were kneeling beside the bed. They bowed their heads and clasped their hands.

They were praying.

One solitary tear slipped out of the younger boy's eye and began to roll down his cheek. He opened one eye and glanced anxiously toward his older brother, then quickly wiped away the tear before his brother could see.

"I wouldn't have done that," Alex objected. Jonah wasn't sure if he was referring to the praying or the crying.

"Oh, but you *did* do that, the first time through history," JB said. "That's what you would be doing right now if Hodge hadn't stolen you away."

The tracer boys were still praying, the picture of piety.

"This is too weird," Chip said. "It creeps me out."

JB laughed.

"Most people have that reaction," he said. "That's one

of the reasons modern weapons aren't allowed in the past. The first time travelers were spooked beyond belief by tracers, and it took a good decade for anyone to be sure what they were. Usually time travelers see duplicates—the real person, thrown off his rightful path, and the tracer. And that's even eerier."

Jonah tried to picture that. When JB came to the twenty-first century, had he been able to see tracers of Jonah and Katherine and Chip? Ghostly shadows doing whatever they would have been doing if JB weren't there?

Then Jonah remembered that he and Chip wouldn't have been in the twenty-first century in the first place if it hadn't been for time travel. Where was Jonah's tracer? What was his proper time period?

JB was still talking.

"We have a saying in time-travel circles, to explain the tracers," he said. "'Time knows how it's supposed to flow.' There's a persistence in the very nature of time, always trying to get back to its original outcomes. . . ."

The ghostly tracer boys were done praying now and had climbed back up on the bed. The older one was looking at the younger one, his eyes serious and sad. And then the older one put his right hand in his left armpit and began pumping his left arm up and down.

"Is he doing what I think he's doing?" Katherine asked.

"You mean, making fart noises?" Jonah said.

"Boys!" Katherine sniffed.

The younger boy on the bed began laughing silently. The older one did too.

He's trying to cheer up his brother, Jonah thought. *He must have known he was crying.*

"I would have thought the fifteenth century would be full of *chivalrous* behavior," Katherine fumed. "Knights and ladies and all that. Not boys acting as stupid as ever!"

"Oh, grow up, Katherine," Jonah said.

Alex was ignoring them. He pushed past Katherine and stepped into the other room. He moved slowly, like each step might be risky. When he reached the bed, he lifted one hand and waved it first through the older tracer boy's shoulder, then through the younger boy's arm.

"Oh," Alex said, his voice flooded with surprise. "That's . . ." He turned back to the others. "Come and try something."

Chip was already walking toward the tracer boys. Something about the way he moved made Jonah think of moths desperately flapping toward flame or—what was it, lemmings?—those creatures that would follow each other off a cliff. Jonah felt like he had to follow too, if only to protect Chip. Katherine lurched unsteadily beside him.

"Put your hand out," Alex directed. "What does that feel like to you?"

It didn't seem to have hurt Alex any, so Jonah obediently shoved his hand into both tracer boys' chests.

He felt nothing. It was just like sticking his hand out into empty air. And the tracer boys didn't seem to notice at all. Now they were shoving at each other, still laughing soundlessly.

"So?" Katherine said, having waved her hand through both tracers too.

"Don't they feel different?" Alex said. "It's like this one seems more . . . real." He pointed to the younger boy, the one who had the same arched eyebrows and hooked nose as Alex.

"No, this one does," Chip argued. He was standing beside the older boy, who had his right arm lifted in the air, emphasizing some point he was making to his younger brother. Jonah wished he could read lips, to tell exactly what the boy was saying.

But Chip wasn't watching the boy's face. He was extending his right arm to match the tracer boy's right arm. Dreamily he spread his fingers so each one occupied the exact same space as the tracer boy's fingers. Chip's hand was bigger, his fingers longer, but that difference seemed to disappear as soon as the two hands joined.

"Whoa," Chip said, a dazed look on his face.

Then he sat down, his legs overlapping the tracer boy's

legs, his chest leaning back into the tracer boy's chest, his face melding with the tracer boy's face.

Instantly the tracer boy stopped glowing.

And Chip disappeared.

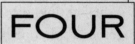

FOUR

"Chip!" Katherine shrieked.

Chip's face lurched forward, momentarily separating from the tracer boy's.

"It's okay," he said. "Don't worry. This is so cool!"

Then he leaned his head back, joining the tracer boy's exact dimensions again.

Now Jonah saw that Chip hadn't completely vanished. Jonah could still see, faintly, Chip's blue jeans and Ohio State sweatshirt and Nikes, coexisting with the tracer boy's black tunic and tights and elflike shoes. And in the boy's blond curls Jonah could see the bristles of Chip's shorter hair. Even Chip's face seemed to be a mix of his own jubilant awe and the tracer boy's more solemn expression. Jonah didn't know how his eyes could see two different things in the exact same space at the exact same time, but they did.

"It's like the mirrors," Katherine whispered.

"Oh, yeah," Jonah muttered. He knew exactly which mirrors she meant. One time when they were on vacation, their parents had taken them to a science museum that had a pair of special one-way mirrors rigged up, back to back, so two people could sit on either side and, by adjusting the lighting, see what their faces looked like blended together. Katherine had loved it, dragging total strangers over to sit opposite her. "So that's what I would look like if I were African American. . . . That's what I would look like Asian," she kept saying. When their parents finally pulled her away, she was scheming: "When I fall in love and want to get married, I'm going to bring my boyfriend here so we can see what our kids will look like. . . ."

"Do *you* look like Mom's and Dad's faces put together?" Jonah had asked grumpily.

"Fortunately, she didn't get my big ears," Dad had joked, while Mom shook her head warningly at Katherine and pulled her aside to have a little talk. Jonah didn't have to hear the words "Jonah . . . sensitive . . . adoption" to know what the talk was about. And he hadn't even been thinking about being adopted—about how he'd never know which of his features came from which birth parent. He'd just thought that Katherine was acting stupid.

But watching Chip and the tracer boy was like watching

a perfect version of those mirrors, ones that completely combined two people.

The tracer boy/Chip began patting the younger brother on his back.

"Forsooth," the tracer/Chip said, his voice coming out loud and strong. "Our father would be proud of us, should we be so brave. And God will reward our courage."

Actually, that might not have been exactly what the tracer/Chip said. That was what Jonah thought he heard, but the words were distorted, oddly inflected.

The king of England is bound to have an English accent, Jonah reminded himself. But even that didn't seem like enough of an explanation.

"Did people really talk like that in the fifteenth century?" Katherine asked. "Is that, like, Old English?"

Oh, yeah, Jonah thought. *Foreign-country accent and foreign* time *accent.*

"Actually, at this time people were speaking Middle English, transitioning toward early modern English," JB's voice came softly from the Elucidator in Jonah's hand.

"Can't you give us a translation?" Katherine asked.

"What you just heard, that *was* the translation," JB said. "The Elucidator does it automatically for time travelers. Otherwise, you probably wouldn't have understood a thing."

"'Forsooth'? That's the translation?" Jonah asked incredulously.

"The Elucidator translates only up to the nearest time period that could be understandable. Time travelers need to remember they're out of place," JB said. "You're not going to hear King Edward the Fifth saying in his rightful time and place, 'Dude! This sucks!'"

"*Chip* would say that," Jonah said, anxiously watching his friend's face, blended with the tracer of the king's.

"Shh!" Alex said. "The other boy's speaking. . . ."

But the younger boy's response was soundless because he was still just a ghostly tracer.

Chip shoved his face away from his tracer boy's for a moment and said, "You guys try it!"

Katherine sat down in the younger tracer boy's lap. Jonah was impressed—he wasn't sure he wanted to be that brave.

But Katherine didn't blend in with the tracer the way Chip did. It was comical how hard she was trying and how badly she was failing: The tracer would lean forward, and a second later she'd lean too. Or the tracer would wave his arm, and Katherine, trying to keep up, would lift her arm just as the tracer was putting his down.

Then the tracer stood up and walked away.

Katherine didn't try to follow.

"*That* didn't work," she said, casting an envious glance at Chip and his tracer, who were still moving completely in sync.

"That's because you don't have any connection to the tracer," Alex said. "He's not you."

"Oh, yeah?" Katherine said. "You try."

Alex didn't have to. Because, just then, the tracer walked into him. It was like watching magnets meet, bonding instantly. Alex melded with the tracer just as completely as Chip had.

The tracer/Alex kept walking, toward a window at the far side of the room. He leaned out the window, his elbows braced against the thick stones of the wall.

"God bless Mother, in sanctuary at Westminster," he said, his voice plaintive and sweet.

Jonah tiptoed over behind the tracer/Alex—somehow tiptoeing seemed to be appropriate. Out the tall window he could see little except inky blackness. It was like being at Boy Scout camp, out in the woods, miles away from streetlights. Wait—was that a torch down there near the ground?

Oh, yeah, Jonah thought. *No electricity. Indoors or out.*

Somehow all that vast darkness was scarier than timesickness, scarier than the tracer boys, scarier than watching Chip and Alex merge with their past selves. This was *real*. This wasn't just some really good special effects in a dark room, maybe a TV show where someone like Ashton Kutcher would burst out in a few moments, crying, "Fooled you! You've been punk'd!"

Something rattled at the opposite end of the room. Jonah noticed for the first time that there was another door besides the one they'd walked through when they discovered the tracer boys. It was the handle of that door that was rattling.

Someone was coming in.

"We're supposed to hide!" Jonah hissed.

It was five steps from the window back to the first door, back to the completely dark room they'd arrived in at the beginning. Jonah covered that distance with amazing speed. He spun around to see that Katherine was cramming herself under the bed. But Alex and Chip hadn't budged. They were still joined with their tracers, Alex at the window, Chip perched on the bed.

Jonah considered racing back and jerking Alex away at least, but there wasn't time. The door was already opening.

A girl stood in the doorway.

"Esteemed sirs," she said—or something like that—and dropped into a curtsy, sweeping her plain, roughly woven skirt off the floor. "I've come for thy tray."

"Another servant already took the tray," the combination Chip/tracer boy said, his tone as haughty as a king's. "It's late. My brother couldst have been sleeping."

"Thou mightest not wish to sleep this night," the girl said.

She winked.

And then she backed away, pulling the door shut behind her.

Jonah waited in his hiding place, holding his breath. When nothing else happened, he dared to step out and hiss, "Didn't she *see* Chip and Alex? She was looking right at them! And what was that winking about? Why shouldn't the tracer boys sleep?"

Katherine rolled out from under the bed.

"I couldn't see a thing," she complained. "Who was it? What do you mean, winking?"

Jonah looked to Chip and Alex for backup—they'd been directly in line for the winking; they would have seen it better. Maybe he'd imagined the whole thing. He also might have just imagined that the conversation of oddly inflected, archaic words made sense. Probably Chip and Alex could understand everything better, since this was their time period.

Chip and Alex gave no sign that they'd heard Katherine or Jonah. They were still completely intact with the tracer boys.

"Come," the Chip/tracer boy said, patting the bedding beside him. "'Tis barely past midsummer, but this night shall be long. *Thou* mayest sleep. I shall keep watch."

The Alex/tracer boy reluctantly pulled away from the window.

"Good night, Mother," he said, blowing a kiss out into the darkness.

He crossed the room and curled up on the bed beside his brother.

"Chip? Alex?" Jonah called, a note of panic entering his voice. "Come out of there!"

Was it also his imagination that the tracer boys' images seemed to be growing stronger as his view of Chip and Alex faded away? Jonah could no longer make out the familiar Nike swishes on Chip's tennis shoes, or the wild-haired picture of Einstein on Alex's T-shirt.

"We're going to have to grab them!" Katherine exclaimed.

She took hold of the Chip/tracer boy's arm and began pulling.

"That's not going to work," Jonah scoffed.

But it was working. A second later Chip slipped off the bed, leaving the tracer boy behind. Unfortunately, Katherine had tugged a little too hard—Chip landed on top of her in the middle of the floor.

"This is how you thank me for rescuing you?" Katherine joked, pushing him away. Then, crouching beside him, she stopped pushing and impulsively wrapped her arms around him, hugging him close. "Oh, Chip, I was so scared—I thought maybe you'd disappeared forever."

Chip squinted at her, as if profoundly puzzled. He sat up and glanced from her to the tracer boy and back again.

"Chip?" Katherine said, sitting back on her heels. "Are you all right?"

"Um," Chip said. He shook his head, like he was trying to clear it. "That was so weird. When we were together, it was like I had his brain. I could think his thoughts."

"So, what does the king of England think about?" Jonah asked. He wanted to make this into a joke. He didn't like the way Chip sounded so serious. He didn't like how scared he still felt, even with Chip away from his tracer.

Chip looked up at Jonah. His expression was more serious than ever.

"He's not sure he's going to stay king," Chip said solemnly. "He thinks his uncle is going to kill him."

FIVE

"No!" Katherine gasped.

"What didst thou expect?" Chip asked. His eyes goggled out a bit. He stopped, pounded the palm of his hand against the side of his head, and tried again. "I mean, what'd you think was going to happen? Weren't you listening when JB and Gary and Hodge said we were all endangered children in history? It's pretty clear that being kidnapped saved our lives. So sending us back means . . ." He got a faraway look in his eyes. He peered out, not at Katherine or Jonah, but toward the dark window at the opposite end of the room. "It means we're supposed to die."

There was a bitter twist to his words, but his face was strangely calm. Accepting.

Jonah crouched beside his sister. He reached out and grabbed Chip's shoulders, and began shaking him, hard.

"Don't say that," Jonah said. "JB promised he'd give us a chance to save history *and* you and Alex. Didn't you hear that?"

"I did," Chip said, still maddeningly placid. "But did you hear him telling us how to do that?"

"I . . ." Jonah realized he'd dropped the Elucidator when he'd reached for Chip's shoulders. He felt around on the dim floor to find it again. His fingers slid over something that felt like a thin rock, maybe the kind you'd skip across a lake. "JB?"

"Yes?"

The voice had definitely come from the rock.

Oooh, Jonah thought. *The Elucidator acts like a chameleon. It tries to blend in with whatever time period it's in.*

The fact that blending in in the fifteenth century meant impersonating a rock was not very comforting. Jonah wanted buttons to push, gadgets and gizmos, high-tech whizzing and whirring.

"We could use a little information," Jonah said. "And advice. Is Chip's uncle—I mean, Edward the Fifth's uncle—is he going to try to kill him? What should we do?"

"I can't tell you the future," JB said.

"It's not the future! It's the past!" Jonah said. "It's already happened!"

"Not from where you're sitting," JB said.

Jonah considered flinging the rock out the window. He wanted to, badly.

"I'm not trying to be mean," JB continued. "I just don't want any of you burned at the stake as witches and warlocks for knowing too much."

Was burning at the stake one of the things that went on in the fifteenth century? Jonah shivered and was glad that JB couldn't see him.

"None of you are trained at time travel," JB continued. "You have to be very, very careful."

"What if we'd already known everything about Edward the Fifth?" Jonah argued. "What if we'd learned all about him at school?"

"Did you?" JB asked.

"No," Jonah admitted. The only English king Jonah could remember learning about was George III, the one who'd been king during the American Revolution. Taxation without representation, and all that. But that would have been in, what, 1776? Long after the fifteenth century.

"George the Third!" Jonah gasped. "And—and Queen Elizabeth. Prince Charles. And William and Harry. See, I already know the future. They're probably Chip's great-great-great—times a lot—great-grandchildren. Right?"

"Not if I die at age twelve," Chip said quietly.

Oh.

"Jonah," JB said, his voice stern again. "I can still yank you and Katherine out of the fifteenth century if I have to. If you insist on being difficult."

"Why don't we get Alex away from his tracer and see what he has to say?" Katherine suggested quickly. She rolled her eyes and frowned at Jonah, one of those annoying girl looks that seemed to say, *Boys! Don't they think before they speak?*

Just for that, Jonah let Katherine approach Alex on her own. If she was so superior, let her pull Alex over on herself too.

Katherine began tugging on Alex's arm, but she seemed to be struggling more than she had with Chip. Maybe Jonah's eyes were playing tricks on him, but it looked like her fingers were sliding right through Alex's arm.

"Can't . . . someone . . . help?" Katherine grunted.

Reluctantly Jonah stood up and joined her beside the tracer/Alex. He pushed against Alex's back. It was such a weird sensation—too cold and too hot, too prickly and too sticky, everything all at once.

"The timesickness," Katherine mumbled. "I . . ."

"Here," Chip said. From the floor, he tugged on Alex's feet. Alex slid out of the tracer feetfirst and banged his head on the floor. Once Alex moved, Jonah fell forward, straight through the tracer, and jammed his chin against the edge of the bed.

Fifteenth-century mattresses were not as thick as twenty-first-century mattresses, so he didn't have much cushioning. Jonah hit hard. His bottom jaw slammed against his top jaw, and he saw stars. When his vision cleared, he saw that Katherine had fallen in the opposite direction, her shoulder striking the stone wall.

If we keep this up, none of us will survive the fifteenth century, Jonah thought. Chills traveled down his spine that had nothing to do with the pain in his jaw.

"Interesting," Alex muttered. He was still lying on the floor, staring up at the ceiling.

"Did you feel like you were someone else?" Chip asked him.

"Yes," Alex said. He blinked. "No. I was me. I am me. It's just—I'm not."

"That's as clear as mud," Katherine said. She was rubbing her shoulder where she'd hit the wall.

"I know exactly what you mean!" Chip said excitedly.

Alex nodded and sat up. He stared toward the window, just as Chip had done.

"I could look at the stars and know that they're light-years away, that they're red giants or yellow dwarfs, that they're the products of nuclear fusion—but also think that they were painted in the sky by God, on a tapestry. I even thought that the stars revolved around the earth!" he said.

Chip nodded.

"Do you know about our uncle?" he asked.

"Lord Rivers, you mean?" Alex asked.

"Gloucester," Chip said, and just the way he said the name made Jonah shiver again.

Alex kept staring toward the window.

"Mother has a plan," he said softly. "She'll take care of us."

"Whoa, whoa, hold on there," Katherine said, stepping between Alex and Chip. "Quit talking like you're *them*." She gestured toward the tracer boys, who were curled up together on the bed again, the older one patting the younger one's head. "You're freaking me out."

"But we are them," Chip said. He started to stand up, as if he intended to rejoin his tracer.

Katherine slammed her hands against his chest, holding him back.

"Stop it!" she insisted. "You're Chip Winston. You live at 805 Greenbriar Court, Liston, Ohio. You're in seventh grade at Harris Middle School. You're from the twenty-first century!" She took one hand off Chip's chest and shoved it against Alex's shoulder. "And you're Alex, uh— what's your last name, Alex?"

Alex seemed to have to think about that for a moment.

"Polchak," he said.

"What's your address?"

"Um, 3213 University Boulevard, Upper Tyson, Ohio."

Katherine nodded.

"What year is it?"

"It's 1483," Alex said.

"No, no! What year are we supposed to be in?"

Alex frowned apologetically.

"I'm sorry," he said. "Chip and I really do belong in 1483. This is where we're supposed to be. I know you're trying to make sure I remember the twenty-first century. And I do. I just remember 1483 better right now."

Katherine had the same look on her face that she'd always gotten when she was a little kid preparing to explode into a massive temper tantrum. Jonah didn't think screaming and pounding her fists on the floor would help.

"Chill," he told his sister. He slipped off the bed and sat down on the floor with the other kids. "Okay, 1483. That's what, about the time Christopher Columbus sailed? Maybe we'll get to be cabin boys on the *Niña*, the *Pinta*, or the *Santa María*. Maybe we shouldn't worry so much. Just think of this as a big adventure."

"Columbus was 1492," Katherine hissed. "Are you forgetting things now too? Remember—it rhymes. In 1492, Columbus sailed the ocean *blue*." A panicked look spread across her face. "Oh my gosh. We're in some godforsaken time when Columbus hasn't even discovered America yet!"

"Technically, it's not really accurate to say he 'discovered' it, since the Native Americans had been living there for centuries," Alex said, sounding much more like himself. "And anyhow, Columbus sailed from Spain, and we're in England, and it's not like the twenty-first century, where you can just hop on a plane and be in another country in an hour."

Jonah was delighted to hear Alex sounding logical again.

"And really, Katherine," Chip said earnestly. Jonah wouldn't have said that Chip was capable of being earnest. Sarcasm was more his style. But—Jonah peered at his friend carefully—Chip's face was as smooth and innocent as a choirboy's. He kept talking. "It's not fair to say that this time period is godforsaken just because Europeans don't know about America yet. God is just about all *he* thinks about." He pointed at his tracer, who now had his head leaned back against the wall. His lips were moving silently. He seemed to be praying again.

"Him, too," Alex said, gesturing toward his own tracer, who was curled up against his brother's shoulder and appeared now to be fast asleep. "And it's so weird, because back in the twenty-first century I thought I was an atheist or an agnostic—I didn't think it even mattered which one. I didn't care. But thinking with his brain . . . well, I could believe. And it wasn't like thinking that the stars revolved around the earth—thinking something I knew was false. It's—I don't know. I can't explain."

"It helps," Chip said simply. "Edward should be terrified out of his skull, he's that certain that he's going to be killed, and that there's nothing he can do about it. But he's just . . . fine."

Jonah considered arguing, *Well, I believe in God too, but I'm still terrified out of my skull—what do you make of that?* But he didn't think that would be very useful.

Katherine took a deep breath.

"You're using third person again," she said.

"Huh?" Chip asked.

"Third person," Katherine said. "Him. His. He. You're not talking anymore like you think you're them."

She swept her hand dismissively toward the tracers, her fingers swiping through Edward V's leg. She didn't even notice.

"It fades a little, doesn't it?" Alex said speculatively.

"The longer we're away from them. We could set up an experiment—see if we experience their minds more intensely with a longer stay in the tracers, see how much our memories fade over time—"

"No!" Katherine and Jonah said together. They exchanged glances.

"What if you forget your real selves completely?" Katherine argued. She looked flushed and frantic, still not far away from some childish tantrum. A long strand of hair had escaped from her ponytail and was plastered to her cheek with sweat. Jonah wondered if she was still feeling the effects of timesickness.

"Which are our real selves?" Alex asked quietly. He turned his head, gazing longingly toward the tracers on the bed.

Chip had the same expression on his face. Jonah could just see the thoughts churning in their heads.

Jonah dived to the right. He rose up on his knees and stuck his arms out straight, his best imitation of a traffic cop refusing to let anyone pass.

"You can't go back to them," Jonah said. He hoped his body was blocking everyone's view of the tracers. "How could you? You said yourself, they're *doomed*."

"But what if that's our fate?" Chip said, just as Alex objected, "*I* didn't say they were doomed."

Chip looked at Alex in surprise. Jonah wondered why he hadn't noticed they were brothers from the very beginning: They had the same blond curly hair, the same blue eyes, the same high cheekbones. *Noble* high cheekbones. Royal looking. Even with their hair cut in a twenty-first-century style, now that they were back in the fifteenth century, both of them did look like they could be princes or kings.

"Really?" Chip was saying. "Your guy—Richard—he doesn't think they're both going to die?"

"I told you," Alex said. "He thinks his mother has a plan. He knows."

"Mother," Chip repeated, as though he was trying out the word. "The queen. Former queen, I mean. Elizabeth."

"Queen Elizabeth?" Katherine shrieked. "The old-timey one? Wait a minute—I know about her. The one Cate Blanchett always plays in the movies?"

Chip and Alex considered this.

"No, that's another Queen Elizabeth," Chip said. "Later on."

Katherine looked defeated.

Chip had his head tilted to the side thoughtfully.

"It's like, I know about the mother's plan, but I don't have much confidence in it," he said. "She's not . . . I mean, I barely know her."

"That's because you were sent to another estate at a young age," Alex said. "To be trained to know how to be king."

Chip bit down on his lip, wonderment traveling across his face.

"I do know how to be king," he said. "Weird."

"But you don't know your own mother?" Katherine asked incredulously.

"I only see her a few times a year," he said, shrugging. He grinned, looking more like himself. "But I've heard things, when people don't know I'm listening. I think she was supposed to be a real babe when she was younger. There was some sort of a scandal when our father married her——like she wasn't good enough because she wasn't a foreign princess who could bring him extra allies, and she'd been married to a Lancaster knight who died, and we're Yorks, of course, and the Lancasters and the Yorks hate each other. . . . Our parents got married in secret, so that was even more scandalous."

"Were people horrified when your mother got pregnant with you? And they didn't know she was married?" Katherine asked. In spite of herself, she was leaning in now, intrigued, like this was just some juicy celebrity gossip.

"Oh, the news came out a long time before that," Chip said. "Our father's advisers were really mad." He thought for a minute. "Anyhow, I have three older sisters, so it's not like I would have been the big surprise, regardless."

Chip still had a stunned look on his face, like it'd just dawned on him that he really did have siblings.

"What happened to your father?" Jonah asked quietly. He couldn't shake the feeling he'd had earlier, when he was thinking about *The Lion King*. There was an uncle in the movie, too. Scar. He gasped, remembering the entire plot now.

"Did your uncle kill your father?" he asked in a choked voice.

But both Chip and Alex were shaking their heads.

"Nah," Chip said. "He just got sick and died."

"Maybe he was poisoned," Jonah said. *Scar killed Simba's father*, he thought. It was awful when remembering Disney movies terrified you.

Alex snorted.

"Nobody had to poison him," he said. "He was kind of a . . . a party animal."

"And bulimic, right?" Chip asked. "Isn't that what you'd call it?"

"Oh, yeah," Alex said. "Hundreds of years before anybody came up with that name. Remember Christmas?" As Chip nodded, Alex turned to Jonah and Katherine to explain. "He ate and drank, ate and drank—roast beef and puddings and everything else—and then he threw it all up to make room to stuff himself again."

"They have bingeing and purging in the fifteenth century?" Katherine asked, making a disgusted face.

"Oh, yeah. We call it 'eating in the Roman style,'" Alex said. "It's a sign of wealth, that someone can afford that much food."

Strangely, Alex and Chip both had admiring looks on their faces. Katherine looked like Jonah felt: like she wanted to gag.

"That's just gross!" she said.

Alex and Chip looked insulted.

"But he was a good king," Chip added quickly. "Don't forget that."

"Of course," Alex agreed, nodding loyally. "Edward the Fourth. Our father."

Our, Jonah thought. So much for Katherine's being excited that they were using third-person pronouns.

The candle by the bedside flickered, as if some new breeze had entered the room. Jonah turned just in time to see the door slowly sliding forward.

"Someone's coming again!" he hissed. "Hide!"

Jonah scrambled up, ready to rush back to the other room. Katherine was right beside him. But Chip and Alex weren't moving at all. Wait—yes, they were. They were both leaning toward their tracers.

"This way!" Jonah whispered, grabbing the hood of Chip's sweatshirt and yanking. "Katherine—get Alex!"

Katherine tugged on Alex's arm, but all that did was counter his forward momentum. She wasn't strong enough to pull him backward. Jonah caught a glimpse of her horrified face as she glanced back toward the door, now open a full inch and still moving.

Katherine bent over and blew out the candle.

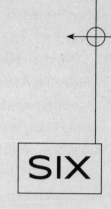

SIX

Jonah could still see—a little, anyway—by the gleaming light of the ghostly tracer boys. They still huddled on the bed, one praying, one sleeping, each still oblivious to the moving door.

Chip and Alex, the modern versions, seemed nearly as oblivious.

"You just changed history!" Chip hissed angrily at Katherine. "Even a single candle extinguished—"

"I had to!" Katherine whispered back. "We have to save you!"

Jonah kept watching the door, still creaking open, slowly, slowly, slowly. . . . Maybe this would just be another serving girl. Maybe she'd see the darkness, assume both boys were asleep, and tiptoe away.

Or maybe it was the uncle, come to murder them.

Maybe his job would be that much easier in the darkness.

"Mother promised she'd send someone to rescue us!" Alex exulted in a loud whisper.

Jonah clapped his hand over Alex's mouth. Never mind saving Alex and Chip from history—how could Jonah save them from themselves? How could Jonah keep Alex quiet, pull Chip back into hiding, get Katherine and Alex safely out of sight too . . . and somehow relight the blown-out candle? All before the door opened another inch wider?

It was impossible. Jonah didn't even have time to take a breath before the figures of two men appeared in the doorway.

They had a candle of their own.

Fortunately, the puny candle glow barely illuminated the floor directly in front of them, so Jonah didn't have to worry about being seen yet. He found himself wishing the men carried a slightly stronger light—he wanted to see their faces. It wasn't that he thought he'd recognize anyone from the fifteenth century. But surely if he could see their expressions, he'd know if they were planning murder or rescue. Wouldn't he?

It didn't matter. The men's faces were cloaked in shadow thicker than beards, their eye sockets like dark holes.

Then one of the men spoke.

"I thought the young prince always had to have a candle burning at night," he said softly. "Afraid of the dark, they say."

And for a split second there was a bit of light around his mouth, the same kind of light that glowed from the tracer boys on the bed.

That isn't what he said in the original version of history, Jonah thought. *That's the only reason I can see his mouth. It's moving differently just because Katherine blew out that candle....*

The other man shrugged and laid a finger on his lips. This must have been the same thing he'd done the first time around, because no tracer light glowed on him.

"Hush," he whispered. "If we can do this whilst they slumber, 'twill be easier."

"I slumber not," Chip spoke up, loudly, boldly.

Oh, no! Why hadn't Jonah put his hand over Chip's mouth too?

Jonah froze. Should he inch back from Chip and Alex—save himself now that he couldn't save them? Maybe grab Katherine, too . . .

Katherine dug her elbow into Jonah's ribs. She pointed, a hard motion to follow in the near-total darkness. But Jonah saw that she wanted him to look at the bed, where Chip's tracer was sitting up straight, his mouth moving precisely in sync with Chip's next words: "Who goes there?"

"Friends," the man replied in a hushed voice. "Your mother, the fair Queen Elizabeth, sent us to rescue you. . . ."

"I told you!" Alex whispered.

The men seemed not to hear him, because they were speaking themselves—Jonah missed their words—and then they bowed low, their flickering candle dipping down, their boots scraping back against the stone floor.

"They're going to walk to the bed," Chip whispered, pulling away from Jonah's grasp. "They're going to walk to the bed, and if we're not there—if they can't see the tracers—they'll . . ."

He was already rising toward the glowing figures on the bed.

"Wait!" Jonah whispered back. "Can't you wait to see if they're really going to rescue you? Are they friends? Or murderers?"

"I can't know that unless I'm in my tracer!" Chip hissed. "Alex, come on!"

The two men were approaching the bed, the glow of their candle growing dangerously near.

Alex was jerking away from Jonah too.

"Let them go!" Katherine whispered in Jonah's ear. "They'll know in a minute if it's safe or not—we can pull them out. . . ."

Quickly Alex and Chip scrambled onto the bed, matching their poses with their tracers'.

Jonah had forgotten that the tracers would stop glowing. He blinked at the sudden darkening. The shadowy men in their little circle of candlelight were advancing faster, rushing toward the bed.

Do you know yet? Jonah wanted to scream at Alex and Chip. *Are they rescuers or murderers?* He reached blindly toward the bed, his fingers brushing fabric. It felt like something more stiff and formal than sweatshirt material— was it velvet, maybe?—but he tugged anyway. If the men really were friends, wouldn't Chip and Alex have recognized them by now? Couldn't Chip separate from his tracer long enough to let Jonah know if he was safe or not?

Before Jonah could get a good grip, Katherine started pulling him back. The circle of candlelight was almost at Jonah's feet. Before he moved away, the plastic tip of his shoelace gleamed dully in the light.

Jonah prayed that neither of the men was looking in his direction.

They weren't. They had their eyes fastened on the tracer/Chip and tracer/Alex, both boys bathed in the light from the candle. It seemed like a 100-watt glow to Jonah right now—it was much too bright for Jonah or

Katherine to dart in and pull either boy away.

The men bowed before the tracer/Chip and tracer/ Alex, the light dipping only briefly.

"Your Highnesses," the first man murmured.

The second man reached his candle toward the candle Katherine had blown out, and a second flame sprang to life. The intensified glow of the two candles, plus the glow of the man's tracer, still hunched in a bow, sent Katherine and Jonah scurrying backward, desperate not to be seen. Just as the man blew out the first candle and rejoined his tracer—dimming the light again—Jonah's head hit something soft. He reached his hands behind him and found that some sort of cloth wall hanging covered the stones near the window, reaching practically down to the ground. *Somewhere else to hide if we have to*, he told himself.

Back by the bed the two men were straightening up from their bows. Then they reached out and grabbed the two boys.

"No!" the tracer boy/Chip screamed.

The man holding him crammed his hand over Chip's face.

"Shh! Someone will hear!" the man hissed. "This is for thine own good! We're helping you!"

Chip struggled against the man's grasp. He seemed to be fighting harder than the tracer boy—his arms and legs lashed out, leaving the tracer's glowing limbs behind. But he couldn't break the man's hold.

Alex was faring no better, and glowing even more. The tracer boy still seemed to be sleeping, even as Alex squirmed, momentarily separating, rejoining the tracer, separating, rejoining. . . .

"What should we do?" Katherine whispered urgently in Jonah's ear.

Jonah watched the men and the struggling boys. Even in the dim, flickering light Jonah could see that both of the men were tall and strong and muscular—he and Katherine could never overpower them.

But maybe they wouldn't have to.

"You try to grab Alex, and I'll get Chip," Jonah whispered back. "They're starting to separate from their tracers already—just pull them away. . . ."

"Without being seen?" Katherine asked incredulously. "Without them noticing? That's impossible!"

She was right. They could either rescue Chip and Alex, or they could stay out of sight and keep up the illusion that history was proceeding along its normal path.

What if that's our fate? Chip had asked just a few moments earlier. The words still seemed to be echoing in Jonah's mind.

"No," Jonah muttered to himself. "We have choices. . . ."

He started to step out of the shadows.

At that exact moment the tracer/Chip gave a particularly hard kick, knocking against his bedside table, toppling the candle off the edge.

The flame vanished, snuffed by the fall to the floor.

Instantly the room was plunged into darkness, except for the dim glow of the night sky outside the window, and the occasional bursts of tracer lights when Chip and Alex briefly separated from their fifteenth-century selves. The candle must have been extinguished in the original version of history too, because no tracers of the men appeared.

"Shall I—," one of the men began.

"Leave it," the other growled back. "It matters not. What we have to do, we can do in darkness."

"So can we!" Jonah whispered delightedly to Katherine. "This is our chance!"

She only stared at him stupidly.

"The men can't see the tracer lights!" Jonah hissed.

In the next burst of light—from a particularly strong squirm by Alex—Jonah saw comprehension flow over Katherine's face.

The men were walking fast now, directly toward Jonah and Katherine, and toward the dim, practically non-existent light coming in the window. Jonah reached out cautiously, feeling for Chip's arm. This time he touched sweatshirt material—surely they didn't have sweatshirts in the fifteenth century, did they? He squeezed tightly, his fingers circling Chip's arm. He tugged, trying to pull Chip away from the tracer, away from the man.

In one quick movement the man lifted the tracer/Chip up. He lifted him up and heaved him toward the window.

SEVEN

Jonah saw the glowing tracers fly out the window and plummet toward the ground, one boy after the other. He couldn't make sense of the sight. Was his mind still slowed by the timesickness? Was he just too flat-out stunned to understand?

They're glowing head to toe, every inch of them, he thought. *Why? They weren't doing that a minute ago. The only things that glowed were the parts that separated from Chip and Alex—hands, feet, maybe an occasional elbow. . . .*

Jonah was working on a grisly calculation, figuring that maybe Chip and Alex, being heavier than their tracers, had separated while falling toward the ground. *No, wait—we studied this at school. Galileo dropping cannonballs—it doesn't matter how heavy two things are, they fall at the same rate. So . . . so . . .*

So Chip and Alex must not have gone out the window with their tracers.

So that was why Jonah still had his hand around Chip's arm.

Relief and understanding washed over Jonah.

He must have pulled Chip away from his tracer at the very last minute, just as the man was trying to fling the boy out the window. Trying to assassinate the king.

Murderer, Jonah thought, his heart pounding faster. *Not a rescuer at all.*

But Jonah had stopped the assassination attempt. Only empty, glowing tracers had plunged toward the ground, not the real, live human boys, not King Edward V, alias Chip Winston, or Prince Richard, alias Alex Polchak. Chip was right there, Jonah clutching him by both arms now—Jonah's hands had somehow known to work together, even though his brain hadn't caught up. And Jonah couldn't see Alex or Katherine over in the thick darkness on the other side of the men, but Katherine must have succeeded too, since Alex's tracer had glowed just as much as Chip's.

Jonah wanted to scream and cheer and beat the air with his fists, as if he'd just scored the winning goal in the last seconds of a soccer game. Childishly, he even wanted to stick out his tongue and taunt the would-be assassins,

Nyah, nyah, nyah, nyah, nyah. You lose! We win!

But more than that, he wanted to make sure that the murderers didn't know that he and Chip and Katherine and Alex were there. He didn't want to have saved Chip and Alex, only to ruin everything with a boast. Or a sneeze, cough, or too-loud breath.

He pulled Chip farther back from the window. If he'd dared, Jonah would have slid behind the heavy cloth wall hanging. But his mind was kicking back into gear, projecting what-if scenarios. *What if the wall hanging's attached to the stones by something metal at the top, and that rattles when we're trying to hide? What if, in the darkness, the men walk right into us, and we can't see them coming because we're hiding behind the wall hanging?* Jonah froze, paralyzed by all the disasters he could picture in his mind.

The men were both leaning over the edge of the window, their figures nothing but dark silhouettes against the sky outside. Jonah stared at them, watching for the first glow of tracer light, the first hint that they were reacting differently than they had in the original version of history. There wasn't the slightest gleam about them; they must not have felt the effects of Chip and Alex being pulled away. Probably that was because they had been jerking back too, reacting to the opposite force from hurling the boys out the window.

"Come along," one of the men growled to the other, both still bathed in darkness. "Hurry. Lest we be seen."

They pushed away from the window and the faint light of the night sky. Jonah could hear their footsteps— cautious, sneaking back through the room—and his eyes burned trying to make out the slightest glimpse of them. But they were dark figures in darkness, as good as invisible. Then the door at the opposite end of the room swung open, turning the men into silhouettes again. There must have been a torch somewhere far down the hallway, providing just enough light to show the men leaving the room, quietly pulling the door shut behind them.

Jonah waited a few excruciating moments to make sure the men weren't coming back. He stared at the darkness that had swallowed the door, willing it to stay darkness.

He felt a hand on his arm and had to stifle a scream.

"We did it!" Katherine whispered in his ear. "We saved them!"

"Katherine, you idiot, you just about scared me to death!" he hissed back. "What if I'd yelped or something?"

"You didn't," she whispered, her old annoying confidence back. "Listen, do you still have the Elucidator?"

Jonah had forgotten all about the Elucidator. He'd dropped it on the floor eons ago, it seemed, back when the tracers were still curled up safely on the bed. When it had seemed a bit like a game, Alex and Chip melding and separating from their tracers for fun.

"JB?" he whispered into the darkness.

"Shh," JB replied.

Jonah figured that if it was safe for JB to whisper "Shh," it was safe for Jonah to crawl across the floor searching for the Elucidator. He let go of Chip's arms, and Chip sagged helplessly against the wall. Was he in shock or something? Was that why he hadn't even said thank you yet?

"Don't worry," Katherine told Chip soothingly. "Jonah's going to get us out of here. We can go home now."

I am? Jonah thought. *We can?*

But now that Katherine had planted the idea in his head, it seemed brilliant. (Not that he would ever admit that to Katherine.) Getting away from the murderers, getting away from this alien time when Columbus hadn't even discovered America yet, getting away from this place where blowing out a candle could ruin history forever—Jonah couldn't wait.

He dropped to his knees and began advancing toward the center of the room, sweeping his hands out in front of him. The floor was made of stone—maybe the same kind of stones as the walls—so it wasn't easy feeling around for something that was essentially impersonating a large pebble. But luck was with him. He'd barely left Katherine and Chip behind when his hand landed on something flat and round. He lifted it toward his mouth so he didn't have to speak so loudly.

"JB!" he whispered into the rock. "You can bring us all back now! Back home! We saved Chip and Alex, and nobody noticed! We saved them and time, just like we said we would!"

"Are you sure?" JB hissed back.

"Oh, yeah," Jonah said. He didn't even have to think about his answer. "Chip and Alex are fine."

"But their originals, the tracers . . ."

"Um, well, I don't think they're going to be having any more impact on history," Jonah said. He found he couldn't quite bring himself to tell JB exactly what had happened. He didn't want to think about it. He didn't know exactly how far off the ground they were, but it had looked a long way down. Far enough to kill. Far enough that no one could survive a fall like that.

"Why not?" JB asked sharply.

Jonah swallowed hard.

"Look," he said. "They're dead. The murderers are still close by. So get us out of here!"

"Can you still see the tracers?" JB persisted.

Jonah stood up, still holding on to the Elucidator. He tiptoed over to the window and looked straight down, into darkness. Then he crouched low again, out of sight.

"No," he told JB. "Is that what happens when some-one's tracer dies? The tracer just disappears?"

"Well, yes, but—"

"Then, there's your proof!" Jonah said. All this talk of death was making him uncomfortable. He didn't want to think about how close Chip and Alex had come to dying, about what the murderers might have done if they'd seen Jonah and Katherine. "Please! It's time! Get us away from here!"

"You really think Chip and Alex can leave without changing history?" JB asked.

"Of course!" Jonah said, raising his voice a bit. Why wouldn't JB listen? Didn't he trust them?

Outside he heard someone shouting.

"What'd he say?" he asked Katherine, who was stand-ing closer to the window. Katherine shrugged, the motion barely detectable in the darkness.

Another voice joined the first. This was the kind of hubbub Jonah would have expected from people discov-ering dead bodies on the ground. Maybe JB was wrong; maybe tracer corpses were visible.

The shouts grew louder, and finally Jonah could make out the words.

"Where are the bodies?" the voices were shouting. "Where did they go?"

EIGHT

Oh, Jonah thought, suddenly feeling so faint he had to brace himself against the stone floor for support. *We already did change history. . . .*

In the original version of history, Jonah realized, anyone looking for the prince and the king would have found them crushed on the ground. Their bodies would have been seen. There would have been proof that they'd died. There would have been bodies to bury; probably hundreds of people had seen the dead boys at their funeral.

Because of us, none of that will happen, Jonah thought dizzily. *Because of us, there's no proof of anything. The boys just vanished. So . . .*

Before Jonah could follow that thought to its logical conclusion, he felt Chip grabbing the Elucidator out of his hand.

"Get us out of here! Now!" Chip demanded. He *sounded* like a king giving orders, a king who expected to be obeyed.

"No," JB said.

Chip hurled the Elucidator toward the floor.

"You wanted us to die from the beginning," he snarled. "That's the only outcome you'll accept! You won't be happy until we're dead on the ground out there!"

Jonah's stomach gave a sickening lurch at the word "dead." *He's right*, Jonah thought, horrified. *No matter what we do, as long as there are no bodies out there, we can't fix time. And JB knew that.*

"JB!" Jonah moaned. "You're as bad as the murderers!"

"No," JB said. "Listen! History—"

"I don't want to listen! I don't care about history!" Chip screamed.

He kicked at the Elucidator—Jonah could feel the breeze from the force of Chip's leg, kicking hard—and the Elucidator skittered across the floor. Then Jonah heard it hit the wall across the room.

Instantly a soft glow appeared in that area.

"JB?" Jonah whispered.

No answer.

Jonah rushed across the room and scooped up the glowing Elucidator. It had a screen now; it wasn't just a rock. The words EMERGENCY REPAIR NEEDED glowed in soft green letters.

EMERGENCY REPAIR NEEDED faded into different words: PRESS RESTORE.

"But where's . . ."

A bluish button labeled RESTORE suddenly appeared on the Elucidator. Jonah pushed against it. The Elucidator seemed to change shapes in Jonah's hand. It looked like a cell phone again—no, it looked like a pocket watch. A club. A pair of dice. A spoon. A book. Jonah blinked, and might have missed a couple of changes, because the Elucidator was zipping in and out of shapes so quickly it blurred.

Then it was a rock again.

The screen still glowed faintly in the center of the rock, holding the words CONSERVATION OF ENERGY NEEDED DURING RESTORATION—CHOOSE OPTIONS and then CONTINUE TRANSLATIONS? Y/N.

"Not that it does much good," Jonah muttered, but he hit the Y.

Those words faded, and now the Elucidator offered him a new choice: MUTE? Y/N.

"You bet we want to mute it," Chip said, peering suddenly over Jonah's shoulder.

"But then we won't be able to talk to JB," Jonah said.

"Exactly," Chip said.

"No! Wait . . . ," JB's voice came from the Elucidator.

Jonah thought about the glowing tracers plunging toward the ground. He thought about how JB had wanted that to be Chip and Alex. He stabbed his finger at the Y.

The Elucidator was just a silent rock in Jonah's hand.

"So there," Chip said.

"I thought you were all for fate," Jonah said. "A few minutes ago you sounded like you were on JB's side. Like you thought you were supposed to die."

"Yeah . . . ," Chip said. His voice trailed off. "I don't know. It was weird how I felt. But now—"

"Um, guys?" Katherine hissed nervously from across the room. She was still standing by the window, peering out at the men in the courtyard below. "I don't think we have time to talk about fate and feelings right now."

Jonah raced over to the window beside her. He looked out cautiously, hunched down so that only his eyes showed over the bottom edge of the window. Down below, he could make out four torches now, flickering in the wind. The men, whoever they were, appeared to have organized search parties. Jonah squinted, trying to make out which of the figures in the courtyard were tracers and which were actual men. But the courtyard was too far away, the light too uncertain.

The first time around, the courtyard probably would have been empty and dark, he thought. *Someone would have secretly dragged the bodies away . . . or left them there to be discovered in the morning. . . .*

He shivered, not wanting to follow those thoughts any further. Two of the torches down below separated from the others. Jonah couldn't see where they went.

"They wouldn't come back up here, would they?" Katherine whispered anxiously. Her teeth seemed to be chattering, but Jonah didn't know if it was from timesickness or fear.

Down below, the men were shouting again.

"Search the chambers!"

Chambers. Chambers were rooms. *The* chambers would undoubtedly be the rooms the prince and the king had been in. . . .

Katherine grabbed Jonah's arm, almost making him drop the Elucidator.

"You've got to turn the sound back on," she said frantically. "JB can tell us what to do. No matter what, he wouldn't want them to find us." She choked back a hysterical sob. "We don't have to listen to him later, but . . . they're coming up here now!"

Indeed, Jonah could hear footsteps echoing outside the door, footsteps that sounded like a whole pack of men tromping up the stairs. They weren't even trying to be quiet.

He crouched down and began stabbing blindly at the Elucidator.

"Where's the unmute?" he hissed.

Words glowed on the screen: CHANGING MUTE STATUS NOT ALLOWED DURING RESTORATION PROCESS.

"Then, stop restoring!" Alex said over Jonah's shoulder.

Jonah was glad to have his help.

"Uh . . . uh," Jonah stammered, trying to feel for a button on the Elucidator—any button, but preferably one labeled ESCAPE.

RESTORATION CANNOT BE INTERRUPTED appeared the screen.

"Can't we do anything?" Alex moaned.

DESIRE TO SEE LIST OF ACCEPTABLE ACTIONS DURING RESTO-RATION PROCESS? Y/N appeared now.

Four kids at once shoved fingers toward the Y. Katherine and Chip were now crouching beside Jonah and Alex, all four of them huddled around the Elucidator.

Jonah could hear the footsteps coming closer. They couldn't have more than a few seconds before the door would burst open and men with torches would swarm into the room.

Words flooded across the Elucidator screen, moving

so quickly that Jonah could barely read them. Or, if he read them, he barely understood. What in the world were "cogency rules"? Or "subtleties of vowel pronunciations"? Why would anyone need "theological arguments" in an emergency like this?

"That one!" Alex said, shoving Jonah's hand aside so he could press a single word glowing in the long list on the screen. Jonah didn't even see the word Alex had chosen until Alex pulled his hand back, letting go.

Jonah could hear the footsteps out in the hallway, so close now. He read the word on the Elucidator screen: INVISIBILITY.

NINE

The entire Elucidator instantly disappeared, even though Jonah could still feel its rocklike form in his palm.

"Was that just invisibility for the Elucidator?" Jonah asked. "Or are we all . . ."

He held his hand up in front of his face. He couldn't see it, but it was so dark in the room that without the Elucidator's glow he wouldn't have been able to see his hand regardless. He thought about standing up, to check in the tiny amount of light coming in through the window. But that didn't seem like a very intelligent plan with the men's footfalls sounding just outside the door.

"I don't know! I don't know!" Alex groaned. "I just thought—we had to hide the evidence of advanced civilization, even if we can't save ourselves. . . ."

"Well, duh! Try to save yourself, too!" Katherine muttered. "Quick! Behind the tapestry!"

Jonah wasn't really sure what a tapestry was, but his sister was already yanking him up, toward the huge wall hanging beside the window. *Okay, tapestry, wall hanging, whatever . . .* His mind didn't seem capable of cranking out anything but short, jerky thoughts. Behind him he heard Chip whispering, "What about the tapestry?" like Chip hadn't figured out the plan either. Jonah crammed the Elucidator in his pocket so he'd have a free hand to reach back and grab Chip's arm.

"This way!" Jonah said, the words barely audible. He pressed in close, into the tight space between the tapestry and the wall, between Katherine and Chip. He hoped that Chip had grabbed Alex, or that Alex was the type of kid who'd taken home ec along with all his science classes. *Is home ec where you'd learn about stuff like tapestry?*

How could he be thinking about home ec at a time like this?

Er, no, Alex would know about tapestry because he can think with his fifteenth-century brain. So Alex ought to be safe. Oh, please, let us all be safe. . . .

On the other side of the room Jonah heard a door slam—slamming open, not shut, he guessed, because suddenly the whole room was flooded with torchlight.

Actually, "flooded" was an overstatement, because Jonah looked down instantly, at the first hint of light, and he still couldn't tell if he was looking down at his own shoes or if he might be able to see straight to the floor—if he and his shoes were invisible. But the contrast between the total darkness and any glow at all made Jonah's heart pound with fear.

They're going to be able to hear me, even if they can't see me! Jonah thought in a panic.

He felt just like he always did in language arts, his hardest class in school, when Mrs. Bodette started passing out tests. He'd get that sinking feeling that he should have studied more, should have been better prepared, but now he was out of time, there was nothing he could do. . . . *If only we'd studied all the options on the Elucidator before we started messing around with the tracers, before the murderers showed up . . . if only we'd scoped out the truly foolproof hiding places . . . if only we'd had time to make sure that these tapestries went all the way down to the floor, that they could hide us completely . . .*

Well, he wasn't going to risk looking down now. If the men searching for the king and prince could see his sneakers peeking out below the tapestry, he'd find that out soon enough.

The glow through the thick tapestry was getting brighter, which meant that the torches were getting closer.

He could hear the searching men muttering to one another: "Seek ye under the bed. . . ." "Aye, and here's another door. . . ." The distorted words were even harder to understand through the sound of his pulse pounding in his ears. This was so much worse than waiting for Mrs. Bodette to slide two or three stapled sheets of paper onto his desk. At least at school he was always able to see Mrs. Bodette coming toward him, instead of just imagining, with every second that passed, that he was only an instant away from staring into the hairy face of some appallingly cruel medieval soldier. Though come to think of it, Mrs. Bodette herself could probably pass for some appallingly cruel medieval soldier. . . .

Oh, no! That thought was going to make him giggle!

Panicked all over again, Jonah bit down hard, trapping the insides of his cheeks between his teeth. The pain barely stopped a laugh.

Think about something that isn't funny! he commanded himself. *Oh, yeah. Impending death. Ruining history for all time. Being burned at the stake for wearing weird clothing . . .*

At that exact moment the tapestry jerked back from in front of his face. The violent motion sent it crashing toward the floor. Torchlight flickered directly into his eyes, from a torch right before him.

Jonah and the others were completely exposed.

TEN

Nightmarishly, the torch kept coming toward Jonah, the flames leaping mere inches from his face.

These men aren't even going to wait to burn me at the stake, Jonah thought, terrified. *They're going to set me on fire now!*

He tried to peer past the flame, to the man holding the torch. Did the man have even a glimmer of possible compassion in his eyes? Would Jonah have any chance to plead his case? Jonah couldn't tell. He could see nothing but the torch blazing toward him.

Reflexively, he turned his head to the side, avoiding the fire. He'd turned toward Katherine, but his eyes were too flame-dazzled to see her.

No. He couldn't see her because she wasn't there.

Thanks a lot! She went and hid somewhere else, somewhere safe—and left me to deal with Mr. Pyromaniac 1483!

Something tugged on his hand, pulling him down. That didn't seem like such a bad idea—Jonah didn't think there were any torches down near the floor. At the last moment before the flames touched his skin, he slid down into a crouch.

Katherine was down there too.

Or—she was *sort of* down there.

In the flickering light of the torches she looked as ghostly and insubstantial and nearly see-through as the tracer boys had. Actually, the only difference between her wispy frame and the way the tracer boys had looked was that she didn't glow. So Jonah could clearly see the stone wall behind her, the dark shadows in the corner. . . . He could feel her clutching his hand—she'd been the one who pulled him down toward the floor. But he still wasn't entirely sure that she was there.

Jonah squinted, trying to make out the lines of Katherine's right arm and hand, trying to tell where her hand ended and his hand and arm began.

His own arm and hand were every bit as hard to see.

Jonah opened his mouth to ask, "What happened? What's going on?" Or maybe, "Do we look like this because Alex pressed INVISIBILITY? Did it have the word 'almost' in front of it, and we didn't see it because we were in such a hurry? What good does it do to be almost invisible? This way, we can't even pretend to be ordinary, normal, *innocent* fifteenth-century kids. . . ."

Katherine clapped her almost-invisible-but-still-quite-strong hand over his mouth. She mouthed the words, "I don't think they can see us!"

Jonah shook off Katherine's hand and tilted his head back to look up. It was true that the man holding the torch had not followed Jonah's motion—he hadn't lowered his torch toward the floor when Jonah jerked his body down. The man was only swinging his torch back and forth along the wall, scanning every crevice and corner.

Okay, I guess that makes sense, Jonah thought. *People who live in this time period can't see the tracers, and we can. So maybe time-traveler invisibility works the same way. . . .*

Just then, as Jonah was peering up, a charred bit of wood broke off from the torch and plummeted down.

It landed on the rim of Jonah's ear.

Jonah barely managed not to scream out in pain. He jerked his right arm up and shoved at the burning ash—he missed it on the first swipe but got it the second time. He sent the tiny bit of ember sailing across the room, into the darkness, and his ear immediately felt better.

But his arm, flailing out to shove the ember away, had struck the leg of the man standing before him.

ELEVEN

"Eh?" the man said. "What the . . ."

Now he bent over, holding his torch down low, closer and closer to Jonah.

Jonah scrambled out of the way. Since Katherine was sitting on his left, he dived to his right. At the last minute, catching a quick glimpse of a shadowy outline, he remembered that Chip was on his right, so he rolled forward, barely managing to pull his legs back so he didn't kick the torch man, too.

Jonah checked over his shoulder—now Katherine and Chip and Alex were struggling to avoid the swinging torch, with its dripping flames. They ducked down low, dodged right, then left, then right again. . . .

The man paused his torch, midswing, and called back to his fellow guards, "Might there be rats in these chambers? Rats big enough to hit a man in the knee?"

Jonah heard an answering chuckle.

"Rats that crawl out of a bottle, mayhap," someone called back.

Jonah relaxed a little, sprawled across the floor. At least if he'd had to hit someone, he'd evidently picked the man that nobody else would believe.

And then he had to roll out of the way again, because the man was stepping back from the wall.

"William," he called. "Come and look at this."

"Did ye find the corpse of one of your giant rats?" another man replied from near the bed. He had mockery in his voice.

But seconds later it was his feet Jonah had to squirm around, his steps Jonah had to dodge.

"Show me," the man called William demanded.

The first man began waving his torch near Katherine and Chip and Alex again, sending them into another flurry of dodging and darting and shoving out of the way of the flames. Jonah watched, paralyzed with fear. *Could* the man see Katherine and Alex and Chip somehow? Even if he just sensed their presence, was he clever enough to reach out and grab them? Was that what he was planning as he waved the torch back and forth so hypnotically?

"See?" the man said. "See how the flames turn the wrong way?"

Jonah saw what he meant. Every time Katherine or Chip or Alex darted out of the way of the torch, they sent up a tiny burst of air, distorting the direction of the flames. Jonah squinted, dimming the light coming into his eyes, so he couldn't really see his sister and friends at all anymore. And then it truly was eerie, watching the flames jump with no apparent reason.

"There's an evil wind along this wall," the first man said.

"I say 'tis evil we're out in the middle of the night looking for princes who should be snug in their beds," William replied.

"Princes"? Jonah thought. *Not "king and prince"? What does that mean?*

But he didn't have time to ponder that, because William began swinging his torch along the wall as well, sending Chip and Katherine and Alex back into their frantic motions. They couldn't just spring out from the wall because both men were moving erratically now; jumping away could easily mean slamming into a man or a torch. So they dodged right and left, narrowly avoiding first one torch, then the other.

The first man stopped his torch midswing, barely an inch above Katherine's shoulder.

"Do you think there's a secret chamber somewhere, where the princes are hiding? Do you think the wind's coming from there?" he asked.

"I think it's dangerous when the likes of you tries to think," the other man said.

The first man didn't move his torch. He seemed to be waiting for an errant flicker, something that would lead him to his suspected secret chamber. The torch burned steadily, the flames flaring evenly in all directions.

One of the flames licked down toward Katherine's shoulder. It wasn't on her shoulder—she didn't need to move yet. Jonah could see by the agonized expression on her face that she was trying not to move, trying not to arouse the man's suspicions even more. But her ponytail was flipped over that shoulder, near the torch. Some force—static electricity, maybe?—was making the individual hairs reach up toward the fire. While Jonah watched, horrified, one of the flames from the torch leaped over onto one of the tiny hairs.

Katherine's hair was on fire, and she didn't even know it.

Jonah rushed forward, heedless of the men. He shoved Katherine down. *Stop, drop, and roll,* he thought crazily. The rush of air made the flame flare up. *No time for stop, drop, and roll.* No space, either. He slammed his arm against Katherine's shoulder, smothering the flames with the sleeve of his sweatshirt.

He looked back at the men, hoping they hadn't noticed anything.

They were stumbling backward, looks of terror spread across their faces, which looked even ghastlier in the torchlight.

"W-witchcraft," the first man stammered.

"Sorcery," the other agreed.

"Or—ghosts?" the first suggested.

Jonah realized that, to them, the smoldering hair would have looked like a flame suddenly appearing from nowhere, floating in midair, and then disappearing just as abruptly.

Jonah had experience of his own with strange appearances and vanishings, out of and into thin air.

The first man turned and called over his shoulder in a slightly shaky voice, "There's nothing to see in this corner. Nothing."

He and William backed away, their eyes trained on the spot where the flame had vanished.

"We're done here, too," a man called from the other side of the room. "Back to the courtyard?"

And then the men with torches left. They pulled the door firmly shut behind them, plunging the room into darkness again.

Jonah sagged against the wall, his body limp with relief.

Then a hand slammed against his shoulder, knocking him to the side.

"What was that all about?" Katherine hissed in the darkness. "Pushing me around in front of those men, hitting me—"

"Katherine, you were on fire!"

"I was?" She sounded skeptical. "How come I couldn't tell?"

"It was just your hair," Chip contributed. "Jonah probably just saved your life."

"My hair?" Katherine wailed. There was a thumping sound, as if she'd slapped her hands down on her head to feel each individual lock. "How . . . how much? Do I have singe marks on the ends? Am I going to have to get it all cut off?"

Incredible. Katherine was almost completely invisible—and sitting in total darkness—and she was still worried about her appearance.

"It was just, like, five hairs," Jonah scoffed. "It won't disqualify you from running for Miss America someday."

"If we ever get back to America," Katherine moaned.

Jonah thought about joking, "I know of three ships that are headed that way in another nine years—and nine years has got to be enough time to get from England to Spain and meet up with Christopher Columbus!" But he didn't really feel like making jokes right now. In the darkness

Katherine sniffled. Great. Was she *crying*? Why did girls do that? Now what was he supposed to do?

Then Jonah heard Chip murmuring, "It's okay. We're all right."

It was too dark to see anything, of course, but Jonah had the really weird feeling that Chip had just put his arm around Katherine's shoulder.

"Alex?" Jonah said softly, to distract himself from thinking about Chip and Katherine. "Are you all right?"

"Oh, yeah. Blindman's bluff with torches is my *favorite* game," Alex said sarcastically. "Aren't most games better with the threat of total immolation? Instant death? Gotta *love* that adrenaline rush."

Jonah wasn't really sure what "immolation" meant, but he could guess.

"Well," he said, "we all survived."

"Barely," Alex said. "This time. We can't do this anymore—just react to one crisis after another. We've got to take charge. Be proactive, not reactive. Make a plan."

"Okay," Jonah said. "What do you suggest?"

"Um . . . ," Alex said.

"Er . . . ," Chip said.

Katherine just sniffled—louder this time, and much more miserably.

What were they going to do?

TWELVE

They fell asleep.

This was ridiculous, of course, because they were still in danger. They were clustered, essentially, in the middle of a crime scene. They were invisible, but they didn't know how that worked—or how long it would last. They'd already messed up time, and fixing it seemed impossible.

But somehow, after traveling back more than five hundred years in time, coping with timesickness, witnessing what appeared to be two murders, being betrayed by JB, and barely escaping being burned to death or discovered, they didn't seem to be capable of doing anything but sleeping. One minute Jonah was slumped against the wall, thinking desperate thoughts (*We need a plan, I can't think of a plan, this is impossible, but, oh, we need a plan. . . .*), and the next thing he knew, it was morning and sunlight was streaming in the window.

The sunlight was also streaming through him.

"Weird," Jonah mumbled.

By daylight, being almost invisible meant that he didn't cast a shadow, that the sunlight from the window illuminated the stone floor directly underneath him—and under Chip, Alex, and Katherine—just as much as it did the bare floor beside them. It was like being made of glass.

Jonah touched his glasslike leg with his glasslike hand. Everything *felt* normal, just like blue-jean material and—he slid his hand down to touch the gap between the bottom of his pant leg and the top of his sock—like ordinary skin. But looking at his own see-through clothes and body made him feel queasy and dizzy again, like the worst of the timesickness was back.

"Chip?" he whispered. "Katherine? Alex?"

The others didn't budge. Deep in sleep, they looked like crystal figurines, finely crafted, with such incredible attention to detail that they each had minuscule crystal eyelashes. Each one of Katherine's long hairs was also individually defined, tangled around her face now that the rubber band around her ponytail had slipped down. Jonah thought maybe he could even make out one strand that was shorter than all the others—the strand that had been on fire.

He closed his eyes dizzily. Last night he hadn't had

time to be scared, but now it was coming back to him: the crackling flames, the swinging torches, the danger. . . .

The sound of footsteps brought him back to the present. His eyes sprang open: A serving girl with a tray had pushed open the door and was approaching a table across the room.

"Breakfast, Your Highnesses," she said, then stopped, looking toward the empty bed. The blanket on the top was mussed, part of it hanging off the mattress and dragging down to the floor. The pillows were lumps half covered by the blanket, but too small to make it look like two boys were still sleeping there.

"Strange," the girl muttered, scratching at her head, under a silly-looking frilled cap. "They's always abed when I come in."

She looked around, her gaze veering toward Jonah and the others. Jonah froze momentarily, but she looked right past him.

"Must be in the privy," she concluded, looking toward the door into the other room, the one Jonah and the others had arrived in the night before.

The privy? Jonah wondered. *Is that, like, the restroom? No wonder it stank in there.*

The girl shrugged, put the tray down on the table, and left.

Almost without thinking, Jonah stood up and walked over to the table. *Food* . . . When was the last time he'd eaten? Breakfast yesterday—well, yesterday more than five hundred years in the future. Mom had made French toast and bacon, one of Jonah's favorite meals, as a special treat because she thought he might be nervous about going to an adoption conference.

If only I'd known what was really going to happen to me that day, Jonah thought, *I would have eaten six slices of French toast instead of only four!*

He looked down at the food on the tray—two mugs, two bowls of something that looked like oatmeal, two bowls of something that might be stewed dates, a charred hunk of something that might be meat, and a loaf of bread that looked hard enough to break a tooth on.

It all looked disgusting, but Jonah's stomach growled anyway.

Nobody would be able to tell if I just took a bite or two of the oatmeal, Jonah thought.

He reached for one of the spoons and scooped up a tiny amount of the runny, grayish cereal. It steamed as he brought it up to his mouth and hesitantly maneuvered it toward his tongue. He closed his lips around the spoon. . . .

And immediately began coughing.

Did they use a whole jar of cinnamon in this one bowl? And then a whole jar of cloves, too?

He coughed, gagged, coughed again. He spit the oatmeal back onto the spoon.

When he finally stopped choking, he realized that Katherine, Chip, and Alex were all awake now, and staring at him.

"*What* are you doing?" Katherine demanded.

Jonah felt a little bit like Goldilocks, except he'd gotten caught eating the porridge, instead of sleeping.

"I just took one bite," he defended himself. "I was hungry, and I didn't think anyone would notice. I just didn't know it'd taste so awful."

Chip stood up, stretched, and wandered toward the table.

"I bet it'd taste okay to Alex and me," he said. "You're right—nobody would miss just a bite or two."

"Plus," Alex said, joining them as well, "it'd be an interesting experiment. Visible food being eaten by an invisible kid—can you see the food all the way down the digestive tract? Or does it disappear once it's in your mouth?" He looked over at Jonah. "I don't see the food in your stomach."

"Didn't swallow," Jonah muttered.

Chip reached for the spoon in the other bowl of oatmeal.

"One small bite for man, one giant science experiment for mankind," he said, dramatically lifting the spoon toward his mouth.

As soon as his lips closed around the spoon, he began gagging too.

"Ugh! That's nasty!" he screamed, spitting even more emphatically than Jonah had. "Water! Must have . . ."

Jonah lifted a mug from the tray.

Chip took a huge gulp—and then spit that out too.

"That's beer! Beer and oatmeal—blech!"

"The king of England drinks beer for breakfast?" Jonah asked curiously.

"Ale," Alex corrected him. "Everyone drinks a lot of ale, even kids. The water isn't always safe."

Jonah shook his head in amazement. Chip was still spitting and moaning.

"Are you guys crazy?" Katherine demanded, coming over to the table to join them. "Making all this noise, spitting things everywhere—do you *want* someone to catch us?"

Chip stopped spitting long enough to say, "Well, we are invisible. They have to *see* us before they can catch us."

"*That's* not invisible," Katherine said, pointing at the tray, with its pools of beer and oatmeal spittle.

"Sorry," Chip said meekly.

Katherine swayed, then dropped down into a chair beside the table.

"I just want to go home," she moaned. "It feels like the whole room is spinning, my stomach hurts, my head aches—and I bet no one's invented aspirin yet!"

"Well," Alex said, "people do know that they can chew on the bark or leaves of willow trees, which contain salicin, which is related to aspirin, so—"

"Shut. Up," Katherine said fiercely.

Alex did.

This was Katherine at her worst: Katherine grumpy, Katherine embittered, Katherine mad at the world and ready to blame everyone else for her problems. Jonah's usual strategy when Katherine was like this was to avoid her like the plague.

(*The plague! Oh, no—had that happened yet? Was it happening now? Were they all going to get bubonic fever because JB had refused to let them go home?*)

To Jonah's surprise, Chip and Alex weren't rushing to get away from Katherine in her venom-spewing mood. Chip actually went over to stand beside her and pat her shoulder. Alex picked up the loaf of bread.

"You would probably feel better if you ate something," he said in a low, comforting voice. "We've already messed up the breakfast tray, so we might as well get some good out of it."

He pinched a piece of bread from the bottom of the loaf, where it wouldn't be so noticeable, and handed it to Katherine.

She put it in her mouth—Jonah saw that it disappeared instantly, as soon as her almost-invisible lips closed around it. But he decided this wasn't the right moment to point out the results of that science experiment.

Katherine chewed, swallowed, and then managed a weak smile.

"That wasn't too bad," she said. "Not as good as Panera or Einstein Bros., but edible at least. Just a little hard and salty." Alex handed her another chunk of bread, but she hesitated before putting it in her mouth. "Maybe we should all eat? So we can keep our energy up and think straight?"

They ended up hollowing out the loaf of bread, so that, on the tray, the crust still looked domed and firm and whole. They also cleaned up the beer and oatmeal spills.

"Okay, so we changed time, but there aren't going to be *that* many people who notice," Katherine said. "Not because of this tray, anyway."

She sneaked a doleful glance at Chip and Alex. She didn't have to say it out loud, that hollowed-out bread didn't matter when a king and a prince had vanished.

Chip clenched his jaw.

"It could have been rats that ate the food," he said in a hard voice. "Those guys were talking about rats last night."

Rats, Jonah thought. *Bread. Oatmeal. Aspirin. Even the bubonic plague* . . . It was so much easier to think about and talk about things that didn't really matter right now. But that left them stuck in a stone room in the fifteenth century forever.

He sighed.

"About last night . . . ," he began. "Was it just me, or did none of that make sense?"

"What do you mean?" Katherine asked in her snippiest voice. Jonah happened to know—only because he'd been living with her his entire life—that she sounded like that only when she was trying not to cry.

"You know," Jonah said. "I'm not exactly an expert on assassination attempts, or the fifteenth century, or anything else. But why were those guys trying to kill Chip and Alex by throwing them out the window? Wouldn't it be easier to just stab them? Or—if you really want to be secret about it—just suffocate them with a pillow?"

Chip and Alex both winced. Katherine only stared down at the secretly massacred bread.

"Those guys were only trying to keep things a secret when they first came into the room," Alex said. "If you want to keep things a secret, you don't stand in a court-yard in the middle of the night yelling, 'Where are the bod-ies?' You don't storm up the stairs with torches and search the royal chambers." He narrowed his eyes. "Maybe . . . maybe they wanted to make it look like we fell to the ground accidentally. Like we died because we were trying to escape."

"Died trying to escape," Katherine said. "Of course!" She looked up now, as if it made her feel better to know at least *some* information. "In dictatorships, when there are political prisoners and the dictator has them executed without a fair trial, they always say they died trying to escape. We talked about that in social studies."

Jonah thought that sixth-grade social studies must have gotten a lot more brutal since he'd taken it. Oh, wait—Katherine had the really hard teacher, Mrs. Hatchett, the one everyone tried to avoid getting.

"England isn't a dictatorship," Chip said stiffly, almost as if he was offended. "A monarchy, sure, but we have Par-liament, too. Representative government." Something like surprise spread over his nearly see-through face. "That's weird. I can still think like *him*."

Nobody had to ask. "Him" was Edward V.

"Did *he* know what was going on last night?" Jonah asked. "Or . . ." He glanced over at Alex. "Did the prince know?"

Alex and Chip exchanged glances.

"Things have gotten very weird lately," Chip said slowly. "It's complicated."

"Maybe if you tell us—when did things start getting weird?" Jonah suggested. He looked down at the trayful of beer and oatmeal, at his own virtually transparent hands. "What's normal around here, anyway?"

Chip frowned.

"It was *normal* that I became king when my father died," he said. "Everybody expected that."

Katherine opened her mouth, and Jonah thought she was going to object to Chip's talking about the king as "I" again. But she only said, "Go on."

"When I heard the news, I was at home—where I lived—at Ludlow Castle with my uncle," Chip said.

"You lived with the guy who wanted to kill you?" Jonah asked, horrified.

Chip squinted, as if remembering. Or as if it took effort to translate his fifteenth-century memories into explanations the other kids would understand.

"No, no, a different uncle," he said. "On the other side. I lived with Lord Rivers, who's my mother's brother. There's kind of . . . bad blood between the two sides. It's like our father's family thinks our mother's family is greedy and ambitious and, I don't know, kind of lower class and tacky."

"But they're not!" Alex interrupted.

"No, no, of course not!" Chip said. "On our grand-mother's side they've got royal blood dating back to Charlemagne!"

Jonah couldn't remember when Charlemagne lived, but he kind of thought he was French. If they were going to skip back to a whole other king, in a whole other country, this was going to take forever.

"Let's go back to you becoming king," Jonah said. "What happened then?"

"Lord Rivers said I needed to travel to London for my coronation," Chip said. "He said it had to happen fast." Somehow Chip sounded younger now, like he really was the twelve-year-old king. And he said "Lord Rivers" in such an admiring tone—no self-respecting teenaged boy would talk that way about anyone but a sports star.

"So Lord Rivers took you to London right away?" Jonah asked.

To Jonah's surprise, Chip's bottom lip began trembling. This was something Jonah would have thought was impossible, when Chip's face looked so much like crys-tal. But, incredibly, Chip seemed to be on the verge of tears.

"No," Chip practically whimpered. "Not because he didn't want to! There were . . . arrangements to make!

Troops to prepare, to make sure I was safe. And so . . . nobody could steal my throne—"

"Wait a minute," Katherine interrupted. "Are we in London now or at that Ludlow Castle place?"

It was funny—Jonah hadn't even thought to wonder that. One scary fifteenth-century castlelike place was pretty much like another, as far as he was concerned.

"London," Chip said forlornly. "Ludlow Castle is miles and miles away. It took five days just to get from Ludlow Castle to Stony Stratford."

Another strange name to keep track of.

"And Stony Stratford is . . . ," Jonah prompted.

The wobbly lip was back.

"Where *it* happened," Chip whispered.

THIRTEEN

Jonah waited. It was hard enough trying to tiptoe around Katherine's feelings, without having to worry about Chip now too. Jonah would rather dodge flaming torches again than see Chip cry.

But, to Jonah's surprise, Chip lifted his head, almost regally.

"We were marching with two thousand soldiers," he said. "All loyal to me. All there to protect me. We were supposed to meet Gloucester and Buckingham"—he said these names sneeringly, without titles—"in Northampton. But Lord Rivers said we should press on to Stony Stratford, fourteen miles away, fourteen miles closer to London."

"Gloucester is our uncle on our father's side," Alex contributed. "Buckingham is his friend."

"Oh," Jonah said. "Where were you for all of this?"

"With our mother," Alex said. "Already in London. But I'm the younger brother, remember? I don't really matter."

It bothered Jonah that Alex could talk like that. But Alex only shrugged and turned his attention back to Chip.

"We stopped at an inn," Chip said. "And Lord Rivers told me to rest for the night while he rode back to meet the others. Gloucester and Buckingham and their men."

"Did he take the two thousand soldiers or leave them with you?" Katherine asked. Jonah was surprised that Katherine would ask that question.

Chip flinched.

"He . . . he left them with me," Chip said. "Practically all of them." He sighed.

"And?" Jonah whispered.

Chip pounded his fist on the table, so suddenly that the mugs wobbled on the tray.

"Gloucester tricked Lord Rivers," Chip said. "They went out drinking together, all nice and friendly. And then the next morning he had Lord Rivers arrested. It wasn't fair. It was . . . it was traitorous!"

Outrage gleamed in his eyes.

"But *you* weren't arrested, were you?" Jonah said. "You had the soldiers."

Chip was staring off into the distance, remembering.

"That morning I was already on my horse, ready to ride on toward London. Everyone said that we should push on, that we shouldn't wait for Lord Rivers. That . . . scared me. I knew Lord Rivers wouldn't desert me. But when you're king, you're not allowed to show fear. So I was sitting up straight, leading the way . . . and then Gloucester came, galloping through my troops."

Jonah, who'd only ever ridden a horse once, at Boy Scout camp, could practically hear the hoofbeats.

"Gloucester's a determined-looking man, you know?" Chip said wistfully. "He always acts like he knows he's right. And he has a way of saying things that you know are wrong, but he makes you feel like you shouldn't argue. You don't think of what you should say back to him until hours later."

"So, what did he say?" Katherine asked.

"He bowed down to me," Chip said. "He said I was the king."

Jonah did a double take.

"What's wrong with that?" he asked. "I thought you were the king."

He wondered if he'd missed some huge chunk of this story.

"It was deceitful," Chip said, his voice wavering. "If Gloucester had just attacked me, straight-out, my soldiers would have protected me. My chamberlain, Thomas Vaughan, would have given his life for mine. But no, Gloucester goes on and on about how *loyal* he is to me, and how my father left him the task of being my protector while I'm underage, and so he's going to accompany me to London, not Lord Rivers. And he said we didn't need all the soldiers, because that might scare people in London into thinking there was going to be some big battle, and so all the soldiers should go home, and I should leave my chamberlain behind too and just go with Gloucester and Buckingham."

"And you *agreed* to that?" Katherine asked.

"I'm just a kid, okay?" Chip said. "And Gloucester was saying all the right things, and I didn't know yet that he'd had Lord Rivers arrested." He hesitated. "It was like we were playing poker, and Gloucester could see all of the cards in my hand, and I didn't know anything about his. But I stood up to him later! Later, as we were riding away, he said that my father had had bad advisers, and that *they* were the reason he'd died, because they'd let him eat and drink way too much, and that's why he was going to protect me. And I said, 'Sir, do not malign my father's memory. I trust his judgment, and I trust the advisers he gave me.'"

Chip sounded so proud and fierce saying that. But then he slumped against the wall.

"That only made Gloucester say, 'Ah, and I'm glad of that, for *I* am the main adviser your father left you.' And he smiled, and it was just like a fox, or a wolf—I should have told my soldiers to attack! I should have fought for Lord Rivers!"

Now Chip was scaring Jonah. Jonah tried to think of something to calm him down, but Katherine was already begging for the next part of the story.

"So then he locked you up and wouldn't let you act like a king?" she asked eagerly.

"Nooo," Chip said. "I was signing documents, I was going to council meetings, we were planning for my coronation, the big ceremony when I'd get my crown. . . . My brother came to join me here so he could play his part in the coronation too!"

"So, what was your problem?" Jonah asked, frustrated. "What do you have against Gloucester? Just because he's your father's brother, not your mother's . . ."

"Everything changed," Chip said. "Nobody would tell me anything! But suddenly there weren't any more council meetings to go to, and I hadn't seen Gloucester in days, and the servants acted like I was sick or something, like I had to stay in my room or the courtyard . . . they even moved my room to another place where I'd be 'safer.' This is the Tower of London, you know? It's the *palace*. But lately . . . lately it started seeming like I was a prisoner here."

"A prisoner someone tried to kill last night," Alex reminded him.

That word, "kill," lingered in the air. Jonah, trying to avoid thinking about it, realized something else.

"The serving girl this morning, the one who brought the tray," he said. "She wasn't acting like she thought the boys had vanished. Or been killed. And I didn't see her tracer, so she wasn't doing anything different."

"Or her tracer was in some other room entirely," Alex said.

"Oh. Yeah."

Jonah frowned. The more he thought about all of this, the more confused he was. Chip's story only made things worse, because it just showed how much Edward V and his brother hadn't known. Where was that Lord Rivers guy now? Was he really so wonderful? And was Gloucester so terrible, or did it just seem that way because Chip had listened to his mother's side of the family?

Maybe all of this is just a misunderstanding, Jonah thought. *A mistake.*

Which was really stupid, because it was pretty much impossible to mistakenly throw two boys out a window.

"Maybe if we check the Elucidator . . . ," Alex suggested slowly.

Chip whirled on him.

"You want to talk to JB again? Somebody we *know* betrayed us? *No!*"

"Not to talk to JB," Alex corrected himself. "For other stuff. JB wasn't the one who made us invisible. We figured that out all by ourselves. Maybe there's some other function like that, that can help us. Or maybe there's, like, some explanation of history on the Elucidator, some button we can click and find out everything."

Jonah wished he'd thought of that.

"Do you still have the Elucidator, Jonah?" Katherine asked.

"Um, uh . . ." Jonah dug in the front pocket of his jeans. You'd think he'd remember something like that, but there'd been so much else to think about. "Here it is." He pulled out a thin, flat disk.

A completely invisible, thin, flat disk. Even though he could feel it, hard against his hand, he couldn't see the slightest shadow of anything in his open palm. He held it up, into the sunlight.

Still nothing.

"Very funny, Jonah." Katherine scrunched up her face in disgust. "This isn't the time for practical jokes."

"No, really," Jonah said. "It's in my hand. It's just . . . even more invisible than we are."

He ran his fingers over the Elucidator, groping for some sort of button, something to use to give it directions. The surface of the Elucidator was completely smooth. The others gathered around him and felt it too.

"Maybe it has an audio activation in this mode?" Alex suggested calmly. "Elucidator, view screen."

Nothing happened.

"Show screen," Katherine said.

"End invisibility mode," Chip said.

"Help?" Jonah tried. "Show help menu?"

The Elucidator stayed invisible.

"Maybe if I throw it again?" Chip asked. "That made it light up."

"Or you might break it completely," Alex said.

Don't panic, Jonah thought. *Don't panic. It wouldn't help to panic. . . .* But it was hard not to when they were all clustered together staring at nothing, and that same invisible nothing was their only link with the outside world, maybe their only hope of ever escaping the fifteenth century.

"Um," Jonah said, his voice cracking. "Anybody got a plan B?"

"I do, but I don't want to do it," Katherine said in a small voice.

Oh, great, now Katherine wasn't making any sense either. No, wait—Jonah hadn't been able to understand her about half the time back in the twenty-first century, anyway, so this was just normal. It was good to have something be normal right now.

"Well?" Jonah said mockingly—mocking was often the best tone to use with Katherine. "What is it?"

Katherine looked carefully at Chip and Alex.

"I think the only way we can get out of here is to fix time," she said. "Even if we can't do anything with the Elucidator, you saw how JB yanked the Taser out of here. Maybe he'd do that with us, too, if we can somehow make it so it doesn't matter that the king and the prince disappeared last night."

"You mean, you're on JB's side. You think Alex and I have to die," Chip said bitterly. "Thanks a lot!"

"No!" Katherine said. She grabbed Chip by the shoulder, steadying him. "I mean, we need to find out how to make it look like you did die, and make the people who wanted you dead think that you are. I want to *fake* your death. But first we need to figure out who tried to kill you, and why. And how they reacted to your disappearance. And for that . . ." She swallowed hard, uncharacteristically hesitant. "For that we have to leave this room."

"You're right," Alex said, sounding surprised. "That's a

good plan." He tilted his head, puzzled. "Why did you say you didn't want to do it?"

Katherine bit her lip.

"You're going to think I'm being a real girl here," she began.

"Katherine, you *are* a girl," Jonah reminded her.

Katherine ignored him.

"Not *that* kind of girl. Not the kind in the movies who's always screaming over every little thing, the kind that everyone else has to rescue." She flipped her long hair disdainfully over her shoulder. "You know I'm not like that."

She was appealing to Jonah now, like she really cared about his opinion.

"Okay," Jonah said grudgingly. "You're not."

"But I'm *terrified* now at the thought of walking out that door," she said. "I know we need to do it, I'm pretty sure it's the best thing, but . . . maybe timesickness makes you agoraphobic? Or maybe it's just because I've already seen murderers, I've already almost been burned to death—and that's without going out into the rest of the fifteenth century. . . ."

Jonah didn't like this. She was scaring him now too.

"Katherine," Chip said soothingly. "We're invisible! We'll be fine."

"Will we?" Katherine asked. "Can you promise that? You're the king here, and you're not even safe!"

Jonah thought maybe Alex was rolling his eyes, but it was hard to tell when his eyes were so close to being invisible.

"Then, maybe you could stay here—see what happens in our chambers the rest of the day—while Chip and Jonah and I go out," Alex said.

Jonah decided that Alex must not have a younger sister back home in the twenty-first century. Otherwise he'd know that that was exactly the kind of thing that would set Katherine off.

It did.

"And that would be even worse!" Katherine said. "I'd be sitting here with no idea what was happening to the rest of you, with nothing to do except imagine all the worst possibilities. . . . We don't even have cell phones to use to stay in touch!"

"We could . . . ," Jonah started to say. "Or if . . ."

But Katherine was right. It was amazing how hard not having a phone made everything.

"Maybe if we promise to come back within an hour?" Alex offered.

Katherine shoved against him.

"No!" she said. "Quit trying to get rid of me! I'm going too!"

And Alex, who seemed to understand scientific concepts so well, just sat there mystified by Katherine.

FOURTEEN

They all took turns using the privy room before they left. This made Jonah feel oddly homesick, because of all those times when he and Katherine were little kids and Mom or Dad would insist, "Make sure you go before we go!"

But the privy bore very little resemblance to a twenty-first-century bathroom. The "toilet" was just a single hole in the stones of the wall. And Chip and Alex had a little too much fun telling Katherine, "Instead of toilet paper there's moss that you can use. See? It's *really* useful!"

They also delayed a bit, looking around the room, trying to make sure that nothing was out of place.

"You didn't leave the Elucidator lying around anywhere, did you?" Alex asked.

"It's back in my pocket," Jonah assured him.

"Should we hang the tapestry up again, or just leave it?"

Katherine asked. "It was the soldiers or guards or whatever those guys were who pulled it down, but probably they wouldn't have done that if it hadn't been for us. . . ."

The hooks for the tapestry were high above their heads, about twelve feet off the ground.

"Never mind!" Jonah said impatiently. "Let's just go!"

He grabbed the door and jerked it open—and found himself staring right into the startled face of yet another serving girl, in the hall outside.

"Wh-wh-who's there?" she called, darting so quickly to peer into the room that Jonah barely managed to step out of the way.

She looked right through Jonah, right through Katherine, right through Chip and Alex. Her eyes didn't focus on any of them.

"Must have been the wind," she muttered. "And the princes must already be outside playing. . . ."

She stepped back into the hall and pulled the door firmly shut behind her.

Jonah stood frozen, his heart pounding in his chest.

"Maybe . . . you were . . . right . . . , Katherine," he whispered after a few moments, after he was sure the serving girl would have moved on. "Maybe it is too dangerous out there."

Katherine reached past him for the door handle.

"Silly," she scoffed. "You just need to be careful."

She pushed the door open a crack, peeked out, and then slipped out into the empty hall. The others followed.

The hall was dim, with little sunlight reaching in from the high windows. Katherine pointed left, then right, then held her hands up questioningly. When everybody else shrugged, she turned to the right. After a few twists and turns in the hall they found a rounded staircase and tiptoed down. Reaching the door at the bottom, Katherine made a dramatic show of peeking out again, looking around carefully before slipping out.

I guess she's not so scared if she can make me look like a fool, Jonah thought. But he was just as glad not to be the first one out this time.

He stepped out into the sunshine behind Katherine and Chip, and blinked a few times to let his eyes adjust. The other three looked even dimmer and harder to see in bright light, and as long as he didn't think about it too much, he found that reassuring.

Beyond them he could see a large courtyard of sorts: grass and greenery and flowering trees. And beyond that he could see soldiers—or maybe guards—standing around. They didn't look like they thought they had anything to worry about; they weren't standing at attention.

One or two of them even had caps pulled down over their faces, as if they might be sleeping.

"*My* soldiers never behaved so sloppily," Chip muttered.

"Maybe if the commanders were away . . . ," Alex whispered back.

Here was another puzzle, Jonah thought. If the soldiers thought the king and the prince had disappeared last night, shouldn't they be running around searching everywhere? Shouldn't they be extra alert, not . . . comatose?

Jonah stepped through an archway to look for other soldiers, other people who might be more awake and more likely to be discussing last night's events.

Two men in fancier clothes walked past, one saying to the other, "Hurry! The last barge is leaving for the coronation!"

Coronation?

Jonah peered back at Chip to see if Chip had heard the man too. Chip's face had gone rock hard with fury.

"So that's how it is," he hissed. "They were trying to kill me or kidnap me, and replace me with another boy at the coronation. One who would probably do whatever Gloucester told him to do. . . ."

"Um," Jonah said softly, because he thought the men were out of earshot now, but he wasn't completely sure. "Wouldn't people notice?"

Alex shook his head.

"It's not like they have TV," he said. "Maybe a few people have seen paintings of me and Chip, maybe a few other people know what's going on. . . ."

Chip had already spun past them.

"I'm getting on that barge," he announced, and stalked away without a backward glance.

"Come on!" Katherine said in a panicky voice, pulling on Jonah's sleeve and reaching back for Alex, too. "We can't lose him!"

Chip was already rushing after the two men, dodging servants with platters and soldiers with pikes and a stray-looking dog that raised his nose and sniffed suspiciously as Chip dashed past.

Jonah felt some of Katherine's panic. *What if we lose Chip? What if he makes it on the barge and we don't? What if he does something really stupid?* Jonah began almost running.

"Jonah!" Katherine whispered. "You're kicking up dust!"

"It's windy," Jonah whispered back. "Who cares?"

Ahead of them Chip had reached a wharf extending out into a river—the Thames? Jonah wondered. He thought that the social studies teacher he'd had in sixth grade (a much, much nicer woman than Katherine's Mrs. Hatchett) would be very proud of him for remembering the name of a foreign waterway at a time like this.

And then there was no time to think, because Chip was jumping from the wharf onto the back of a low boat.

"That idiot!" Alex whispered.

"No, no, he's all right—he'll catch that pole . . . ," Jonah said.

Alex shot him a disgusted look.

"What?" Jonah said.

The answer was instantly clear. Chip did indeed grab on to a pole holding up a canopy over the well-dressed people crowding onto the boat. But he had landed on the outer edge of the boat, throwing everything off balance. The canopy wobbled; his corner of the boat dipped low in the water. Women in ridiculously elaborate skirts fell against elegant men, all of them separating from calm, unaffected tracers. It was eerie how the number of people on the boat seemed to instantly double, as Chip's one action changed everyone's movements. People laughed and shrieked—and stared. A man holding an oar left his tracer behind to creep toward Chip, a mystified expression on his face.

Katherine peered in distress from Alex to Jonah.

"Well?" she whispered. "Do I have to do everything?"

Jonah just looked at her blankly.

Katherine took off running. She broke through the

crowd like a star basketball player determined to score the winning point before the buzzer. Then, at the wharf's edge, behind the loading area, she eased down into the water and—Jonah craned his neck to watch—disappeared with only a small ripple. Seconds later she resurfaced at the far side of the boat, climbed up, and clutched the pole on the opposite side from Chip.

Instantly the boat righted itself.

The man with the oar shrugged and went back to his position, rejoining his tracer.

"Oh," Jonah whispered. "I would have figured that out. Eventually," he told Alex.

Alex grinned.

"When should we tell her that people dump their sewage into the Thames?" he whispered.

"Never," Jonah whispered back.

One by one, all the tracers vanished from the barge, as everyone settled down. Jonah and Alex waited until the rest of the people had crowded on, and then, just before the barge pulled away, they gingerly stepped down to grab other poles. They were careful to balance their weight, so the barge barely swayed.

And then they were gliding along the river.

FIFTEEN

It wasn't bad on the barge. Clinging to the pole, balanced on the outer edge of the boat, Jonah was at least certain that he wouldn't accidentally jostle into someone. And Jonah could hear bits and pieces of the conversation under the canopy.

Mostly people seemed to be talking about the weather.

"What a lovely day . . ."

"Perfect for the coronation . . ."

Jonah noticed that, although the people in the boat all had on fancy clothes, a lot of them were missing teeth or had pockmarked skin or bad scars. One man was even missing both an eye and a hand, like he was an extra for one of the *Pirates of the Caribbean* movies. Jonah started thinking about how in movies about old times it was only the pirates and the outlaws who ever had any deformities or blemishes, while the heroes and heroines all had perfect teeth and perfect skin and perfect hair and bodies—as if they all had time-traveling plastic surgeons and ortho-dontists and hair stylists and personal trainers to take care of them. While in real life . . .

Oh, my gosh, Jonah thought. *Some of these people are hideous!*

A woman had turned toward him, exposing a cheek eaten up with some sort of infection, with pus oozing copiously from the side of her face. And she hadn't even bothered to cover it up, hadn't even bandaged it. Flies hovered above the pus.

Jonah turned his head to see how the others were reacting. Chip and Alex were staring straight ahead, com-pletely unfazed.

Oh, yeah, Jonah thought. *They'd be used to it.*

Katherine had her jaw clenched and looked like she was trying very hard not to throw up. But really, she'd looked like that ever since they arrived in the fifteenth century, because of the timesickness.

Huh, Jonah thought. *As long as I don't look at Lady Pus Face, I don't feel sick at all anymore.*

Maybe twelve hours of breathing fifteenth-century air had cured him. Maybe eating the fifteenth-century bread had helped. Jonah remembered a little bit of a Greek myth his sixth-grade social studies teacher had told his class—she'd been really into Greek myths. This one was something about someone going to the underworld and being offered food. And the food was really important because . . .

Suddenly Jonah got chills. He'd remembered the rest of the myth.

Because once you ate the food, you could never leave.

Jonah started practically hyperventilating, breathing much too loudly. A man turned toward him, a puzzled expression on his pockmarked face. Jonah clamped his teeth together, trying to hold his breath instead. But this only made him dizzy.

He tilted his head back and stared up at a single wispy cloud in the bright blue sky. *What a lovely day . . . lovely day . . . lovely day . . .* Nice weather *was* something to focus on, to distract yourself with, when all your other thoughts were dangerous.

So, maybe . . . Jonah dared to glance back at the crowd on the barge. He tried to look past the pus and the pockmarks, the missing teeth and limbs. There was something fake and strangely shallow about the conversation on the barge. As far as Jonah could tell, no one was saying, "What a fine king we'll be crowning today!" No one said, "Can someone explain why we're going to a coronation today when the king disappeared last night?"

Jonah looked around. The river was crowded with barges, all headed upriver. And whenever Jonah got a good glimpse of the shore, it looked like people on the streets of London were streaming in the same direction as well. Everyone was going to the coronation. Were people acting so artificially in all the barges, on all the streets?

"Do you see the spires yet?" a man asked his boy as he pointed off into the distance.

"There?" the boy said. "That's Westminster Abbey?"

"Yes," the man said. "Kings are always crowned there." He paused. "It's fine weather for a coronation, isn't it?"

The barge docked at another wharf, and people began streaming off toward the church. Chip started to rush forward with the crowd, but Jonah and Alex held him back, keeping him in the barge. Chip struggled against them.

"I must . . . ," he hissed. "I have to—"

"Shh!" Jonah whispered back. "You can't walk through that crowd, even invisible. People would freak out if they bumped into you."

When everyone but the oarsmen had gotten off the boat, the four kids stepped cautiously onto the wood dock. They skirted the edge of the crowd, surging forward, then stumbling back to avoid elbows, shoulders, feet.

"This is impossible!" Katherine whispered. "We're never going to get anywhere!"

But then soldiers came through the crowd, commanding, "Clear the way! Clear the way! Make way for the king!"

By twisting and diving and dodging, all four kids managed to land in the open area when the crowd parted.

"Sweet!" Alex muttered.

They had a clear path ahead of them, right up to the soaring cathedral.

Chip stood in the exact center of the open space, looking around.

"This is the path I would have taken," he whispered. "I would have worn cloth of gold, there would have been a silk canopy. . . ."

Chip sounded calm, but he had a strange expression on his face. He had his eyes narrowed and seemed deep in thought, reminiscing. But he kept clenching his jaw, as though he was fighting some internal struggle. He ran his hand through his short hair, and then something like bafflement spread over his face, as if he'd expected to feel long, flowing curls.

Or as if he'd expected to touch a crown.

Jonah was so busy watching Chip, he failed to notice the hubbub behind him.

A procession was advancing toward them, toward the cathedral. Jonah could see knights in armor on horseback; he could see the peak of a white canopy, probably made out of silk, just as Chip had described. And then Jonah could hear what the crowd around the procession was yelling:

"Long live the king! Long live Richard the Third!"

Those words apparently reached Chip's ears at the same instant. A change swept over Chip's face, leaving only one emotion behind: pure fury.

"Usurper! Thief! Murderer!" Chip shouted. "You do *not* deserve to be king!"

And then he took off running.

SIXTEEN

Jonah could see exactly what Chip planned to do. He planned to dart invisibly past all the knights and horses and nobles. He planned to scream the entire way. And then he planned to tackle the impostor king and take the crown for himself.

Jonah shot a quick glance at Katherine and Alex. Katherine was just standing there, horrified. Alex looked strangely baffled and was mouthing the words, "Richard? Richard the Third? But that's . . ."

Jonah decided that if anyone was going to do something, it'd have to be him.

He took off with a burst of speed behind Chip. Back in the twenty-first century Jonah could outrun Chip easily—he did it all the time playing basketball. But this time Chip had a head start.

And maybe an advantage anyway, since he fits in the fifteenth century and I don't? Jonah wondered.

Jonah fell farther behind.

Then Jonah got lucky.

Chip darted around a horse but skidded in a pile of mud. *No, probably horse manure, given that it's right behind that horse,* Jonah thought. Jonah pushed off harder with his big toe, the way his soccer coach had told him to run. He was making up ground now.

But Chip was righting himself, aiming toward the crowd under the canopy, all those people in gleaming clothes. In jerky glances Jonah could see that one of the people under the canopy was carrying a crown on a tasseled pillow. If Chip got under that canopy, near that crown, Jonah wouldn't be able to stop him.

Jonah lunged.

For a moment Jonah was sure he'd missed. Something squished beneath him—*Ugh! Manure!*—but his hands wrapped around something solid: Chip's leg.

Jonah pulled Chip back from the people under the canopy. He rose up so he could shift his grip, grabbing Chip by the waist, then the shoulders. Finally he clapped his hand over Chip's mouth and hissed in his ear, "This is not the way to do this!"

"You don't understand!" Chip hissed back. At least he

wasn't shouting anymore. "He's stealing my throne! That crown belongs on my head!"

"No!" Jonah whispered fiercely. "*You* belong in the twenty-first century. Here you're supposed to be dead. Remember?"

At that, the fight went out of Chip. He sagged against the ground, as if he had no intention of ever getting up. Not even if a thousand horses and knights marched over him.

"Come on," Jonah whispered. "I think I know what you can do to get some revenge. It might even help fix time."

Chip frowned but stood up stiffly. Then the two boys dodged horses and knights again to get back to Katherine and Alex.

"How many people do you think heard him?" Jonah asked Katherine grimly when they reunited.

"Honestly, only the four or five who were right beside him," Katherine said. "They're the only ones who looked startled. Everyone else was cheering so loudly . . . these people believe in ghosts and sorcery and that kind of thing anyhow, so they wouldn't be too suspicious, would they?"

"That's what I'm counting on," Jonah muttered.

While the procession was still advancing, slowly, Jonah and the others slipped into the church.

"Where can we go to get out of the way?" Jonah asked, pausing at the back of the huge sanctuary.

"I don't want to get out of the way!" Chip said. "I—"

"Just so we can talk," Jonah assured him. "And plan."

"That way, then," Chip said reluctantly. He pointed down a dark hallway.

They ended up huddling in a corner near eerie statues and flickering candles. In the dim light Jonah finally got a good look at Alex's anguished face.

"What's wrong with you?" Jonah demanded, tact having deserted him about the time he tackled Chip in the manure.

"I didn't know it was Richard the Third," Alex said. "I didn't know who he was."

"Because he's *not* Richard the Third," Chip said cuttingly. "He's only Richard, Duke of Gloucester. Our *uncle*. Stealing the throne for himself." He glared at Alex. "You knew his first name was Richard."

"But not the *Third*."

"So?" Jonah asked quickly, before Chip had a chance to interrupt again.

"Because Richard the Third—that's Shakespeare," Alex explained, grimacing. "There's a whole play about him. He's, like, one of the worst villains in literature."

Jonah suppressed a shiver. *Literature*, he told himself. *Not history*.

"We already know he's a villain," Chip complained. "He tried to have us killed! He's usurping the throne!"

"Wait a minute," Katherine said. "Shakespeare wrote a play about this guy, and Alex remembers it? That's great! Now we'll know what's supposed to happen in reality!"

The light from the prayer candles glowed through her.

"Well . . . um . . . that is . . . er . . . ," Alex stammered.

"What?" Katherine demanded.

Alex winced.

"My mom's a high school English teacher, okay?" he said. "She *loves* Shakespeare. She's always trying to get me to read the plays or go to the plays or just listen to her quoting the plays. But—they're all really boring, all right? I never pay any attention. I just know Richard the Third's an awful villain, because she always says, 'You'd think I was raising Richard the Third, the way you're acting!' any time I do something wrong." He frowned. "Is Richard the Third the one where there's something rotten in the state of Denmark?"

"We're in England," Jonah said flatly.

"Oh, right . . . I think that's *Hamlet*," Alex said. He made his hands into fists and pounded them against his forehead. "Think, think, think. . . ." He took his fists away from his forehead for a moment. "I can recite all of Einstein's greatest formulas. Would that help?"

"Not right now," Jonah said. "Not unless you can use those formulas to get us out of here."

"And then Einstein probably wouldn't ever exist because of us," Katherine said gloomily.

"No, wait, I do have a plan," Jonah said.

He'd kind of hoped that everyone would turn to him and fall silent, in awe. But Alex was pounding his fists against his forehead again, muttering, "Is 'winter of our discontent' from *Richard III*? Doesn't matter, it's summer now. 'Parlous youth'? Maybe, but that's no help. . . ." Katherine was frowning and watching Alex. Chip was staring off into the distance, toward the light coming from the open door. His eyes were narrowed to slits now, as if he was listening to the ongoing cheers outside: "Long live the king!" "Long live Richard the Third!"

"It doesn't make sense," Chip muttered.

"*What* doesn't make sense?" Jonah asked, giving up on announcing his plan for the moment.

"It was just last night that someone tried to kill me, the real king," Chip said. "They didn't even succeed. There's no proof of it, anyway. So how could they be having Richard's coronation today?"

Jonah shrugged.

"Fast planning?" he suggested. "Overconfidence?"

"It takes a long time to plan a coronation," Chip said.

"That's why I hadn't been crowned yet. They were still working on all the details, all the invitations. . . ."

"Are you sure you were king?" Jonah asked, then flinched because he thought that might set Chip off again. "Can you be the king before you're coronated—or whatever it's called?"

"Crowned," Chip said emphatically but without anger. "And I *am* the king, regardless. A coronation's just a formality. A show, for everyone to see. I was supposed to have a grand one. But I was already king. I became king the minute my father died."

"Oh," Jonah said. "So how do you explain . . ." He gestured weakly toward the hubbub coming from outside.

"I *can't*," Chip said. "Did you see how much cloth of gold our evil uncle was wearing—the shimmery stuff, with real gold woven into it? And that purple velvet cape—I bet there was at least eight yards of it trailing behind him. . . ."

"So?" Jonah asked. He wouldn't have expected Chip to care about fashion at a time like this.

"So—it all had to be woven and sewn by hand," Chip said.

Jonah still didn't understand.

"We haven't had the Industrial Revolution yet. No mechanical looms or sewing machines," Alex contributed before going back to muttering, "And I know it's not *'Et tu, Brute?'* because that's *Julius Caesar*. . . ."

"Oh," Jonah said. He thought it had been only about twelve hours since the mysterious intruders tried to throw Chip and Alex out the window. *Maybe* a team of seamstresses, sewing through the night, could produce eight yards of velvet cape that quickly. But Jonah couldn't quite imagine the murderers coming back from their job, rushing into a roomful of seamstresses, and announcing, "Okay! That job's done! Get to sewing!"

And coronation clothes made to fit Chip definitely wouldn't have fit his uncle. Chip's uncle—the guy Jonah had seen in a purple cape, anyway—was taller than Chip, more muscular.

More grown-up.

"You think he had everything planned and arranged ahead of time?" Jonah asked.

"He must have!" Chip snapped. "But how did he convince everyone to go along with him? All the knights and nobles in that procession with him . . . all those people cheering in the crowd . . ."

It was pain and sorrow that filled his expression now, not just hurt pride and outrage.

"No wonder you wanted to grab his crown," Jonah said grudgingly.

"Yeah. Probably not the best idea, right? Not in front of hundreds of people, anyway," Chip said. "I don't know what came over me. I felt different again, kind of like I did when I was around the tracers last night. I wasn't thinking like myself at all."

"That's weird," Alex said, finally giving up on Shakespeare. "I wasn't feeling like myself either when we were standing outside. But for me it just felt like I, uh, missed my mother."

He sounded embarrassed.

"Fifteenth-century mother the queen, or twenty-first-century mother the Shakespeare teacher?" Katherine asked.

Alex didn't have time to answer because the coronation procession had arrived at the threshold of the cathedral now. The royal horns were almost deafening; the cheers of the crowd overwhelming.

"You said you had a plan?" Chip said.

Jonah leaned over to whisper it in his ear.

Chip smiled.

"I'll really enjoy that," he said.

SEVENTEEN

Jonah barely had time to whisper his plan to Alex and Katherine, too, before the procession was streaming toward their dark hallway.

"This is perfect!" Chip said. "They'll go to the shrine of the saints first. It's right over there. Come on!"

He began rushing toward an opening between pillars, several yards down. It was lucky that Jonah, Katherine, and Alex followed him quickly, because seconds later royal pages were shaking out wide swaths of finely woven cloth for the royal party to walk on. One bolt of the cloth landed right where the four kids had been standing.

"They take their shoes off to be respectful to the saints," Chip explained. "Crazy, isn't it?"

He walked on through the opening into the saints'

shrine, a grottolike enclosure with a row of statues and an altar at the front.

"We can stand by the statues while they're coming in," Chip said. "Richard will come to the front and kneel, and everyone else will stay behind him."

Jonah moved back between two statues with equally fierce expressions on their stone faces. He thought they looked more like soldiers than saints.

"Hi. How you doing?" Jonah muttered to the statues. "Do you know you're missing a nose?"

Katherine shot him a look that clearly said, *How can you make jokes at a time like this?* Jonah shrugged.

The royal procession began entering the shrine. Richard—Duke of Gloucester, King of England, whichever he was—did indeed have the most luxurious clothes. Even in the dim candlelight everything about him shimmered. Only a small number of the noblemen followed him into the shrine—probably the highest-ranking ones. The man carrying the crown on the pillow was one of them.

"That's Buckingham," Chip whispered. "His good friend. And fellow traitor."

A woman came into the shrine too, followed by another nobleman with a smaller crown on a pillow.

"Richard's having his wife crowned today too?" Chip muttered. "That's different."

The queen—or queen-to-be—was a frail, sickly-looking woman with thinning hair and deep lines in her face. But the way she smiled at her husband almost made Jonah feel bad about what they were about to do to him.

Some guys in robes—priests?—began chanting, and then Richard and his wife went to kneel at the altar.

"Maybe you shouldn't . . . ," Jonah began in a soft voice.

Chip flashed him a dirty look and went to crouch beside Richard. From his position by the statues Jonah could hear every word Chip said.

"You do not deserve to be king," Chip hissed directly into his uncle's ear. "After what you had done to your nephews, you don't deserve to live. All this pomp and ceremony—bah! It is for naught. The crowd may cheer you now, but they will jeer when they know your sins. . . ."

Richard stayed on his knees, but he jerked to attention. Separating from a calm, devout-looking tracer, he peered around, something like panic on his face.

"Oh, yes, you *will* be found out," Chip murmured. "And then . . . then you will die a terrible death, as terrible as the death you gave your nephews."

"Begone!" Richard muttered through clenched teeth, glancing around again. "Plague me not!"

"I will plague you anytime I want!" Chip said, his voice rising.

Jonah thought maybe a few of the priests had heard him too, because they stopped in the middle of their chanting, creating more tracers.

Richard looked back at them.

"Leave me," he commanded. "I require time to pray. Alone."

The priests and the nobles exchanged baffled glances. This was evidently an unusual request.

"I . . . I am adding a new part to the coronation ceremony," Richard said. "I was inspired, kneeling here, to know that a king needs time alone in communion with God."

"But—," a priest ventured timidly.

"Go!" Richard ordered.

At that they began filing out of the shrine, leaving their tracers behind. Only the man with the crown remained.

"You, too, Buckingham!" Richard commanded.

"Oh, er, I thought I . . ."

Richard pointed at the door, and Buckingham scurried out with the others.

Jonah wasn't sure what he expected Richard to do next. But as soon as everyone else was gone, he threw himself against the stone altar, completely apart from all the ghostly tracers.

"Dear Father," he moaned. "Thou knowest—"

"God knoweth everything you've ever done!" Chip interrupted.

"Please! I am a godly man!" Richard begged.

"Do godly men kill children?" Chip sneered.

Richard slowly raised his head, his brown hair splaying out on his shoulders.

"I didn't . . . it was not I who . . ." He was almost weeping now, deep in anguish. "What wouldst Thou have me do?"

"Renounce the throne!" Chip commanded.

Richard froze. When he spoke again, he sounded like he was trying very hard to control his voice.

"Renounce it in whose favor?" he asked. "Who else could protect England so well as I? All I have done, I have done for the good of my country."

"That's what traitors always tell themselves," Chip said scornfully.

Jonah was amazed that Chip could sound so strong and authoritative. Anytime Jonah tried to sound like that, his voice cracked. In a weird way Chip was even starting to seem less see-through.

It makes sense, Jonah thought. *If someone sounds strong, your brain and your eyes start thinking that they look strong too. A nearly transparent kid just couldn't look that powerful.*

"But that is the truth!" Richard protested.

"Your version of truth," Chip scoffed. "God will judge you based on, uh, the true truth."

Jonah hoped that Richard wouldn't notice that Chip had faltered. "True truth" didn't sound authoritative. It just sounded stupid.

But Richard was staring up, right at the place where Chip was standing. A look of horror was spreading over his face.

"I see you," he whispered.

EIGHTEEN

It was hard to tell who looked more stunned now, Richard or Chip.

"I . . . I . . . ," Chip stammered, looking helplessly down at his hands.

Katherine started to bolt toward Chip, almost knocking over one of the stone statues in her haste. Jonah reached out his arm to stop her.

It's just an illusion, he wanted to assure her. *A trick of the eye. I thought I was seeing things too, just because Chip is doing such a great job. . . . Richard can't see Chip. Chip's invisible to everyone in the fifteenth century. Remember? So are we.*

But Richard's eyes followed Katherine's motion, and Jonah's.

"There are more of you?" he murmured. "Children? And in such strange garb . . ."

Now it was Jonah's turn to look down at himself. He wasn't see-through anymore. He wasn't translucent. His hands were flesh colored again, not crystal. He could even see that the *H* of the HARRIS MIDDLE SCHOOL on his sweatshirt was starting to peel off. A thread stuck out from a worn place on the knees of his blue jeans. The glow-in-the-dark green stripes on his tennis shoes gleamed.

Jonah felt paralyzed.

How could we not be invisible anymore? he wondered in agony. *We shouldn't be standing here in twenty-first-century clothes in the middle of the fifteenth century. It's too dangerous to time. And . . . to us.*

Richard half turned, like he was about to call for his guards.

But Katherine stepped forward, calmly now.

"This is what people wear in heaven," she said. "Don't you . . . I mean, do you not recognize your own nephews?" She pointed first at Chip, then Alex, who was standing among the statues as still as if he, too, were made of stone. "They were changed by, uh, what they went through. Dying so tragically . . . they were transformed. That's how it works." She lowered her voice and glared at Richard. "Not that you'll ever get to see heaven, after what you did."

Richard looked from Chip to Alex.

"My nephews?" he murmured, his voice cracking. "Haunting me?"

"And we plan to do a lot of it!" Chip threatened.

Footsteps sounded at the back of the shrine.

"Richard?" a voice called softly. "Everyone's waiting."

"Buckingham," Richard murmured. Determination gleamed in his eyes—maybe it was a determination not to believe in ghosts. "My lord," he called back to his friend. "Wouldst thou . . ."

Jonah didn't want to stick around to see exactly what he was going to say.

"Run!" Jonah cried.

"This way!" Alex agreed.

He led the others behind the statues to a small door in the wall at the back of the shrine. He yanked on it, hard, and it swung open—*Maybe they don't have door locks yet*, Jonah thought disjointedly. And then he couldn't think anything else because he was concentrating so hard on scrambling down dark, winding stairs. And he was listening so hard for footsteps behind him—footsteps of people who weren't wearing tennis shoes. He could hear only Chip's Nikes pounding on the stone steps, Katherine's panicked panting. . . .

The stairway opened into a long, dark hallway lit solely by intermittent torches propped on the wall.

"Is anyone following us?" Alex stopped to ask.

"I can't hear anything but Katherine breathing," Jonah

complained, breathing hard himself. "Hold your breath!"

She gasped and puffed out her cheeks, silently. Jonah did the same. Now he could hear only his own pulse pounding in his ears. He gave up.

"We've got to get out of here!" he said, looking around frantically.

"Not looking like this, we can't," Katherine countered.

"Calm down," Chip said. "Richard isn't going to send his guards after ghosts."

"Do you think he really believed we were ghosts?" Jonah asked.

"Well, once he saw us, he wasn't going to believe it was just his conscience speaking to him," Chip said disgustedly.

Jonah leaned back against a damp wall. Since no guards had shown up yet, he was inclined to believe that they were safe. For the moment.

"But *why* did we stop being invisible?" Alex asked. "What changed? I would have thought it'd be like Newton's first law of motion—anything in motion will remain in motion, anything at rest will remain at rest, anything invisible will remain invisible. . . . Jonah, let me see that Elucidator."

Jonah dug the rocklike object out of his pocket. Now

that it was visible too, he could make out a screen full of glowing words: RESTORATION COMPLETE. ALL SYSTEMS RETURNED TO ORIGINAL SETTINGS.

"Oh," Jonah mumbled, holding the Elucidator out to Alex so he could see the screen too. "Great timing."

Alex shook his head.

"We should study this," Alex said, peering down at the Elucidator. "See if we can find some instructions for using it . . ."

"Don't you think we should hide first?" Katherine asked. She paused. "Is someone coming?"

Jonah tilted his head back into the stairwell, but the footsteps he heard weren't coming from above. They were far down the hall, in the shadows.

"Hurry!" Jonah said, pointing in the opposite direction. "That way!"

It was ridiculous to try to combine tiptoeing and running, but that's what they all attempted as they scurried away. When they'd gone several yards, the hallway branched. Jonah peeked around the corner into the new corridor, which was equally dark and shadowed.

Er—no. Some of those shadows were men in dark robes.

"Hasten your steps!" a voice called far down the hallway. "The king wishes you monks to line his path through the church."

Jonah threw a glance over his shoulder at the men advancing behind them, then looked down the other corridor again.

"We're trapped!" Jonah whispered. "We can't walk past this hallway without those monks seeing us. And we can't go back. . . ."

Chip surprised him by dropping down to the ground and half crawling, half wriggling forward.

"Come on!" he whispered. "It's darker down on the floor. They won't see us here."

Jonah, Katherine, and Alex followed his example. None of the monks cried out, "Wait! Who's that crawling on the floor? And why are they wearing such strange clothes?"

When they were safely on the other side of the corridor, and back on their feet, Jonah leaned over and whispered in Chip's ear, "How'd you figure that out so quickly?"

Chip snorted.

"Used to do it all the time sneaking out of the nursery when I was a little boy, back at Ludlow Castle," he muttered. "There are some advantages to bad lighting."

It was so hard to understand how Chip could have memories of two completely different childhoods, separated by more than five hundred years. Jonah was just as glad that there wasn't time to think about it. They had to keep rushing forward, turning shadowy corners, advancing from one flickering pool of torchlight to the next.

And then they ran out of hallway.

Stairs lay before them, as dark and winding as the ones they'd used before.

"Should we . . . ?" Katherine asked.

Jonah could hear the footsteps approaching behind them: closer and closer and closer. . . .

"It's our only choice," he decided.

He began scrambling up the stairs tripping on the uneven stones. He fell. He got up. He fell again. He got up again.

"Speed it up!" Alex hissed from the back of the line. "Those monks are moving fast!"

At the top of the stairs Jonah spun around the corner. . . .

And slammed right into yet another monk.

NINETEEN

"Oof," the monk said.

He was a large man with a distended belly. Jonah practically bounced back.

"Sorry," Jonah muttered. He thought that maybe if he kept his head down and brushed on by as quickly as possible, the monk wouldn't notice his twenty-first-century clothes. It was almost dim enough by the stairs. The monk wouldn't be able to see the glow of the tracer moving past them, and who could tell, maybe the monk was nearsighted, maybe they hadn't invented glasses yet. . . .

Then Jonah saw that there were four other monks behind the first one, all also stopped in their tracks while their tracers glided forward. And all of them were staring, openmouthed, at Jonah.

So much for the possible benefits of myopia.

Alex, Katherine, and Chip rounded the last corner of the stairs behind Jonah and slammed to a halt, each one bumping into the next. The combined forward motion of all three of them shoved Alex against Jonah's back. Jonah lurched forward and back, trying to keep his balance.

Incredibly enough, the five monks were capable of letting their jaws drop even farther toward the floor.

For a moment everyone just stared at one another. Then Katherine stepped out past Jonah and Alex.

"Hi!" she said, as perky as a beauty contestant. "Uh, greetings! Nice to meet you!"

Five pairs of medieval monk eyes blinked incredulously.

Jonah hadn't given much thought to what his sister was wearing. It wasn't something he usually paid attention to, and he'd been a little preoccupied lately. But he noticed now. She was wearing blue jeans with some sort of weird stitching near the bottom, with shiny red thread. She had a sweatshirt knotted around her waist, and a T-shirt with sparkly beading on the front that spelled out CHEER!

She looked completely and utterly wrong next to all those black-robed monks. Jonah still knew almost nothing about the fifteenth century, but even he could tell that not a single part of her outfit would have been possible in 1483.

"Ah . . ." The big-bellied monk had to clear his throat

and try again. "Art thou a female creature or a male creature?" he asked Katherine.

Katherine giggled.

All the monks must have had younger sisters who giggled in the same way, because they seemed to relax a little bit.

"Oh, I'm a girl," Katherine said. She looked down at her clothes. "I just . . . uh . . ."

"We're travelers from a foreign land," Jonah said quickly. He felt like grinning at his own brilliance. "That's why we're dressed so strangely. We must look really freaky to you."

All five monks looked at him blankly. "Freaky" must not be a fifteenth-century word.

Jonah went on, trying to cover his mistake.

"We came to London for the coronation," he said. He had another flash of brilliance. "But we were surprised when we arrived this morning. . . ." He tried to make his voice sound innocently confused. "We had heard that the new king was a young boy, Edward the Fifth? But now we hear the crowds cheering for Richard the Third. Who is this Richard? What happened to Edward?"

The big-bellied monk narrowed his eyes.

"You are a foreigner and you dare to question our ways?" he asked.

Jonah took a step back, bumping into Chip and Alex again.

"Oh, we're not *questioning* anything," Katherine said quickly. "You can have whoever you want as king."

The monks continued to look at her as if she'd suddenly appeared from Mars. Jonah realized they wouldn't take anything she said seriously.

"It's just . . . it's just . . . ," he began. But he couldn't think of anything else to say.

Alex shoved Jonah aside.

"We're just attempting to comprehend your ways," he said, holding his hands out in front of him, like someone trying to show he wasn't carrying any weapons. "'Tis humility to know one's own ignorance, is it not? 'The fool doth think he is wise, but the wise man knows himself to be a fool.'"

"So true," one of the monks murmured. "So true."

"Well, you know, that's a quote from Shakesp . . ." A panicked look spread over Alex's face. "Uh, never mind," he muttered.

Jonah guessed that meant Shakespeare wasn't famous yet. Maybe he hadn't even been born.

The oldest-looking monk—a bald man with bushy eyebrows—stepped forward.

"I'll give you some advice, since you appear to be

innocent fools," he said. "It's never wise to question the circumstances of a king's ascension whilst he yet sits on the throne. A short memory can be a gift."

Now, what did that mean? Jonah really needed a better translator. *"Ascension" means . . . what? "Rising"? What's that got to do with kings? Oh. Rising to become king?*

"But Edward the Fifth *was* king," Chip said in a hard, unyielding voice. "What happened to Edward the Fifth? Does he not yet live?"

Okay, so now I need a translator for Chip, too, Jonah thought. *"Does he not yet live?" would be the same as . . . uh, let's see . . . "Isn't he still alive?"*

The old monk glanced over his shoulder, as if afraid of being overheard.

"Dead or alive, it matters not," he said softly. "He is king no more."

"'It matters not'? 'It matters not'?" Chip repeated. His face was so red suddenly he looked like he might explode. "How can it not matter if a king is alive or dead?"

One of the younger monks let out a snort of laughter.

"That's like one of those riddles they ask us," he said in an overly loud bumpkin's voice. "Even I know the answer to that one. Being alive or dead don't matter if he's not going to be king, neither way." He chuckled again, at the apparently stunning possibility that he might be wiser than the strangely dressed "foreigners." Then he stopped and looked back anxiously at the older monk. "Of course, his soul would be in heaven if he was dead."

One of the other monks, a tall, thin man with ears that stuck out like jug handles, leaned in conspiratorially.

"See, what happened was, they found out the boy's parents hadn't even been married," he said, whispering gleefully, like this was the juiciest gossip he'd ever heard.

"They were too!" Chip retorted instantly. He sprang forward, his hands balled up into fists, like he intended to start throwing punches at the monks. Jonah grabbed his arms, trying to hold him back.

"How would you know, if you are foreigners who only arrived this morning?" the old monk asked, pursing his lips thoughtfully.

"It's . . . it's what we heard," Jonah said, struggling with Chip.

Katherine began tugging on Chip's arm too, and that helped some. Jonah wished that Alex would help as well, but he was just standing there muttering, "Not married? Not married?"

"Well," the jug-eared monk said, lowering his voice again. "I don't know when you heard that, but Dr. Ralph Shaw preached on June twenty-second, two whole weeks ago, that Edward the Fourth was pre-contracted with another woman before he married Elizabeth Woodville. So none of their children are legitimate. So of course Edward the Fifth couldn't inherit the throne."

Chip stopped struggling. His face instantly went from furious red to ghostly pale.

"People heard this?" he whispered. "People believe this?"

Katherine stopped tugging on Chip's arm and began patting it comfortingly.

"That's crazy," she said. "Even if, uh, Edward's father thought about marrying someone else first, that shouldn't change anything about who he ended up marrying. Or about Edward being king."

The old monk frowned at Katherine.

"I don't know what it's like where you're from," he said in a tone that implied that she must be from someplace awful. "But here marriage is a sacred rite. Do you take the sacraments lightly? Do you mock the sanctity of holy matrimony?" His voice was getting louder and louder, more enraged. "Are you even Christian?"

How had it come to this? Jonah wondered. One minute they were listening to gossip about people getting engaged and married, and now this old monk was towering over them, glaring, shaking his finger at them.

"I'll have you know I—," Katherine began indignantly.

She was standing on her tiptoes, like she was ready to face off with the old monk, nose to nose, glaring eye to glaring eye.

"Womenfolk," Alex interrupted her, shaking his head and rolling his eyes. He gripped her arm warningly. "You know how their feeble minds fail to grasp the subtleties of proper doctrine. She's a little weak minded anyway, as you can tell from her choice of apparel."

Now Katherine's jaw dropped. Her eyes bugged out. She seemed stunned beyond words.

"Indeed," the old monk agreed, sounding calmer now.

"Perhaps we should remove her from the cathedral during this sacred ceremony," Alex said. "We apologize for any disruption we have caused."

Still clutching Katherine's arm, he bowed low and backed away, off to the side.

Jonah decided it was probably wise to follow. He grabbed Chip's arm, just in case Chip was prepared to start arguing where Katherine had left off. But Chip came along dazedly.

Ahead of them Katherine struggled with Alex as he pulled her into the shadows.

"Come on," Alex was murmuring. "Argue with me later. It isn't safe here. . . ."

Jonah picked up his pace.

He threw a quick glance over his shoulder, to see if any of the monks were following them, but they'd already been engulfed by a whole new crowd of monks, coming up the same stairway that Jonah and the others had used. The man whose voice Jonah had heard before was calling out, "Move along! We are supposed to be taking our positions. . . ."

Alex was almost running now that he was out of sight of the monks. In the near darkness Jonah was having trouble keeping track of him.

"Wait for us!" Jonah hissed. "Where are you going, anyway?"

"I know this part of the cathedral," Alex whispered back. "I just figured out where we are. I used to play here sometimes—I know a crypt where we can hide until the crowds clear out."

A crypt. Great. That sounded like a wonderful place to go.

TWENTY

The crypt turned out to be just a dark space with pillars in the bowels of the church. Jonah couldn't see any bones or dead bodies lying around, like he'd half expected. The dead bodies were probably tucked away behind the stone tablets on the walls, but Jonah was not going to ask about that.

He couldn't have gotten a word in edgewise anyway. Katherine, freed from the need to be careful around the monks, was all but screaming at Alex.

"How dare you!" she spit out. "Saying I'm feebleminded? Saying it's because I'm 'womenfolk'? 'Womenfolk'—bleh! Just the word is sexist!"

"Katherine, calm down," Alex said, sounding amazingly calm himself for someone getting his ears blistered. "I don't think you're feebleminded. I don't think girls in general are feebleminded. That was just the only thing I could think of to say to keep them from stringing us all up as heretics. I knew that's what those monks believed, anyway, that females are stupid."

"And you think that makes it all right?" Katherine complained. "It's okay to perpetuate a stereotype if the people you're perpetuating it to are already idiots?"

Whoa—"perpetuate a stereotype"?—Katherine really was mad.

"I'm sorry, okay?" Alex said pleadingly. "It's not my fault 1483 wasn't a great time to be female. Those monks don't really think of girls as human beings, exactly. Men in 1483 think of women more as just . . . uh . . ." His voice trailed off.

"What?" Katherine demanded.

"Uh . . . breeding stock," Alex said apologetically.

Katherine kicked one of the tablets in the wall.

"I am *so* getting out of here," she said. "I am not spending my whole life in this godforsaken time. And don't any of you correct me! This *is* a godforsaken time if women are just treated like *breeding stock.*"

She kicked the wall again.

"It's not really such a great time to be a male, either," Chip said weakly. "Remember? Somebody tried to murder me and Alex last night. My own uncle cheated me out of my crown. And it sounds like the whole country's letting him get away with it."

Dimly, distantly from up above, they could hear the cheers of the huge crowd. Either Richard III had just had the crown placed on his head, or he'd just walked out in front of his subjects, or . . .

It didn't really matter. Either way Chip wasn't king anymore.

Chip kicked the wall just as angrily as Katherine had.

"I still don't understand," Jonah admitted. "What's that whole story about your father being 'pre-contracted' to someone else before he got married? What's that got to do with anything? Who cares?"

"It's just a lie," Chip said bitterly. "An excuse."

"Well," Alex said. "Maybe . . . knowing our father . . . maybe he was engaged to someone else before he married our mother."

"So what?" Katherine said, still sounding angry. "Maybe the woman dumped him. Don't tell me women aren't allowed to do that in the fifteenth century!"

Even in the dim light of the crypt Jonah could tell that Alex was frowning.

"Um . . . kind of not," Alex said. "For someone who's the king of England, it's not like getting married is a romantic thing. It's strategic, all about uniting powerful families, getting the rights to land and titles. Except our father, Edward the Fourth, he did have this thing about falling for women. And he might have promised to marry someone that he never married. And making that promise, it would be legally binding."

"So when he married our mother, it would be like bigamy," Chip said gloomily. "Not a legal marriage. So we wouldn't be legal, legitimate offspring of the king. So Alex and me—neither one of us could inherit the right to be king."

Jonah thought about that. Being adopted, he'd always kind of figured that his birth parents weren't married when he was born. *He* didn't care. It wasn't like it was his fault.

But in 1483, people must have cared about that kind of thing a lot, if it determined who became king.

"So if everybody was saying that you weren't king after all, why'd they bother throwing you out the window?" Jonah asked.

"Just because Richard can convince everyone that I'm not the king now, that doesn't mean that he can keep them convinced," Chip said. "Any time he does something people don't like, they can start plotting to get rid of him. As long as I'm alive, they could say, 'Oops, we were wrong. Edward's parents really were married after all. He's the *real* king! Let's get rid of that Richard guy!'"

Jonah thought about this. Being king didn't sound so great, really. It sounded like you'd spend your whole time worrying that someone was going to knock you off.

"Ooooh," Katherine said. "It's just like fifth grade."

"What?" Jonah said.

"Remember?" Katherine said. "Last year when Kelly Todd was kind of the queen of all the fifth-grade girls? And then Courtney LaRosa moved in from California, and everyone thought she was really cool, being from California and all. But that wasn't enough for her, and she had to make sure that everyone started hating Kelly Todd too, so it wouldn't be like Kelly ever got back her power. And then—"

"Katherine! The royal family in England is not like a bunch of stupid fifth-grade girls!" Jonah said.

"But it is!" Katherine said. She sounded excited now. "See, Chip, this is what ended up working for Kelly, what you ought to do about your uncle. You should—"

"He shouldn't be trying to get the throne back," Jonah said sternly. "We're supposed to be making everyone think that he's dead. Remember?"

"Oh. Yeah," Katherine said.

They all fell silent for a moment. Jonah could hear the cheers from up above again.

"We must have convinced Richard that Alex and I are

dead," Chip said. "Since he didn't chase after us. Do you think that's good enough?"

"Our mother needs to think that too," Alex said forlornly.

It was funny how Alex could sound so sure of himself, so expert when it came to talking about scientific facts or details about 1483. But whenever he talked about his mother, the queen, he sounded like a little boy again.

"So we figure out how to turn invisible again," Jonah said. "We go haunt your mom. Do you think that will fix time enough? Do you think after that we can just go home?"

To his embarrassment, his voice broke on the word "home." He wasn't going to be like Katherine. He wasn't going to think about how much nicer it would be to go back to a time when people didn't consider you heretics just because you dressed a little funny. He wasn't even going to think about how nice it'd be to have a thick, juicy twenty-first-century cheeseburger right about now.

But when Alex said, "Why don't we all look at the Elucidator now?" Jonah had it out of his pocket instantly.

TWENTY-ONE

They decided to wait until dark to leave the crypt. It seemed safer that way, even though Alex figured out how to make them all invisible again.

Oddly, that was just about all they could figure out about the Elucidator. None of them could get the Elucidator to show the long list of choices they'd seen before. No matter how much they poked, prodded, pressed, rubbed, turned, tossed, or even shouted at it, the Elucidator's screen showed only one option: INVISIBILITY? Y/N.

"Maybe it caught a computer virus, going through time?" Alex suggested, his voice thick with frustration.

"Or maybe it's still broken from Chip throwing it at the ground," Katherine said.

"It *said* the restoration was complete," Chip argued.

"At least the invisibility works," Jonah said, trying to

calm everyone down. He amused himself by pressing the Y, then the spot on the screen where the N had been, when it was visible. Then Y again. . . . He could *feel* himself turning invisible, then visible, then invisible.

"Stop that!" Katherine said. "Now you're going to break it!" She swallowed hard. "And . . . turning invisible, going back and forth—that makes me feel sick."

"Really?" Jonah asked. He resisted the urge to hit N again, just to show her that he could.

"Timesickness, remember?" Katherine said. It was dark enough in the crypt that Jonah couldn't be entirely sure, but he thought he saw her stick out her tongue at him. She went on in a scolding tone, "And what if there's a limit to the number of times we can become invisible? What if you run down the batteries—or whatever that runs on— and then it doesn't work when we need it to?"

"Stupid thing doesn't work very well anyhow," Alex muttered, taking the Elucidator from Jonah, turning it upside down, and shaking it. He turned it over once more—the screen still said, INVISIBILITY? Y/N.

"Maybe you're just doing it wrong," Chip said, jerking the Elucidator away. "Let me try."

Pizza, Jonah thought. *If we just had a big pizza in front of us, this wouldn't seem like such a big problem. Or a big bowl of spaghetti. Or lasagna.*

Maybe his true identity, whatever it was, had something to do with Italy, since all he could think about was Italian food?

Alex was yanking the Elucidator back away from Chip.

"Oh, no," he said. "You'll just end up throwing it on the floor again."

"Stop it!" Katherine said. "Stop fighting! If we've got any hope of getting out of this place, we'll all have to work together."

"Fighting? Who's fighting?" Chip said.

"Squabbling, then," Katherine said. "You know what I mean."

"We're in the fifteenth century. In 1483 even squabbling involves bows and arrows or giant spears," Chip said harshly.

"Or lances," Alex said.

"Swords," Chip said.

"Battering rams," Alex said.

"You're not making me feel any better about the fifteenth century," Katherine said.

Alex stopped shaking the Elucidator for a moment.

"The funny thing is, I remember being really happy here," he said softly.

"Me too," Chip said. "Everybody at Ludlow Castle was always pretty nice to me."

"Well, *duh*," Jonah said. "They knew you were going to be their king."

"No," Chip said, shaking his head. "It wasn't just that. It was . . . we all belonged. We all had a place." His voice got husky. "This probably sounds stupid, but I wanted to make my family proud of me. It's not like in the twenty-first century, when Mom and Dad . . . uh . . . well, you know. It always seemed like they had their own lives that had nothing to do with me. And my life had nothing to do with them."

Jonah didn't know Chip's parents very well. But he knew that they hadn't even bothered telling Chip that he was adopted until he guessed it.

"Chip," Jonah said. "Nobody in the twenty-first century ever tried to *murder* you."

"JB did, by sending me back in time," Chip said.

"JB isn't from the twenty-first century," Jonah said. "He's from the future."

"What's it matter?" Alex asked, poking uselessly at the Elucidator again. "It's not like we have any control over anything."

"We *are* going to convince the queen that you two are dead," Katherine said stubbornly. "And then we're going home."

Home, Jonah thought longingly. He refused to think

about how hard it might be to get there.

"Do you suppose it's dark outside yet?" he asked.

"I'll go check," Alex said.

"No. We go together," Katherine insisted.

Nobody argued with her.

It was barely dusk when they poked their invisible heads out of a side door of the cathedral, but they agreed that that was dark enough. The crowd from the coronation had melted away.

"I bet they're all feasting now," Chip said bitterly. "Feasting on the foods that were ordered for *my* coronation."

Jonah refused to think about food.

Go haunt the queen, he told himself. *Then go home.* The words seemed more like a prayer than a plan. *Please let it work that way. Please let it be that easy.*

"Um," he said, a new thought occurring to him. "The queen's not at some castle five days away, is she?"

"Nope," Alex said. "She's right in there."

He pointed at a squarish stone building that looked more like a fortress than a castle. It was practically within spitting distance of the cathedral door.

"She was there the whole time the coronation was going on?" Katherine asked, horrified. "Within earshot? When everyone was shouting . . . did King Richard know that?"

"Oh, yeah," Alex said grimly. "He knew."

"But—why?" Katherine asked. "Why wouldn't she go somewhere else? For the day, anyway . . ."

"Because she's in sanctuary," Chip said.

"I thought the coronation was in the sanctuary," Jonah said.

"No, no," Alex said. "Not that kind of sanctuary. She's in *political* sanctuary. After Gloucester—Richard—had her brother arrested and took control, she moved in there, where she'd be safe. Where he couldn't arrest her."

"But—she's his own sister-in-law," Jonah objected. "Right?"

"So?" Chip said.

Jonah decided he didn't like Chip's fifteenth-century family any better than he liked Chip's twenty-first-century parents.

"That doesn't make sense," Katherine objected. "Why would staying in that building make any difference if someone wanted to arrest her?"

"Because it's sacred ground," Chip said. "Church property. Even a king has to bow to church authority."

Jonah was about to say, "What about the separation of church and state?" Then he realized that that would sound really, really stupid. This wasn't America. This wasn't the twenty-first century.

"I was staying there with her," Alex said softly. "Until Gloucester came and said he wanted me to be with Chip for Chip's coronation."

"So he tricked her into letting you go?" Jonah asked.

Alex shook his head slowly.

"No," he said. "She's really smart. She knew what she was doing. That's why I was sure she had a plan to rescue us. Me and Chip both."

"Well, let's go pay her a visit," Katherine said grimly.

They tiptoed across a stone path, though there was no one nearby to hear them if any of their shoes squeaked. They rounded the corner of the stone fortress and discovered two guards in front of the only door.

"Now, how are we going to get past them?" Jonah muttered.

"I have an idea," Alex said.

He tiptoed close to the guards, but Jonah couldn't really tell what he did after that. He seemed to be lifting his arms over the guards' shoulders. Was he dropping something on them? What good would that do?

Moments later a cluster of large black crows swooped down from a nearby tree and began to peck at the guards.

"Begone!" the guards screamed. "Shoo!"

The birds flapped their wings in the guards' faces; the

guards separated from their tracers to wave their arms and spin around, trying to shove the birds away.

"Now!" Alex whispered. "Hurry!"

While the guards were fighting with the crows, Alex shoved in through the door. Jonah walked right behind him, with Chip and Katherine on his heels.

Once the door creaked shut, they found themselves in a small alcove outside a dark chapel.

"How did you know that would work?" Jonah asked.

"Think about it," Alex said. "I was stuck in this building with my mother and sisters for a month and a half. Don't you think I had to figure out a way to get in and out?"

"But what did you put on the guards?"

"Bread crumbs," Alex said, grinning triumphantly.

Jonah thought about asking why Alex was carrying bread crumbs around in his pockets, but that reminded him of food, which he really shouldn't be thinking about, because it made him too hungry. He wished he'd thought to bring some of the bread crumbs in his own pocket. He wouldn't have wasted it on birds.

"Come on," Alex said. "Our mother's chambers are upstairs."

They tiptoed up a dark, winding staircase—were all the stairways in the fifteenth century like that? Jonah wondered. He thought about what it would be like to be trapped in this dreary building for a month and a half.

"No TV, huh?" he whispered to Alex. "No video games?"

"Are you kidding?" Alex whispered back. "We just got the printing press in England six or seven years ago. We barely have books!"

They reached the top of the stairs and tiptoed into a sparsely furnished room. A blond woman in an elegant black dress and five blond girls—also in black—were all leaning against a bed, their faces buried in the comforter.

All of them were sobbing.

"Uh, Chip?" Jonah whispered. "If that's your mom and sisters, I think they already know you're supposedly dead."

The sobbing was especially hard to watch and listen to because Jonah could see the tracers of the queen and her daughters, the way they would have been if nobody had interfered with time. The tracer queen was seated regally on the bed, silently smiling, laughing, and talking. The tracers of the five girls, who all looked so much like Chip and Alex, were seated beside their mother. One of them flipped a cascade of blond curls over her shoulder and giggled silently.

Wait a minute, Jonah thought. *The tracer queen and princesses shouldn't look so happy. The tracers should be the ones crying.*

Wouldn't they be certain that Chip and Alex are dead? Shouldn't the queen and princesses now, after the tampering, still have some hope that Chip and Alex are okay?

He was confusing himself, getting mixed up between how things should be with and without the tampering.

I'd think a lot more clearly if I had some pizza or spaghetti or lasagna in my stomach, he thought grumpily.

Katherine was tapping him on the shoulder, very annoyingly.

"L-l-look," she stammered, pointing to the opposite side of the room from the sobbing queen and princesses and their eerily happy tracers.

Jonah turned, ready to tell Katherine not to bug him when he was hungry.

But turning, he saw what Katherine was pointing at.

Two chairs sat on the opposite side of the room from the bed. And two more glowing tracers sat in the chairs, laughing just as uproariously as the tracers of the princesses and queen.

One of the tracers was Alex's. The other was Chip's.

Even in the original version of time the prince and the former king had survived.

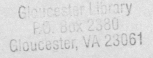

TWENTY-TWO

"What?" Jonah exploded, loudly enough that the queen stopped sobbing for a moment, lifted her head, and looked around, a mystified expression on her face. Then, seeing nothing, she buried her face in the bedding again and sobbed even harder.

Jonah pushed Katherine back out into the hall. Chip and Alex had just turned and caught their first glimpse of the tracer boys, and now they were leaning toward the tracers, as if they were being pulled in that direction.

"Oh, no," Jonah muttered. "Don't even think about it."

He grabbed the back of Chip's sweatshirt and the back of Alex's T-shirt and tugged. It took a lot of effort, but eventually he had them back out in the hallway too. He forced them down toward the ground.

"We've got to talk," he whispered. "How can this be?"

"They didn't die," Katherine murmured. "They never died. We were wrong all along."

"But how did they survive?" Jonah asked. "That was, like, six stories down to the ground."

"No, it wasn't," Chip said. "Don't you remember, we only climbed down one or two sets of stairs?"

Jonah thought about this. Chip was right—there hadn't been that many stairs when they were leaving the Tower of London.

"But I looked out the window," Jonah said. "The ground looked a mile away."

"Could that be because of the timesickness?" Katherine asked. "Messing us up? When I jumped into the river to swim to the barge, I thought I was going to have to swim forever. But then it only took three or four strokes."

Through raw sewage, Jonah wanted to add, but he restrained himself.

Were his perceptions so badly off too? He remembered how, when Chip was running toward Richard III's procession, Jonah had managed to tackle his friend even when he was sure Chip was too far away. He thought about how high and echoey the ceilings had seemed in the tower room, how far he'd had to run to hide behind the tapestry. . . .

"But . . . but . . . Chip and Alex never had timesickness,"

Jonah protested, still not convinced. "They saw how far away the ground was."

"I never looked out the window," Chip said.

"And I just looked *up*, toward the stars," Alex said.

Both of them spoke in dreamy, distracted tones. Both of them were looking back over their shoulders, gazing longingly toward the tracers.

It's like mind control, Jonah thought. *Any time they're near their tracers.*

Did that explain why both Chip and Alex said they felt strange as soon as they got close to Westminster Abbey? Maybe the tracers had been moving right past them, just out of sight, heading toward their reunion with their mother. . . .

Katherine was focused on a more immediate problem.

"But what do we do now?" she asked. "This changes everything!"

Chip and Alex started to stand up, edging toward their tracers once more.

"No, no, you can't do that!" Jonah said. "We've got to figure this out. Logically."

"What's to figure?" Alex asked. "We can stop our family's sorrow. We can bring joy to our mother's heart."

He gestured toward the queen and princesses, who were, indeed, sobbing as though their hearts were broken.

"But they'll see you change!" Katherine objected. "It'll look like you just appear out of nowhere. . . ."

"They're not looking," Chip said. "That's why we've got to meld with our tracers now, while they're all crying on the bed."

"No, wait!" Jonah called out.

It was too late. Chip and Alex broke away from Jonah's grasp. In four quick strides they were beside their own tracers.

"It's okay!" Katherine hissed in Jonah's ear. "They're invisible, remember? They'll just stay invisible! They've just got to find that . . . out. . . ."

Her voice trailed off because she was wrong. As soon as Chip and Alex sat down on the chairs, occupying the same space as their tracers, their forms sprang back into living color.

"It must be like multiplying negative numbers," Jonah muttered. "Two negatives make a positive. So, invisible tracer, invisible time traveler—fully visible boy."

"*What* are you talking about?" Katherine demanded.

"Never mind," Jonah mumbled.

Chip pulled away from his tracer long enough to grin broadly at Alex. Alex grinned back. And then he called out in a high, sweet, pure voice that sounded a lot younger than his usual voice, "Mother?"

The sobbing queen on the bed—and all five of the sobbing princesses—jerked to attention and whirled around.

"Oh, no, their clothes!" Katherine moaned. "They look all wrong!"

But the queen and the princesses didn't seem to notice that Chip and Alex were a strange blend of fifteenth century and twenty-first century. *They must not be able to see the jeans and the Nikes and the short hair,* Jonah thought. *Maybe just time travelers can see that. The serving girl back at the Tower of London didn't notice anything weird either. . . .*

And then Jonah forgot to wonder about clothes or hair or anything else. The queen let out a shriek of pure joy and cried out, "My sons! Oh, my sons! I thought you were lost to me forever!"

She sprang up and dashed across the room, burying both boys in a hug. The princesses raced after her, their arms outstretched. They grabbed their brothers too. They were all so overjoyed that their laughing, giggling tracers back on the bed seemed downright solemn by comparison.

"But how did you get here?" the queen asked when Chip and Alex finally pulled back from the embrace. "My faithful servants said something went wrong with our plan, and you vanished. I thought we'd been betrayed, and you'd been carried away by the enemy. . . ."

"We thought you were surely dead," the tallest princess added.

"We hid and came here on our own," Chip said. "We distracted the guards and tiptoed up the stairs. We . . . we knew you had a plan, but we weren't sure who we could trust."

The queen gave a most unladylike snort.

"Is not that the story of our time?" she asked, and a hint of sadness crept into her voice. "Whom do we have left to trust?"

"Lord Rivers will come to us now, will he not?" Chip asked. "We can mount a campaign against Gloucester. We will defeat him."

But the queen was peering over Chip's head now. The sadness had taken over her face again.

"You do not know," she murmured.

"Know what?" Alex asked.

"We know that Gloucester had himself crowned king," Chip said in a hard voice. "We know that he is spreading slander about . . . about . . ."

The queen waved this news away, as though it was inconsequential. Or as if she had much worse problems to worry about.

"He had Rivers beheaded," she said in a numb voice. "Rivers, and Grey, and Vaughan . . . he had Hastings executed too, because he said he was plotting against him."

Jonah had no idea who any of those people were, except the Rivers guy—wasn't he Chip's uncle? The one on his mother's side that Chip liked? As soon as the queen said "beheaded," Chip slumped in his chair and clutched his face in shock and horror.

"No . . . ," he moaned.

Beside him, Alex was shaking his head in disbelief. With each name the queen recited, both boys gasped. Finally Chip dropped his hands from his face and peered up at his mother.

"Has he left us no one?" he whispered.

"He has left us ourselves," the queen said with great dignity. "My daughters. My sons. Myself."

Chip's face showed what he thought of princesses and a queen as their only allies. Jonah hoped Katherine didn't notice.

"Some of this conversation . . . it must have partly been what they were talking about anyway," Katherine whispered.

Jonah noticed that the tracers on the bed had stopped laughing and giggling and rolling about. The queen's tracer had the same expression of sorrowful nobility as the queen herself.

"But we shall prevail," the queen said, her head held high. "We are in the right."

Like an echo, the tracer queen on the bed mouthed the same words. The tracer princesses sat like statues beside her.

"I missed you, Mother," Alex said, throwing his arms around his mother's waist. "I missed how you always know the right thing to do."

Alex couldn't have seen his mother's expression because he had his face buried in her skirt. But Jonah saw how the corners of her mouth trembled, how the pain and fear settled deep in her eyes.

"I can't watch this," Katherine murmured. "It's like watching Holocaust movies, where you know everyone's going to die."

She pulled Jonah away from the doorway into the room so he couldn't see either.

Jonah was busy trying to work something out in his head.

"They're all going to die anyhow," he said. "They lived more than five hundred years before we were born." He remembered that he actually had no idea what time period he'd been born in. "Before you were born, anyway."

"But can't you feel it? In that room? The way it seems like really, really bad things are going to happen?" Katherine asked.

Jonah could. *Foreboding*, he wanted to tell Katherine. *That's what it's called. What we feel.* But what good did it do just to know the right word? Action was what counted.

"We promised we'd save Chip and Alex," Jonah muttered. "We promised."

"Why aren't we saving the princesses, too?" Katherine asked. "Why didn't Gary and Hodge kidnap them when they kidnapped Chip and Alex? Just because they're girls, not boys?"

Jonah was getting sick of Katherine thinking everyone was prejudiced against girls.

"Gary and Hodge kidnapped lots of endangered girls from history," Jonah argued. "Remember? There were about as many girls as boys in the cave that day. Maybe . . . maybe the princesses aren't in any danger. Maybe it's just Chip and Alex."

Katherine clenched her fists.

"This is driving me crazy, not knowing what's going to happen. What's *supposed* to happen," she said.

"But this is no different from regular life," Jonah said. "When have you ever known what's going to happen in the future?"

Katherine glared at him.

"You know what I mean," she said. "I'm used to the future being the future, not the past being the future. Or—you know. It's weird that the future already happened once, but we don't know what it was. Er—will be." She was getting so tangled up in verb tenses that she stopped trying.

She gulped. "How can we save Chip and Alex if we don't know what we're supposed to be saving them from?"

Especially when we thought we'd already saved them, Jonah thought dizzily. His stomach churned. What if they'd "haunted" the queen before they noticed Chip's and Alex's tracers? What if they'd managed to convince her that her sons were dead? What if King Richard III did something differently because he'd seen the boys' "ghosts" at the Westminster shrine? How come it seemed like everything they did messed up time?

"Maybe JB was right," Jonah muttered. "Maybe it is dangerous for us to be here."

"JB—oh!" Katherine suddenly sat up straight, practically banging her head on the wall. "He didn't want Chip and Alex dead on the ground after all! He didn't betray us!"

Jonah stared at her. She was right. They'd been so upset thinking that JB wanted Chip and Alex dead that they hadn't given JB a chance to explain. Chip had cut him off and kicked the Elucidator across the room. And then they'd muted it.

Jonah dug in his pocket for the Elucidator. He expected it to be completely invisible again or, at best, still stuck on the words INVISIBILITY? Y/N. But it held a full sentence now, in tiny, barely glowing type:

WILL YOU LISTEN TO ME NOW?

TWENTY-THREE

Jonah immediately felt annoyed for all those hours they'd spent trying to get the Elucidator to say something besides INVISIBILITY? Y/N. When JB's question faded into another one—SAFE FOR ME TO TALK OUT LOUD? Y/N— Jonah hit the Y with an angry stab of his fingernail.

"Thanks a lot," he muttered. "So you could have communicated with us all along? You can do anything you want through the Elucidator?"

"Not while you had the Elucidator muted, during the system restore," JB's voice came softly out of the mostly transparent "rock" in Jonah's mostly transparent hand. "You cut off all contact with the outside world."

Jonah suppressed a shiver at that.

"But ever since the Elucidator reset, back at the cathedral— you could have talked to us then?" Katherine demanded.

"Did you want me to?" JB asked.

Jonah decided to leave that question alone.

"So talk now," he said brusquely. "Tell us everything." The word "everything" came out a little mockingly. Jonah was proud that he could make it sound like he didn't really care whether JB talked to them or not.

"It's hard with you right there, near the royal family," JB's voice was barely a whisper. "Will you give me permission to pull you out of time for a little bit?"

Jonah exchanged glances with his sister.

"*All* of us?" Katherine asked, peeking back toward the room where Chip and Alex were still talking to the queen.

Even across the centuries Jonah could hear JB's frustrated sigh.

"I can't pull Chip and Alex out right now," JB said. "It'd be too . . . complicated. And they're not really Chip and Alex at the moment. They're Edward and Richard, two very critical players in history."

"You promised we could try to save them!" Katherine's voice rose a little too high. "Was that all a lie? Is it even possible?"

"It's possible, it's possible," JB said soothingly. "The fact that you're there proves I'm giving you a chance."

"But you want to pull us out now," Katherine said.

"Some chance." She grimaced. "Sure, Chip and Alex weren't killed by being thrown out the window—but what happens when King Richard finds out where they are now?"

Jonah hadn't thought that far ahead.

"I promise you," JB said, his voice cracking with seeming earnestness. "Nothing bad will happen to Chip and Alex while you're away." A hint of steeliness entered his voice. "Now, *please*, before someone hears you—can I pull you out of time?"

Jonah raised an eyebrow at his sister. She frowned back at him.

Jonah wasn't quite sure what thoughts were tumbling through his sister's head, but his were a frantic tangle. *Should we say just one of us can go, and the other one stays here to watch out for Chip and Alex? No—that would be too awful, not knowing what the other one was dealing with. Or what was happening with Chip and Alex. So should we refuse and never know anything? That's not any good either. If JB's really sure Chip and Alex would be all right without us for a while . . .*

Jonah thought of something else.

"Wait a minute," he said. "How can you promise they'll be safe? I thought we weren't allowed to know the 'future.'" He said "future" sarcastically, just to let JB know that he and Katherine weren't nervous at all.

Katherine was biting her lip now. Jonah began tugging on the ragged edge of his left thumbnail.

"You can know more now," JB said. "Now that you're not with Chip and Alex."

"We're still with them!" Jonah said.

"They're not within earshot," JB said with exaggerated patience.

Jonah wanted to pull Katherine over to the side and confer with her, out of JB's earshot. But if JB could make the Elucidator work again from the distance of centuries away, he could probably hear anything they said, no matter where they were.

Actually, if he wanted to, he could probably just yank them out of time, like he'd done with the Taser. Why wasn't he doing that? Why was he asking permission? Somehow the fact that JB had given them a choice made Jonah more inclined to trust him. But what if JB knew that and was just asking in order to trick them?

Jonah shook his head, trying to clear it.

"I'm going to ask Chip and Alex what they think," he said firmly. "Whether it's okay with them if we leave for a while."

"You don't have to do that," JB said. "Really, that's not the best—"

And then he broke off because Jonah shoved the Elucidator in his pocket and stood up.

"This should be quick," he told Katherine with a confidence he didn't feel. Katherine stared up at him, wide eyed.

"I'm coming with you," she said.

They tiptoed silently back into the royal family's room. This was hard to do, since the floor was covered with mats of woven rushes that rustled easily. But Chip and Alex didn't seem to see or hear them approaching.

Chip and Alex were eating now, scooping up handfuls of berries and grains—maybe the fifteenth-century version of granola. Jonah had never been a granola fan, but it sounded almost as good as pizza right now. Had Chip or Alex thought about how Jonah and Katherine might be starving too? Were they making any attempt to save some food to give to Jonah and Katherine later, when the queen and princesses weren't watching?

The answer to that, clearly, was no. The boys were tossing strawberries in the air and catching them in their mouths, very dramatically. There was no way to hide food doing that. It was almost as if they were trying to show off how they had food and Jonah and Katherine didn't.

Jonah stopped a few inches from Chip's ear.

"Chip, listen," he whispered quickly. He hoped he could say everything he needed to say before an errant strawberry landed on his head and appeared to bounce off empty air. "Find some excuse for you and Alex to get away from everyone for a few minutes. Say you have to go to the bathroom or something."

Chip turned his head toward Jonah, but his blue eyes focused on a point far past Jonah. Chip caught a berry in his mouth and turned his head back in the other direction. He seemed every bit as oblivious as the serving girl and the men with torches back at the Tower of London. He, too, seemed to be looking right through Jonah.

Jonah felt his heart clutch with fear.

"Chip? Can you hear me?" Jonah whispered. "Do something to show you know I'm here. Blink three times, or . . . or . . ."

Chip didn't blink.

"You're just acting, right?" Jonah pleaded. "Because the queen and the princesses are watching you? That's okay, I understand, but . . ."

It was too agonizing to just stand there waiting for Chip to react. Jonah grabbed Chip's arm. Though Jonah could see Chip's red sweatshirt faintly, along with his tracer's fifteenth-century clothes, all Jonah could feel was stiff velvet. Jonah tightened his grip.

Chip didn't seem to notice.

"Katherine, please, help," Jonah whispered urgently.

Katherine grabbed Chip's other arm. Jonah hadn't

exactly told her what he wanted her to do, but she began tugging, as if she was determined to separate Chip from his tracer. Jonah forgot about the queen and the princesses sitting on the other side of the room. He began yanking on Chip too.

And then suddenly Jonah's hands held nothing but air.

TWENTY-FOUR

Chip was gone. So was Alex. So were their chairs. So were the woven rushes on the floor. So were the stone walls. Jonah looked around to see if Katherine had disappeared too, but seeing required light, and in a split second all of that had vanished too.

But a second later—a second or an eternity, who could say?—Jonah felt bathed in light. He wasn't conscious of moving, but somehow he was sitting down now, his legs dangling from an oddly contoured chair, his back cushioned by soft pillows. He turned his head, and Katherine was there in another chair beside him. He turned his head back because he'd missed something.

JB was standing in front of them.

Jonah had gotten so used to JB as a disembodied voice coming from a rock that he had to blink a few times to make sure that it really was him. Same dark hair flopping over his forehead. Same intelligent green eyes and handsome face that had made Katherine call him "cute janitor boy"—back when they thought he was only a janitor for the FBI. Same nondescript clothes he'd been wearing the last time they'd seen him. Vaguely Jonah wondered if regular time travelers like JB had special clothes that blended in no matter what century they were in.

"You pulled us out of time, didn't you?" Katherine accused, blinking in the unexpected glare. "Weren't you waiting for us to give you permission?"

"I don't need your permission if you're caught breaking a time law," JB said, a slight smirk traveling across his face. "Trying to separate Chip from his tracer right in front of his mother and sisters—that's a clear violation of Time Code 6843J6. I was just waiting for you to do something like that."

The smirk turned into a cocky grin.

"We did practically the same thing in front of the murderers at the Tower of London last night," Jonah said. "Er—last night in 1483." They could not possibly be in 1483 anymore. The lights were too bright, the room too clean and angular and antiseptic. "Why didn't you pull us out of time then?"

"That wasn't a violation because you were in the dark

then, and the so-called murderers didn't notice anything different," JB said. "And remember—they weren't murderers after all. They didn't kill anyone."

"Not yet," Katherine muttered. "How do we know they're not sneaking up on Chip and Alex right now?"

"You mean, right at the moment you just left?" JB corrected. "Look."

He pressed a button on the wall beside him, and the wall slid back to reveal a view of Chip and Alex with their mother and sisters. The view was so clear and distinct that it was like looking through a window.

No, Jonah thought. *Clearer than that. It's like a window without glass. Just an opening. It looks like I could walk right back into the room with them.*

No, that was wrong too. If the medieval room were really that close, the division between them really that nonexistent, the bright light of the room Jonah was in would be illuminating every corner of the sanctuary room at Westminster. And that room was just as dim and dusky as it had been moments before, lit only by candlelight.

TV, Jonah concluded. *Really, really, really good TV.*

"One second after you left," JB said. "Two seconds after you left." On the screen, or through the window or whatever it was, Chip and Alex continued to eat strawberries. The queen and princesses watched them from across the room with great relief and love written all over their faces. "Three seconds after you left. Four—"

"Okay, okay! We get it!" Jonah said grumpily. He squinted up at JB. "But why are you here?" The last time they'd seen JB, he'd been in a cave with thirty-two other kids he intended to return to history. "What happened at the cave? What'd you do with the other kids?"

"To your way of thinking, they're still in the cave," JB said. "And so am I."

"Huh?" Jonah said at the same time that Katherine muttered, "What?"

JB laughed.

"If you're going to do much time traveling, you're going to have to stop thinking of time as a line," he said.

Jonah thought about telling JB how many time lines he'd had to draw in school over the years—all his social studies teachers had certainly acted like time was a line.

"And," JB continued, "you've got to stop thinking of your experience of events as the only sequence."

Jonah knew the expression on his face was dead blank.

"Come again?" Katherine said.

"Exactly!" JB congratulated her. Then he did a double take. "Er—you weren't demonstrating your understanding of the Principle of Simultaneous Time?"

Katherine rolled her eyes and shook her head.

"I knew I should have spent more time boning up on bizarre twenty-first-century American expressions," JB muttered to himself. He cleared his throat. "Look. To your way of thinking, you were in the cave. Then you were in the Tower of London. Then you were on the barge. Then you were at the coronation. Then you were in sanctuary at Westminster. Then you came here. Right?"

Jonah shrugged.

"Sure," Katherine said.

"But if you remove the element of time, then you could be in all those places in any order, even simultaneously," JB said. "To quote: 'Time is what keeps everything from happening at once.' And if you mix up time with time travel, it can seem like everything *is* happening at once. I stayed in the cave with the other kids. But I also left the cave to contact my fellow time protectors, and we've been doing everything we can behind the scenes to keep the fifteenth century on course."

"So you, like, stopped time in the cave to deal with us?" Katherine asked doubtfully.

"Time wasn't moving in the cave anyhow. Remember?" JB said. "What actually happened, if you want to be technical, is—"

"Can we just think of it this way if it makes us feel

better?" Katherine asked. "Because I want to talk about the really important questions. And then we can get back to Chip and Alex before they completely forget who they are."

"But . . ." JB stopped and seemed to be reconsidering. "Okay. Fine. I'll dispense with the technicalities for now."

Jonah shifted in his chair. Oddly, the chair seemed to shift with him. It figured that he'd have a funky, futuristic chair to go with the futuristic TV in front of them. *Focus,* he thought. *Past, not future.* He narrowed his eyes, watching the queen on the screen watching her sons so carefully.

"So, what's the deal with 1483?" Jonah asked. "You say Chip and Alex are safe right now, but . . . I know they weren't when we first got here. I mean, there. To that time." He pointed at the dim scene in front of him. "Those guys who came into Chip and Alex's room in the Tower of London—you can't tell me they were some brave heroes who the queen sent in to rescue her little boys. You can't tell me Chip and Alex would have been fine if we hadn't intervened. I don't believe it."

JB nodded slowly.

"That's very astute of you," he said. "You're right about that. Somewhat."

Jonah stared at JB. Now he was confused.

"But Chip and Alex were supposed to survive being

thrown out that window?" Katherine asked, sounding baffled too.

"Oh, yeah," JB said. "Which made it a big problem that Gary and Hodge did some rather incomplete historical research and yanked them out of time shortly before the—shall we call them window-throwers, for lack of a better term?—before the window-throwers stepped into the Tower of London. It turns out that you four kids arrived almost exactly at the same moment that Edward and Richard vanished, the first time around."

Jonah was trying to picture this in his mind. Gary and Hodge, the unethical time travelers from the future, had probably arrived in the same dark room that Jonah and his friends had landed in. They'd probably been very gleeful when they snatched Edward/Chip and Richard/Alex, because they had two famous members of British royalty to carry off to the future, to be adopted by families who could then brag about their children's lineage. Gary and Hodge just hadn't known how far JB and his friends would go to stop them.

"So if Chip and Alex hadn't come back, the . . . the window-throwers would have rushed into an empty room? They wouldn't have found anyone to throw?" Katherine asked, grimacing.

"Exactly," JB said.

"So what?" Jonah said.

JB and Katherine both whirled on him, mouths agape, brows furrowed. Jonah wondered if he sounded heartless or just stupid.

"I mean," Jonah hurried to explain, "if Chip and Alex were going to disappear either way, why does it matter if they disappeared from their room or from the courtyard down below?"

"Ah," JB said. "That's a very good question."

Katherine rolled her eyes.

"You have to understand how complicated everything was in the room that night, and in the courtyard down below," JB said. "There were five or six different layers of plots being carried out simultaneously—you'd practically need a graph to map out all the conflicting interests."

Jonah sincerely hoped JB wasn't going to produce a graph. Or a map.

"Shall I just give you the headlines?" JB asked.

Jonah and Katherine both nodded.

"It was about a week ago," JB began, "when the queen heard that Richard had been proclaimed king and was planning his coronation—"

"What?" Jonah interrupted. "You told us last night that Chip was king—I mean, that Edward was. You told us!"

"Were you lying to us?" Katherine accused.

JB held his hands up in a show of innocence.

"Would you let me explain?" he asked. "I told you what Edward would have believed about his own identity, at that point in time, the first time through history. It wasn't exactly a lie—things were very much in flux. Edward didn't know what Richard was saying out in public. And Edward/Chip still believes he's king, don't you think, even now, even though Richard is wearing the crown?"

Jonah glanced at the screen, at the superior expression on Chip/Edward's face, even as he tossed strawberries in his mouth.

"But the guards last night said they were looking for princes, as if Chip and Alex had the same rank," Katherine said. Jonah was impressed that she'd noticed that, since she'd been dodging flames at the time.

"The serving girl this morning said 'princes' too," Jonah added. He'd been too distracted to really think about that before. "Does that mean even the servants were on Richard's side?"

"That means they thought it was safest to act like they were," JB said grimly. "Now, can I please get back to my story?"

Jonah shrugged. Katherine nodded.

"When the queen heard that Richard had claimed the throne for himself, she knew that her sons' lives were in danger," JB said. He pointed to the regal woman in the scene before them, her head held high and proud. "Queen Elizabeth Woodville—now, there's another person whose talents were never fully appreciated by history! To think what she could have done in a time when women had equal rights . . ."

"What did she do?" Jonah asked quickly, before Katherine could get started on this topic. "In real history?"

JB seemed to shake himself back from gazing adoringly at the queen, who was, now that Jonah thought about it, much prettier than anyone else he'd seen in the fifteenth century. For a mom, anyway.

"Oh, yes . . . she had her people infiltrate the plot against her sons' lives," JB said. "In the room that night, those men you saw? The window-throwers? One of them thought there was another man on the ground waiting to bash the boys' brains in, to make it look like they died trying to escape."

"I knew it!" Katherine said, sounding much too triumphant about such a grisly theory.

"The other window-thrower thought that there was a man waiting below to spirit the boys away to safety," JB said. "But he knew he had to act like a murderer, to convince his partner."

"And *were* there men on the ground?" Jonah asked.

JB nodded grimly.

"Two were there, planning to catch the boys, if they could, or bind up their broken limbs and carry them off if they hit the ground and were injured," JB said. "You see how desperate the queen was, that she would agree to such a dangerous plot?"

"I guess it's better than letting your sons be killed," Katherine muttered.

"But there were other men on the ground whose job it was to claim that they'd seen the boys jump and innocently discovered the bodies afterward," JB said. "They were the ones who mistakenly called out, 'Where are the bodies?' when they didn't see the boys—they were so stunned they forgot that *that* wasn't information they should broadcast."

"So in the original version of history . . . ?" Jonah asked.

JB chuckled.

"In the original version of history both boys landed in bushes and took off running before any of the men on the ground saw them, friend or foe," he said. "This left both sides in confusion. The officials in the tower pretended for quite some time that the princes were still there—but they were also systematically interviewing everyone who might have heard or seen anything. So, as you can imagine, rumors began to fly."

"Rumors that the boys were dead?" Jonah asked.

"That they were dead, that they were alive, that they'd sprouted wings like angels and flown away . . . name the theory, and somebody was trying to pass it off as gospel truth," JB said. He shook his head in amusement. "Meanwhile, the boys were being quite resourceful evading capture—it was one of the greatest adventures of their lives. I feel rather bad for Chip and Alex that they missed it."

"Sor-ry," Katherine muttered, stretching out the word so she didn't sound apologetic at all. "Call me crazy, but when you don't know what's *supposed* to happen, and you see someone trying to throw your friends out a window, it's just kind of natural instinct to want to stop it."

"If you didn't want us to save Chip and Alex, you should have told us," Jonah said grumpily. Though he wasn't sure what he would have done if JB had commanded, *"You're going to see two guys who act like murderers come in and throw Chip and Alex out the window—but don't worry. They'll be fine. As long as you stand back and watch and don't do a thing."*

"No, no," JB said. "You don't understand. The two of you saving Chip and Alex was the best outcome. We ran computer models on this. If the boys had landed just a fraction of an inch differently, they could have been maimed or killed. Or been caught by the murderers on the ground. Or been found by the rescuers, who were then caught by the murderers, who would have killed everyone. Or—"

Jonah didn't want to hear any other ways everything could have gone wrong.

"So why didn't you tell us ahead of time what we had to do?" he asked.

"If you'd known that those men were going to try to throw Chip and Alex out the window, would you have been able to wait until the last possible second to try to save them?" JB asked. "Or would you have jumped the gun a little, grabbing them too soon because you *really* didn't want to wait until you were too late? And then the men throwing them out the window would have noticed the difference, and . . ."

JB didn't have to finish his sentence. Jonah felt breathless just thinking about it. He and Katherine had had a split second to save Chip and Alex. A fraction of a second either way and they would have failed.

Jonah turned toward Katherine, expecting her to look as awestruck as he felt. But her expression was gripped with rage.

"And you didn't even want me and Jonah to come!" she spit out. "How could you! What did you think was going to happen?"

"We thought history would repeat itself," JB said. "We thought Chip and Alex and time itself would proceed exactly as they and it had the first time around."

Katherine continued scowling at him.

"You were taking a lot of chances, weren't you?" she said. "Chip and Alex are bigger than their tracers. That could have thrown things off. They were struggling a lot more than their tracers did. Flailing about. Couldn't that have made them land differently? And—"

JB cut her off.

"We're doing the best we can, all right?" he said. "This is the first time we've ever tried to return missing children to history. It's not easy trying to account for every possible variable. We weren't expecting the two of you to go jumping into the past, for example, so we had to rerun all our calculations. And you saw for yourselves what a dicey time 1483 was. . . ."

He gestured toward the scene of the royal family, the queen and her children holed up in sanctuary. But then his voice trailed off and his eyes goggled out slightly.

"No," he moaned. "That's not supposed to happen yet."

Jonah immediately looked toward Chip and Alex, or where they'd been. The scene before him had changed. He no longer had a clear view of the queen and princes and princesses sitting in their private chambers. Instead he could see the outside of their sanctuary building, where guards stood forbiddingly on either side of the front door. Some of the guards held torches, waving them out into the night as if they were trying to ward off evil. In the dim torchlight Jonah could see a lone man approaching the guards.

The man moved briskly, authoritatively—he didn't seem the type to be frightened off by guards or torches. At first Jonah could see only his shoulder-length brown hair, the tip of his strong nose, his long, swinging dark cape. The man walked right past the guards and the torches, unimpeded. Then the man turned, his hand on the door, and Jonah could see his face.

It was King Richard III.

TWENTY-FIVE

"No!" Jonah screamed.

He sprang up and raced toward the king. Jonah would have to tackle him and then yell loudly enough that Chip and Alex would hear and have time to hide, up in their sanctuary room. Or no, maybe Jonah wouldn't be strong enough to knock down the king—maybe Jonah would have to settle for grabbing the king's cape and hollering at the guards, "Don't you know who this is? Aren't you supposed to be protecting the queen and her kids from this man?"

But how good could these guards be if they were fooled by Alex's bird trick? Jonah thought. *I'll have to try something else. Maybe—*

Jonah ran smack into the wall. Instantly he remembered that he was only watching 1483 on an unnaturally realistic TV. Evidently the TV was part of a very hard wall, one that was quite painful to run into at full speed.

Jonah hit so hard he bounced back, lost his balance, and slammed into the floor.

"Are you all right?" JB asked, bending over him.

"Jonah!" Katherine shrieked, right behind JB.

"Chip. Alex. Must warn . . ." Jonah made his eyes focus on JB's face, made his brain focus on what really mattered. "Send me back to 1483. Now. I have to tell them. Let them know—"

"Shh, shh," JB said. "They're all right. Remember? I promised they'd be safe. You're the one who probably just gave yourself a concussion."

JB was poking at Jonah's eyes, pulling the lids back, one after the other, and peering deep into his pupils, just like Jonah's soccer coach had done that time Jonah banged heads with another player in the championship game.

Jonah turned his head and struggled to sit up.

"But you said this wasn't supposed to happen!" he argued.

"I said it wasn't supposed to happen *yet*," JB said. "The king's just a little early. I'm very confident about this . . . let's watch it play out. . . ."

Jonah jerked away from him, rolled over on his side, and began digging in his pocket.

"That's right," Katherine cheered him on. "Try getting out of here using the Elucidator."

Jonah pulled the Elucidator out, but before he could even glance at the screen, JB wrapped his hand around Jonah's wrist. In one motion JB jerked the Elucidator away, stabbed a button on its surface, and tossed it toward the ceiling. It turned invisible in midair, but Jonah scrambled up and ran over to where he thought it might land.

JB threw it a little sideways, so let's see, a normal trajectory would end up right about . . . Jonah listened closely, hoping he could hear the Elucidator hit the floor. But any sound it made was lost in the echo of the footsteps from 1483, King Richard III walking up the stairs toward the room where Chip and Alex sat, unaware.

Jonah dropped to the ground and began sweeping his hands right to left, left to right, groping for the Elucidator. At least he wasn't searching for a stone on a stone floor again—this floor was smooth as glass. His hand hit something . . . but it was only Katherine's hand. For the first time Jonah realized Katherine had also dropped to her knees and was searching.

"You two are indomitable," JB said, sounding amazed. "I'm glad we're on the same side—I just wish I could get you to believe we're all on the same side."

Neither Jonah nor Katherine answered him. They

just kept sweeping their hands across the floor. Jonah was starting to feel discouraged. The Elucidator had to have hit the floor somewhere. Didn't it? *Could JB have activated some other function besides just invisibility—something that made the Elucidator impossible to feel, too?*

JB let out an exasperated sigh.

"Look," he said. "Just watch what's going on in 1483. The king's at the top of the stairs. . . ."

Jonah lifted his head and stared at the scene before him. A servant was greeting the king, promising to tell her mistress that he was there.

"See?" JB said. "The king came alone. He didn't bring soldiers to carry out any murders. He isn't brandishing knives or swords—he wouldn't do that, anyway. Kings usually want other people to do their dirty work for them. At least . . . well, I know this is still the Middle Ages, but . . ."

Jonah stopped listening to JB. He also stopped searching for the Elucidator. He could only watch the screen as the king stepped into the chambers where Chip and Alex had been talking with their mother and sisters.

Chip and Alex were no longer there.

The queen—ex-queen, really—sat straight-backed and regal on her bed, her daughters arranged like miniature versions beside her. Amazingly, even the youngest had mastered their mother's air of contemptuous hauteur.

"Richard," the queen said. It was hard for Jonah to believe that one spoken word could sound so accusing and yet still polite, both at the same time.

Jonah noticed that the queen did not call him "king."

"My dear, grieving sister-in-law," Richard said, taking her hand and kissing it. "And my lovely nieces."

He kissed their hands as well, then sat in the same chair Chip had occupied only a few moments earlier.

"I would have thought you would be feasting yet," the queen said with an air of feigned interest. "Celebrating your coronation."

The way she said "coronation" was masterful, implying in four short syllables that he didn't deserve a coronation, and that everyone knew he had stolen the crown, and that if he had any shame at all, he would be throwing himself at her feet and begging her forgiveness for tarring her good name and his dead brother's good name on his way to the throne. And yet, she smiled politely.

"My brother would have been feasting still," Richard conceded, sounding only slightly humbled. "Feasting and drinking and dancing with all the most beautiful women in the kingdom. But"—his gaze was steely—"I am not my brother."

The queen's eyes narrowed slightly, but she gave no

other sign that Richard had just insulted her dead husband.

"More's the pity," the queen said, and just enough grief throbbed in her voice that Richard could hardly have claimed that she was insulting him, though she clearly was.

"I'm sorry he's gone," Richard said softly, and just those four words seemed to turn the conversation from a nasty fight veiled in politeness to something more like a condolence call.

Had Richard really liked his brother? Jonah wondered. Was Richard maybe even sorry that Edward IV was dead, even though it meant that Richard himself got to be king?

"That is not what you came here to say, the night of your coronation," the queen said. But her voice was softer now, and kinder. "You've told me that before."

"It's no less true today, milady. I assure you," Richard said.

"Liar," Katherine muttered under her breath. "You're probably glad your brother died, so you could be king."

"Shh," Jonah hissed, afraid he'd miss something.

Richard and the queen sat silently for a moment, but Jonah glanced quickly around, wondering where in the room Chip and Alex were hiding. They hadn't had time to go anywhere else, had they?

Richard leaned forward suddenly.

"Milady, this morning at . . . at Westminster, I was gifted with a vision," he said.

"Indeed?" the queen said coldly.

"Indeed," Richard said. "A vision of your two sons, in a happier place. Away from the struggles and travails of our mortal lives."

"Oh. My. Gosh," Katherine practically shrieked. "Is he trying to tell her that her sons are better off dead? Because he thinks they *are* dead. Because he hired murderers. Because we convinced him he saw their angels. This is incredible! This is better than a soap opera!"

Before them, the queen froze at Richard's words.

"Right, right, that's what you have to do," Katherine coached. "Pretend that you're devastated so he'll think that you think that Chip and Alex are dead. That way he won't try again to kill them. And—"

"Katherine, she can't hear you," Jonah said disgustedly.

"I know, I know," Katherine said excitedly. "But . . ." She broke off because the queen was speaking again.

"You had a vision of my boys," the queen repeated numbly. "In heaven?"

"They were such saintly boys," Richard said, bowing his head slightly, as if in tribute.

"He's using past tense now!" Katherine screamed. "Don't let him get away with this!"

The queen inclined her head slightly.

"Henry the Sixth was a saintly man," she said with studied casualness. "Too saintly to be king, don't you think? And yet, others fought to restore him to the throne."

"What?" Katherine screeched. "Henry the Sixth? Who's that? What's he got to do with anything?"

"Former king of England," JB said quickly. "Very holy, occasionally crazy. But he took the throne from Edward the Fourth for a few years. Because of Henry, Edward the Fourth was in exile when Edward the Fifth—er, Chip— was born."

However Henry VI was connected, King Richard definitely recognized the name. His face drained of color; he opened his mouth and then shut it again without speaking.

"You remember?" the queen said almost airily. "You remember what a painful experience that was for my husband?"

"Wow," JB muttered. "She's really good at this."

In the scene before them Richard seemed to be struggling to regain his composure.

"E-everyone knew where Henry was," Richard finally said. "Until your husband ensured his death."

"Richard's not bad at this either," JB said.

"Wait. Is he accusing his brother of murder?" Katherine asked. "To make it sound better that he's murdering people too?"

JB waved his hands quickly at her, signaling for silence. "Later," he whispered. "I'll explain later."

The queen raised one elegant eyebrow.

"You wish it to be a fight to the death, then?" she said. "Very well. I assure you, others do as well."

Richard bolted upright in his chair.

"You dare to threaten me? Me, the king of England?"

"Game over," JB muttered. "See? Right there? He just lost his cool."

The queen looked shocked, though Jonah thought it was probably fake shock.

"You think I could threaten anyone?" she asked, her voice tremulous. "Me, a defenseless widow?"

"Defenseless, my foot," JB murmured.

Richard looked like he wanted to say the same thing. He grimaced, as if struggling to regain his composure. Finally he gave a tight nod.

"I see my sympathies were unnecessary," he said in a clipped voice. "I should return to the festivities."

"Aye," the queen said. "For who but God knows how long any mortal has left to celebrate?"

JB began clapping.

"Bravo!" he cried. "What a performance!"

Jonah sank back on his haunches, his search for the Elucidator completely forgotten.

"Performance?" he repeated numbly. "You mean that wasn't real? It was just a play or something? Just . . . acting?"

"Oh, it was real, all right," JB assured him. "But incredible acting, too, couldn't you tell? Neither one of them could come out and say what they were really thinking, but they both got their messages across."

"Like at school, when Caitlin Deets tells Alexis Raypole, 'Wow, that shirt is really flattering on you. Very slimming,' she's not really giving her a compliment," Katherine said. "She's really saying, 'You're fat and ugly and nowhere near cool enough to be my friend.' And then when Alexis tells Caitlin—"

"Katherine, stop!" Jonah said. "Nobody cares about that right now!"

JB grinned.

"She's right, though," he said. "It's the same kind of double-talk. Richard left his own coronation to tell Elizabeth, 'Look, your sons are dead. I'm the king now. Give up.' He expected to find her weak and sobbing, and then he could be charitable and comforting, as if he'd had nothing to do with her sons' deaths. But she told him, 'Hey, you can't bully me. How can you be so sure my boys are dead? Even if they were, how can you be so sure that I wouldn't pretend that they're still alive and have my friends mount a campaign to put them or some impostor on the throne? You may have the Crown tonight, but that doesn't mean you'll still be alive next week!'" JB grew so animated acting out each side's hidden message that he swung his fists, punching the air. "And they said all that without actually uttering a single discourteous word."

Jonah frowned. Did people do that kind of double-talk all the time—not just sixth-grade girls and medieval royalty? Why hadn't he noticed? Most of the time he just said exactly what he meant. Who needed the complications?

Katherine scrunched up her face.

"Yeah, well . . . Caitlin Deets is really nasty, but even she's not threatening to kill anyone," she said doubtfully.

JB shrugged.

"What if she lived in a society where certain types of murder were considered perfectly acceptable—would she be making death threats then?" he asked.

"Caitlin Deets? Oh, yeah, in a heartbeat," Katherine said. "She'd probably start strangling other kids with her bare hands."

Jonah couldn't quite remember which girl in Katherine's class was Caitlin Deets—the really skinny one with the big nose, long blond hair, and triple-pierced ears? The tall girl who always wore platform shoes and pink clothing? He decided, whoever she was, he'd want to avoid her if he ever got back to the twenty-first century.

JB gestured toward the scene before them, King Richard slowly climbing down the winding stairs.

"There's a lot of blood on the English Crown at this point in history," JB said. "The York and Lancaster families have been fighting for thirty years over who deserves the throne."

"But Richard and Chip and Alex are all in the same family, right?" Jonah said. "And anyhow, Chip and Alex aren't dead. Why didn't the 'murderers' tell the king the boys escaped? Is Richard supposed to think they're dead? Or does he think they're dead just because we made him think he saw their ghosts?"

"If you worked for a king who ordered people killed in the middle of the night, would you tell him you'd messed up?" JB asked.

In the scene before them Richard stepped out of the building and nodded curtly at the guards around the front door. Then the scene shifted: Chip and Alex were climbing out of a cupboard of sorts, one that blended neatly into the stone wall. They were grinning triumphantly.

"So they knew to hide," Katherine said. "Somebody warned them the king was coming."

"Elizabeth Woodville has very loyal servants," JB said, nodding. "She may be out of power, but she's not out of plans."

As the princesses gathered around them, Chip raised his right hand and smacked Alex's right hand in a very dramatic high five.

"They had high fives in 1483?" Jonah asked, surprised. Had Chip's arm separated from his tracer's arm for just that long?

"No," JB said disapprovingly.

"Then, they're still in there," Jonah said. "The real Chip and Alex."

"No doubt," JB said, though he didn't sound as happy about it as Jonah.

The princesses, who had gathered around Chip and Alex, were shooting them puzzled glances. One girl flipped a long lock of blond hair over her shoulder and whispered to her sisters. Jonah imagined she was saying, "Methinks our brothers have gone crazy. Wherever did they learn those bizarre hand signals?"

"Well," Jonah said. "Katherine and I had better get Chip and Alex out of there before they corrupt the princesses with their twenty-first-century habits. You couldn't have *princesses* starting to do high fives."

Huh, Jonah thought. *Maybe I do that double-talk thing too.* He didn't care about whether or not high fives caught on in the fifteenth century. He just wanted to get everyone home.

"You think you can just snatch them away now?" JB asked harshly. "Just because you want to?" He glowered. "You sound like Gary and Hodge."

"It's for their own good," Jonah said. "Chip and Alex's."

"How do you know that?" JB asked. "How do you know that in the twenty-first century they're not going to step in front of a car tomorrow and be killed instantly? How do you know that Chip's not going to get his throne back in the fifteenth century and reign for fifty years, in happiness and prosperity?"

"Does he?" Jonah asked. "Is that what's supposed to happen?"

"Uh, no," JB said. "Probably not."

Jonah gaped at JB.

"Probably?" Jonah repeated. "You don't know for sure?"

JB shrugged.

"Everything's uncertain now."

Jonah looked to Katherine for reinforcement. At home

she was usually the one who raged and blustered and told their parents their rules were insane, no kid should be expected to have to do *that* . . . Jonah could usually count on her to do all the screaming and complaining, so he didn't have to.

But Katherine was wincing and biting her lip.

"How long?" she asked softly. "How long until we know what's going to happen? How long do Chip and Alex have to stay in the fifteenth century?"

JB turned and faced Jonah and Katherine squarely.

"You want my best guess?" he asked. "The most likely time span, assuming we haven't changed events too greatly from the original version?"

Jonah and Katherine both nodded.

JB tilted his head to the side, calculating. Or else delaying delivering the bad news.

"If everything goes the way we hope," he said, "it's two years."

TWENTY-SIX

"Two years?" Katherine wailed. "That's forever! I'll be fourteen in two years! I'll miss everything about middle school!"

Jonah considered telling her, "No, you'll just be a fourteen-year-old sixth grader." Or, "Don't you think it might be a good thing to miss middle school?" But he had his own distress to deal with.

Two more years before I get pizza again? I'll die! Strangely, he wasn't hungry right at the moment—*Oh, yeah, people aren't hungry or thirsty or anything else when they're in Outer Time*—but if breakfast was any indication, he'd starve with nothing but fifteenth-century food for two years.

JB held up his hand like a traffic cop.

"I didn't say the two of you were going to stay in the 1400s for two years," JB said. "Just Chip and Alex."

"That is *so* not fair," Katherine ranted. "You promised us they'd be safe. You promised we could rescue them. You—"

"I promised you could *try* to rescue them," JB corrected her in a steely voice. "There's a difference. I never promised you'd succeed."

Katherine gulped, turned pale, and stopped talking for a moment.

"But if they're stuck in 1483 for two years—or I mean, 1483 and 1484—" she began tentatively.

"The first half of 1485, too," JB interrupted, though his voice was almost gentle now.

"Okay, they're there until 1485 . . . well, isn't there more danger that they'll do something to contaminate the time period?" Katherine asked. "Something like high fives, only worse? Or—what if the opposite problem happens? What if Chip and Alex forget the twenty-first century? What if they forget Jonah and me? What if—"

"Katherine," JB said. "I already told you we were facing a lot of risks." His expression was severe, then softened. "When we ran our first projections, we thought we had no choice but to let Chip and Alex ultimately meet whatever fate was waiting for them in 1485. I'm a time officer, sworn to uphold the sanctity of history. I *had* to send Chip and Alex back. But we never want to sacrifice anyone on the altar of authenticity. We never intended to return missing children to history just to see them die. We just . . . knew that that might be the inevitable outcome, in some cases."

Now it was Jonah's turn to gulp. He was a missing child too. What fate waited for him in a foreign time?

"Then you and Jonah grabbed Chip's elbows back in the cave," JB said, a hint of amusement creeping into his voice. "You should have seen the panic you caused at time headquarters! If it weren't strictly forbidden by thirty-two separate time regulations, I'd show you a clip of it someday. But then everyone scrambled to run new projections and . . . you might have changed things just enough. If the time projections had shown you introducing rap music or the theory of evolution or, I don't know, Coca-Cola, we would have yanked you out instantly. But they didn't. They showed you having a chance to rescue your friends."

JB sounded so earnest it was impossible not to believe him. It was impossible not to believe that he wanted to see Chip and Alex safe just as much as Jonah and Katherine did.

"What do we have to do?" Jonah asked.

"You probably need to know what's going to happen between 1483 and 1485," JB said. "We need to make sure that everything goes as projected, anyhow. And then . . ." He cleared his throat. "How do you feel about wearing armor?"

TWENTY-SEVEN

Jonah felt hideous wearing armor. It was heavy. It was hot. And it smelled like a locker room full of sweaty teenage boys. Trying on the suit of armor JB gave him, Jonah sniffed surreptitiously, almost gagged, and resorted to holding his breath.

JB said this was brand-new armor—could I really be producing that smell all by myself?

Jonah lifted the visor of his armor.

"Look," he said. "You're from the future. Can't you give us something that just *looks* like fifteenth-century armor, but really weighs nothing—and has air-conditioning?"

JB laughed.

"Good idea," he said. "But no."

"Why not?" Katherine demanded. She had on armor of her own and was awkwardly trying to walk wearing, essentially, a forty-pound tin can.

"Against time regulations," JB said curtly, bending over to examine a squeaky knee joint on Katherine's armor.

"Why?" Katherine said again.

JB sighed. He straightened up but somehow wouldn't meet Katherine's gaze.

"Because I'm sending you into a dangerous area. And if . . . something happens . . . we can't take the risk of having anachronistic items discovered," he said.

"What? You mean if klutzy Katherine trips and loses one of her metal gloves, you couldn't just yank it out of time, like you did with the Taser?" Jonah asked.

JB gave him a rueful half smile.

"That kind of thing isn't as easy as it looked from your perspective," he said. "And . . . we can't do it in a battle zone."

Those words, "battle zone," just hung in the air.

"We could die, couldn't we?" Katherine asked quietly. "That's what you're talking about. 'If something happens'— you mean, if we're killed, and we lie there with all the other dead bodies, in wrong-time armor . . . that's the problem, right?"

Why did Katherine always have to say things like that? Jonah would have been perfectly fine not thinking about the fact that people died in battle zones.

"Nothing's going to happen," he scoffed. "We'll be

invisible, remember? JB's just being crazy overprotective. It's like Mom and Dad practically making us wear bike helmets just to cross the street."

JB stared off toward the wall where Chip and Alex's fifteenth-century life was on display. They were still in sanctuary with their mother and sisters.

"I won't lie to you," JB said. "Death rates were high on medieval battlefields."

"But you wouldn't send us back there if you really thought we were going to die," Jonah argued. "Right?" He adopted a joking tone. "Because then that'd ruin our time periods—Katherine and the twenty-first century, and me and, well, whatever time period I'm really from."

JB winced.

"All the projections show the two of you surviving," he said. "We wouldn't risk this otherwise. It's not worth it to just trade your lives for Chip's and Alex's. Or . . . to lose all of you. But I have to tell you . . . the projections aren't always right."

Jonah gulped and was glad that the armor still covered his throat so no one would see his Adam's apple bobbing nervously up and down.

"We're not scared," he said.

"Speak for yourself," Katherine said. "I am."

"You don't have to do this," JB said. "Neither of you do.

This is not a moral or an ethical dilemma. Chip and Alex are not entitled to any more time than fate gave them to begin with. They both believe in heaven—or, at least, their fifteenth-century selves both do. So neither of them would blame you if you chose the safe route. You could go home right now."

Home . . .

Jonah was ashamed of how tempted he was.

"Chip and Alex are our *friends*," Katherine said. "We're not abandoning them."

She jerked her chin up in the air and was probably trying for a noble pose. But for all those stories about knights' chivalry and honor and nobility, armor was actually a very difficult thing to wear while striking a noble pose. Jonah heard a muffled *thunk*, then Katherine jerked off the top part of her armor and began rubbing the back of her scalp.

"Ow," she said sheepishly. "I hit my head on the armor. It's not bleeding, is it?"

Jonah leaned over to look.

"You're fine," he said. And, he vowed, she would be fine. Even if they were in a battle zone. He'd make sure of it.

"So," he added with studied casualness. "Just what battle are we going to? Does Chip's army attack Richard the Third, or does Richard's army attack Chip?"

"Neither," JB said. "You've got to remember, this is fifteenth-century England. None of their political battles are simple. Here. We'll get you up to speed."

He reached up and plucked something out of midair. He ran his right hand over it like a magician revealing his latest trick, and the thing appeared in the palm of his left hand: the Elucidator.

Jonah groaned.

"It was up there the whole time?" he asked. "In midair? That's not fair. We didn't know you had antigravity powers too."

"Defying gravity is actually easier than defying time," JB said. "But that's not something I'm going to explain to you. Watch."

He pointed the Elucidator toward the fifteenth-century scene on the far wall. Instantly, everyone began moving faster, like a DVD on fast-forward. Chip, Alex, the princesses, and the queen zipped around their small room, sleeping, waking, eating, conferring with guests, sleeping, waking, eating. . . .

"Okay, even I'm starting to feel claustrophobic with that room," JB muttered. "Wait, wait—here—now the queen's sending the boys away, to safety."

The scene slowed momentarily as Chip and Alex were bundled into a cart in the dark of night and hidden under blankets. Then—quickly—they rattled down rutted roads, out into the countryside. Jonah caught a final glimpse of them joyfully running through a field, playing with wooden swords, before the view blurred.

"They do a lot of that the next several months," JB said. "Meanwhile, King Richard isn't having much fun trying to consolidate his power." The scene shifted to a grim-faced king. "His own friend, Buckingham, betrays him four months after the coronation."

Jonah watched men hunched over tables, battle plans scattered before them. Soldiers gathered together, whispering plans for treason.

"Supposedly Buckingham is throwing his support to a rival for the throne, Henry Tudor, who's in exile in France. But is that the point? Or does Buckingham really want to put Chip back in power?" JB asked. "Buckingham's wife is Chip's aunt—his mother's sister."

The soldiers flocking together, oddly, seemed to be facing disastrous rain and floods rather than a battle.

"In the face of extreme weather the rebellion fails," JB intoned. "King Richard has Buckingham executed."

King Richard appeared again, not demanding his friend's death, not watching his friend's execution, but sitting stonily at a table, staring off into space. He was completely alone.

The scene shifted to festivities, people dancing and feasting.

"Oh, wait, I'll back up a little—I missed showing you one of the happiest moments of King Richard's reign," JB said. "He had his son named Prince of Wales, heir to the throne."

A frail-looking blond boy of seven or eight beamed happily at the crowd from the seat of honor at the feast. Eerily, he looked a lot like Chip and Alex, only younger and more fragile. His father stepped up behind him and gave him a hearty, proud slap on the back. The feeble boy lurched dangerously—the slap seemed much too hard for his brittle bones. But he turned back to grin up at Richard.

"Seven months later the sickly boy dies," JB said. "Richard and his wife have no other children, and his wife is too ill to give him any more heirs."

Now Jonah saw the king sobbing beside a bed. He was clutching a woman's thin, bony hand and crying out, "Anne! Anne! Oh, please, no . . ."

"Richard's wife dies less than a year after her son," JB said. "Richard is heartbroken."

More scenes of Richard sobbing, Richard on his knees praying to God: "Is it because of my sins, O Lord? Is this my punishment? What wouldst Thou have me do? Am I unforgivable?"

"Please," Katherine interrupted. "Do we have to watch this? I'm starting to feel sorry for him. That kind of makes it hard to keep hating him."

JB froze the action on the scene of the grief-stricken king. Jonah could see each individual tear rolling down his face, each deeply etched furrow in his anguished brow. Katherine was right: It was impossible not to feel sorry for someone in such obvious pain.

"Why is it necessary to hate him?" JB asked quietly.

"He's the enemy, isn't he?" Katherine asked.

"Is he?" JB replied, raising an eyebrow. "Shall I also show you the queen's conniving and plotting during this same time period?" Scenes flickered past quickly: the queen meeting again and again with clusters of solemn men. "Would you like to consider how much she's willing to endanger her children in order to regain political power? Nobody in this story has pure motives. Not even your friends."

Once again the scene changed. Now they were back to Chip and Alex, parrying back and forth with wooden swords in a meadow. Chip swung hard, knocking the sword from Alex's hand. Then Chip used the broad side of his sword to push his brother down; he thrust the sword's point against Alex's chest to pin him to the ground. Chip threw back his head and laughed.

"They're playing," Jonah said. "They're just playing."

"Of course," JB said. But he looked like he wanted to say something else.

Jonah stared hard at his friends, trying to discern any hint of an Einstein T-shirt showing through Alex's tunic, any trace of a Nike swish on Chip's black shoes. He couldn't. He stared at their faces: Were they thinking fifteenth-century thoughts or twenty-first-century thoughts? It was impossible to tell.

Then he noticed something else.

"Is that *hair* on Chip's lip?" Jonah asked. "Has he started growing a mustache just in the couple of days he's been there?"

JB glanced down at the Elucidator, checking the date.

"That's 1485 you're watching," he said. "Summertime again. Chip and Alex have been there two full years. Chip's fourteen and a half now—closing in on fifteen."

Jonah fingered his own lip. Back home sometimes he'd lock the bathroom door and stand there staring into the mirror, searching for his first signs of facial hair. If he stood in just the right light, at just the right angle, it was possible to see at least six faint hairs on his upper lip. He would have said Chip's crop of mustache hair was about the same.

This new, 1485-era Chip had enough hair on his lip

that it showed up at any angle, in both sunlight and shadow.

"Chip's the same age as me," Jonah argued. "Thirteen."

"If you pull Chip away from the tracer, he'll be thirteen again," JB corrected. "But right now . . ."

Chip lifted his sword triumphantly in the air, and the sleeve of his tunic slid back on his arm, revealing well-defined biceps. His hair streamed back in the breeze—somehow the shoulder-length blond curls didn't look girly at all anymore.

"Wow," Katherine whispered. "He looks like he could be in high school. On the football team. Varsity."

On the ground Alex started to sit up. In a flash Chip had the wooden sword back down, aimed at his brother's throat.

They aren't playing after all, Jonah realized, chills traveling down his spine. *They're practicing.*

TWENTY-EIGHT

"You have a very narrow window of opportunity," JB said.

"Really?" Katherine said sarcastically. "You never mentioned that before."

They were finally ready to go rescue Chip and Alex. JB had been through their instructions a million times, repeating again and again how important it was that Jonah and Katherine separate the boys from their tracers at exactly the right moment. Too soon and they'd mess up time.

Too late and Chip and Alex could die.

It was that possibility that made Jonah's stomach churn, his skin prickle, his mustacheless face break out in a cold sweat.

I'm a thirteen-year-old kid, he thought. *Katherine's not quite twelve. Why would anyone trust us with life-or-death decisions?*

He knew the answer to that. He knew, because JB had told them, that the time experts had run computer projections checking out every possible scenario. The only way Chip and Alex could survive the fifteenth century was if Jonah and Katherine saved them.

It didn't make Jonah feel any better to know that he and his sister were Chip and Alex's only hope.

"Well, let's go, then," Jonah said gruffly.

"Wait! Just make sure that . . ." JB broke off. A rueful grin spread over his face. "Oh, never mind. What I was about to say—you already know that, too. Just . . . be careful, all right?"

"Aye, aye, Captain," Katherine said, rolling her eyes.

"Are you *sure* you want to do this?" JB asked, hesitating, with his fingers poised on the Elucidator.

Jonah nodded so vigorously that his armor rattled.

"Send us already!" Katherine demanded. "Now!"

Everything vanished from before Jonah's eyes.

Traveling back into the fifteenth century was not quite so distressing this time. There was the nothingness again—*Yeah, yeah, seen that before*—and then the distant lights far below, zooming closer. Once again Jonah felt as though his whole body was being tugged apart during his reentry into time. But maybe the armor helped; maybe he was protected because he'd been in the fifteenth century before. He didn't feel quite so miserable and disoriented when he landed.

Darkness? Check.

Spinning head? Not really.

Churning stomach? Nope. If anything, it was more like his stomach had just awakened and was crying out, *FEED ME!*

He'd forgotten how hungry he'd been when he left 1483. His stomach almost felt like he'd lived through an entire two years without food.

"Katherine?" Jonah whispered. "How's your timesickness?"

"It's . . ." She hesitated. "Not too bad. Not bad at all." She sounded surprised.

"Good," Jonah whispered back. "I'm going to go look for some food."

He scrambled up, swaying only slightly.

"Jonah!" Katherine whispered. "Are you crazy?"

Jonah shrugged, which wasn't the easiest thing to do while wearing armor and dealing with even a mild case of timesickness.

"The battle's not until dawn, remember?" Jonah asked.

JB had sent them back early so they'd have some time to adjust, in case their timesickness was extreme. Also, the battle they were about to witness had always been something of a historical mystery, so many, many time travelers had watched it over the years. That made travel in and out during the battle difficult—there was always the danger of running into someone from another time, someone equally out of place.

"JB said to hide," Katherine reminded him. "That's the safest thing to do."

"I can't hide when I'm starving," Jonah said. "My stomach will growl."

He half expected JB to start yelling at him too, but they hadn't brought the Elucidator this time around. That would have been too dangerous, too potentially anachronistic. Half of the time projections of them bringing the Elucidator showed that it would lead to a curious wave of English peasants turning invisible during the 1500s. Somehow that completely messed up the Protestant Reformation, changed the outcome of dozens of witchcraft trials, and, strangest of all, led to an invisible ship crashing into the Massachusetts coastline in the early 1600s.

So—no Elucidator. This meant that Jonah and Katherine had had to get "translation shots," a sort of vaccination against the problems they would have had understanding Middle English on their own. (Jonah wished this alternative was possible in the twenty-first century—it would make Spanish class *so* much easier.) But not having the

Elucidator also meant that they had no way of communicating with JB or anyone else outside of 1485.

Right now that was a good thing.

"Look," Jonah said. "It's the middle of the night. Everyone's asleep. We're already invisible—and in a tent. Nobody's even going to know if I creep around a little looking for something to eat."

"Fine," Katherine said. "I'm hungry too."

She stood gingerly. Through the armor Jonah felt a jerk on his arm, as if she'd needed to hold on to him to pull herself up. It was just like being back in elementary school, Katherine always wanting to tag along with whatever Jonah was doing. Her armor clanked softly against his.

"Katherine!" Jonah scolded. "We've got to be quiet, remember?"

"Then, quit running into me," Katherine retorted.

"I didn't run into you. You grabbed my arm," Jonah accused.

"I did not!" Katherine said.

"She's right," another voice said. "She did not. It was I."

TWENTY-NINE

The voice was deep and adult, and for one long moment Jonah dared to hope that it was only Chip, with a two-years-older grown-up voice to match his grown-up muscles and facial hair. But then there was a scratching sound in the darkness, and a candle sprang to life.

Jonah found himself staring directly into the face of the king, Richard III.

"Ahh! JB!" Jonah cried, forgetting in his surprise that they'd left the Elucidator behind. Jonah wanted to talk to JB now. No—Jonah wanted to yell at him.

How'd JB mess up so badly? Jonah wondered. *I thought we were landing somewhere safe and quiet and out of the way. Not in the king's tent!*

Now that it was too late, Jonah noticed a ghostly shape—the king's tracer—glowing softly on a bed at the far end of the tent. The king's tracer tossed and turned, his expression anguished.

"What's that?" the real Richard said, leaning closer. He was blinking in the sudden light, and swinging his hands out before him. Jonah barely managed to jump out of the way of the candle.

At least it's only a candle, not a torch, Jonah told himself.

Katherine was making a similar dodging maneuver to avoid Richard's other hand. In her haste to get away she threw back her arms and hit her own chest, the armor ringing loudly this time.

King Richard's eyes stayed wide and awed and unseeing.

"You will not show yourselves to me this time?" he asked sadly. "But I know you are there. I hear you moving. I heard your voices. I *touched* you. I know who you are."

Somehow it seemed wrong not to answer. The king just looked so desperate. And . . . hopeful.

"Who do you think we are?" Jonah whispered.

The king's face was amazingly calm.

"You are the angels who appeared to me at Westminster," he said. "The ones who carried my poor nephews off to heaven." He hesitated. "The ones who said I would never see heaven myself because of what I'd done." A sob seemed to catch in his throat. "My wife and precious son are in heaven."

"Uh, yeah," Jonah said. "We know."

Katherine glared at him, her face all but see-through in the candlelight. Jonah held up his hands helplessly in a *What was I supposed to say?* gesture.

"You've seen them, then?" Richard said eagerly. He reached out like he wanted to clutch Jonah's arm again, but Jonah edged backward just in time. "Are they well? Are they happy? Have they been blessed by God?"

"That's what heaven's all about," Katherine said softly. She shrugged at Jonah, as if to say, *Okay, you're right—it's hard not to answer back.*

Richard's shoulders sagged.

"But I will never see them there," he said. "I can never enter heaven myself."

Katherine leaned over and whispered in Jonah's ear. "What kind of religion do these people have?" she asked. "Don't they believe in forgiveness or anything?"

Richard must have heard at least the word "forgiveness," because suddenly he fell to his knees and clasped his hands together, the candle clutched between his fingers.

"Oh, please," he begged. "I could do penance, I could offer indulgences. . . ."

Katherine snorted.

"Right," she said. "That's easy for you to say now. Now

that you're wearing the crown. Now that you think—I mean, now that you know your nephews are dead."

Richard peered up earnestly toward her, even though he still couldn't see her.

"I had to take the throne, for the good of England," he said. "You are heavenly creatures, you may not know the evil deeds of men. A boy king is an invitation for rogues and thieves and usurpers—"

"And you were the first in line," Katherine muttered.

"No, no!" Richard cried, shaking his head violently. "It was the Woodvilles, the mother's family. They were grasping and greedy, and had I not stepped in, they would have stolen everything. . . ."

"*You* were the one who hired murderers," Katherine said scornfully. "How many people have you had killed?"

"A king must show strength," Richard pleaded. "I know it must seem strange to a heavenly being like yourself, but that's how these things are done on earth."

"But to want to kill boys," Katherine said. "Boys. Innocent children."

Tears began streaming down Richard's face.

"If I could, I would atone for that," he said. "I know that is why my son died—a child for a child, a son for a son. That is no more than I deserved, but much worse than my son deserved. And yet . . . and yet . . ." He raised his tearstained face toward Katherine, toward heaven. "I swear to you, upon my dead son's soul, if my nephew Edward could be resurrected, I would put the crown upon his head myself. I would give everything back."

Jonah tugged on his sister's arm.

"Katherine!" he whispered. "We're not trying to get the Crown back for Chip. We're trying to get him out of here!"

"I know!" Katherine whispered. "But—just look at that face!"

Richard's countenance was twisted now, drowning in anguish and grief and guilt.

"Oh, please," he cried. "Pray do not fall silent now!"

"Uh," Jonah said. "Uh . . . I'm sure, if you are sincere, there is a way for your sins to be forgiven."

"And what is that way?" Richard asked eagerly. "Tell me!"

Jonah tried to think about what he'd heard in church. Then he tried to think about whether what he'd heard in church would be the right thing to say in 1485, or if it'd ruin time forever. Was this maybe why "theological arguments" was one of the choices on the Elucidator? Was this maybe why they should have begged to bring the Elucidator with them, no matter what?

"We can't tell you everything," Katherine finally said.

"Some things you have to figure out for yourself."

Richard nodded slowly.

"I see," he whispered. "I will think. I will pray. I *am* sincere. . . ."

Jonah pulled Katherine away. He noticed for the first time that the flap of the tent was pulled back, open to the outdoors.

"This way," he whispered in his sister's ear.

They wove their way out the door, past the king's guards, past knights and soldiers sleeping on the ground. And then, under a bright, starry sky, Jonah collapsed against the thick trunk of a widespread tree.

Katherine collapsed at his feet.

"Oh. My. Gosh," she moaned.

Jonah peered down at her.

"What did we just do?" he asked.

THIRTY

"Maybe it doesn't matter," Katherine said.

Jonah frowned at his sister.

"Katherine, I think, from what JB said, Richard's probably going to die tomorrow. What if we just changed whether or not he goes to heaven?"

"Well, what if we did?" Katherine asked fiercely, glaring up at him. "Wouldn't it be a good thing if Richard got to see his wife and son again?"

Jonah didn't answer. He tilted his head back, leaning it against the tree trunk so he could stare up at the stars. He thought about saying, *But maybe that's not what is supposed to happen. Maybe that's not what happened the first time around.* But that seemed heartless, almost, much too cruel. And what did he know? He wasn't used to worrying about who was going to get into heaven and who wasn't. At his church back home there was a lot more talk about who was going to collect for the food pantry, who was going to volunteer to help out with games at Bible School.

"What if Richard does something different tomorrow before he dies?" Jonah finally said. "What if he acts so differently, because of talking to us, that he doesn't die at all?"

"You want me to feel bad for trying to help?" Katherine demanded. "What were we supposed to do—just let him keep crying?"

Jonah looked back down at his sister. The moonlight shone through her. For the first time in his life Jonah could see how she could be mistaken for an angel.

Jonah swallowed hard.

"What if what we said changes things so much that we can't rescue Chip and Alex?" he asked.

"JB would have yanked us out of time," Katherine said confidently. "He wouldn't have let us talk to Richard if it was going to ruin everything. Remember? All the projections show us saving Chip and Alex."

Jonah decided not to remind her what else JB had said: that sometimes the projections were wrong.

Katherine rolled over.

"Hey, what's this?" she muttered, feeling around on the ground. She scooped something up, holding it toward the dim moonlight. "Look—pears! This is a pear tree!"

"Food!" Jonah said, remembering his empty stomach.

It wasn't pizza, but at least it was something to eat. He began pulling down pears from the lowest branches.

"See, this could change time too," Katherine said as they sat together chewing on the fruit, which was a little hard but still good. "What if this seed right here was supposed to drop to the ground right over there and then grow up to be a huge tree? And then someone built a road that curved, to go around the tree? And then, five hundred years from now, someone important misses the curve and crashes into the tree and dies? Only, none of that will happen now because I'm dropping the seed . . . right . . . here." She made a dramatic show of lifting the seed high, then releasing it and letting it fall into the grass. "Or what if it's the change that leads to people dying? What if the tree grows here, and here's where the road curves, and then—"

"Katherine?" Jonah said. "Quit talking about people dying."

He didn't want to tell her yet, but he could see a thin line of pink on the western horizon. It was almost dawn, almost time for the battle. Their tree—and Richard's tent—was on a bit of a hill, so as the sky brightened, he could see the whole landscape laid out before him. Were those banners off in the distance, announcing an army's approach? That twang he just heard—was that the first bow sending the first arrow arcing through the sky?

"Should we go find Chip and Alex?" Katherine asked.

Jonah glanced to the right, where he knew Chip and Alex were hiding with other troops. Very few people knew they were there; the battle brewing before them was going to be between Richard III and Henry Tudor, his rival who had invaded from France. Chip and Alex were just waiting in the wings, waiting to see if they could take advantage of shifting loyalties or shifting fortunes on the battlefield.

"Nooo," Jonah said slowly. "Not yet. Let's go see what Richard's up to first."

Katherine shrugged, wiped her sticky hands on the grass, and stood up to follow him. In their noisy armor they had to be so careful walking past the knights and soldiers and guards, now that the men were all up and stirring about.

What are these men thinking, knowing any one of them might die in the battle today? Jonah wondered. *How is it that they're not turning around, running away?*

He and Katherine dodged two guards and stepped back into Richard's tent.

Richard was dressed in armor now, transformed from the sobbing, grief-stricken, guilt-ridden man of the night before into a cold, efficient military leader.

"We can certainly count on Norfolk's men," he was telling a cluster of other men in armor. "What think ye of Lord Stanley?"

"Your Majesty!" A breathless page sped into the tent. "Lord Stanley's reply!"

Jonah stepped back, out of the page's way, as the young boy placed an envelope in the king's hand.

Lord Stanley . . . Lord Stanley . . . , Jonah thought. JB had given him and Katherine a crash course in all the different noblemen leading men into the battle. Jonah had found it hard to keep track of them all. But Lord Stanley's name stood out because of what Richard had done to him. Richard wasn't sure he could trust Lord Stanley to fight on his side, so the king had kidnapped Stanley's son Lord Strange and was holding him hostage. He'd threatened to kill Lord Strange if Lord Stanley's men didn't fight.

Richard was opening the letter. His eyes darted across it, then he let out a short, bitter laugh.

"Your Majesty?" one of the other armored men said.

Richard crumpled the letter in his hand.

"He says he doesn't care—he has other sons," Richard said in a dead voice. He let the letter drop to the ground.

"Shall I tell the guards you've ordered Lord Strange's death?" one of the armored men asked, edging toward the tent opening. He sounded like he wanted to get away.

Richard turned and stared at the man.

"No," he said, his voice still flat and emotionless. "I will not let another boy die because of who his father is."

The man's jaw dropped in astonishment. The other men in armor began whispering, "Another boy? *Another?*" Jonah could tell that they all thought he was referring to Edward V—to Chip. They acted like they thought Richard was confessing to his murder.

But Jonah saw the sorrow in Richard's eyes.

He's talking about his own son, Jonah thought. *He thinks that his own son died because of him. Him and his sins.*

The man who'd suggested ordering Lord Strange's death shifted uncomfortably.

"Then . . . shall I have the guards set him free?" the man asked incredulously.

"Not now," Richard said. "We've got a battle to fight."

Jonah wondered if Richard and the armored man had said the same words the first time through history. Was Richard refusing to kill Lord Strange because of what he'd talked about with Jonah and Katherine the night before? Had Jonah and Katherine saved Lord Strange's life? Jonah was at the wrong angle to see if Richard's mouth separated from his tracer's, or if he'd simply repeated the same words he'd said the first time. And Jonah hadn't been watching the other man closely enough to tell if his words had changed either.

Richard whirled around and stalked out of the tent. The other men in armor followed.

Jonah and Katherine were left alone.

"Maybe we should just stay close to Richard," Jonah whispered. "Remember? JB said we can't pull Chip and Alex out until after Richard sees them."

"I want to talk to Chip and Alex first," Katherine said stubbornly. "To make sure they'll be ready to go."

Jonah shrugged and muttered, "Okay." He wasn't sure if it was lingering timesickness or the inadequacy of eating nothing but pears for breakfast, but he felt light-headed and confused, his thoughts jumbled.

What if Chip and Alex aren't ready to go? Jonah wondered. *What did JB say to do, again?*

"Come on," Katherine said, tugging on his arm.

They stepped back out of the tent. They didn't have to dodge any guards this time because the guards, like everyone else in sight, were clustered around Richard. He sat high above them on a tall horse, his armor gleaming in the sunlight, his crown perched on the helmet of his armor.

"Dismiss all fear," Richard was telling his men, "and like valiant champions, advance your standards!"

Standards, Jonah remembered, were the flags that

represented each leader on the battlefield. Far below, down the hill, Jonah could see a huge flag with a red dragon advancing across the field.

It was the flag of Henry Tudor, Richard's enemy. Coming closer.

Richard glanced over his shoulder and apparently saw the dragon banner too.

"Everyone give but one sure stroke, and the day is ours!" he proclaimed. "Onward!"

Richard's men cheered, and then they began rushing down the hill.

"That was the pregame pep talk, wasn't it?" Katherine whispered.

"Sure," Jonah said. "Same thing."

But it wasn't. Jonah had played lots of sports—soccer, basketball, even baseball for a few years—and he'd had coaches who really, really wanted to win. But they hadn't been sending their players out to kill anyone.

Far down the hill the first man fell. Then the second. The third. All across the field before them men were collapsing. Dying.

Jonah noticed that Katherine's lip was trembling. She'd heard the bloodthirstiness in the cheering too. She saw the blood on the field. She knew they weren't just watching a football game. She knew they weren't just watching a movie, where all the blood was fake. She turned her head, looking away from the battle.

"Chip and Alex won't be near the fighting yet," Jonah said gently. "Let's go."

They skirted the edge of the battle, walking far behind the archers launching arrow after arrow from their bows. Jonah had done archery at Boy Scout camp one year, and it'd seemed so pointless and silly. He and his friends laughed about how rarely any of their arrows ever hit the targets.

These archers were grim and serious. Their muscles flexed, their bowstrings sang . . . and out on the field more men sank to their death.

Arrows can pierce armor, Jonah thought with a chill.

Right in front of them one of the archers keeled over, an arrow embedded in his side.

Jonah didn't stop to look for the archer who'd sent his arrow so far across the field. He grabbed Katherine's hand.

"Run!" he shouted, pulling her along.

It didn't matter that they were noisy, rushing down the side of the hill. Out on the battlefield men were screaming, men were crying, swords and lances and knives were crashing. The sounds seemed to burrow deep into Jonah's bones.

Beside Jonah, Katherine fell.

THIRTY-ONE

"Katherine!" Jonah screamed.

He crouched beside her, looking for the arrow. *Pull it out or leave it in?* he asked himself. Why hadn't JB foreseen this? Why hadn't he warned them?

"JB!" he screamed, because surely JB would have to yank them out of 1485 now, surely . . .

Katherine lifted her head, her nearly transparent face now covered with nearly transparent mud.

"Would you shut up?" she asked. "I just slipped. Don't you see how muddy it is here? It's like a swamp or something."

Jonah hadn't noticed. It was amazing what you could tune out when you were panicked and scared. He looked down at his feet, caked with mud, and wondered why he hadn't noticed how hard it was to run. Was he thinking clearly about anything?

Jonah drew in one unsteady breath. Then another. He forced himself to look around. A thin line of trees stood between them and the archers now. And none of the soldiers were venturing in their direction, probably because of the swamp. As long as Jonah and Katherine stayed low, out of the way of arrows, they weren't in any more danger than they would be at home, standing in their own front yard.

"We've got to stay calm," he told Katherine. "There's no reason to panic."

"*I* wasn't the one telling *you* to run," Katherine complained. "I wasn't dragging you through the mud."

She stood up and began brushing off the rapidly drying mud. In another mood Jonah would have laughed to see how the mud was nearly invisible, along with Katherine, until it fell away from her armor. Then it turned brown and clumpy. Jonah felt like he was watching mud flakes rain from thin air.

"We better hope no one sees that," Jonah said, glancing around. "Anyhow, it doesn't matter what you look like—no one can see *you*, remember?"

"Chip and Alex will be able to see me," Katherine said.

"Ooh, *Chip*," Jonah teased her. "Can't have Chip see you with a hair out of place."

That wasn't a fair thing to say, since Chip had already seen Katherine with her hair on fire, in the throes of timesickness nausea, and, back home, all sweaty and gross from biking to the library to try to solve the mystery of where Chip and Jonah had come from. Their adventures with time travel hadn't really made it possible for Katherine to be the prissy, perfect-hair cheerleader type.

Katherine stopped trying to brush the mud away.

"What if he can't see us?" she asked. "What if he and Alex are . . . totally fifteenth century now? What if they don't even remember us?"

"JB said they'll remember," Jonah said.

"But he said they have to choose to come with us," Katherine said. "We can't force them. What if we can't convince them?"

"We'll figure out the right thing to say when we get there," Jonah said impatiently.

He stepped forward, straining because it took so much effort now just to pull his feet through the mud. This portion of the swamp was even wetter, the mud even deeper.

What if it's really quicksand? Jonah wondered. *What if we get stuck out here, and we die and nobody discovers our bones for hundreds of years?*

He wasn't sure why this bothered him so much—not just the dying, but the not being found. What did it matter, if it was going to be hundreds of years before anyone he knew was even born?

I'd want Mom and Dad to know what happened to us, he thought. *I'd want them to know we were trying to be brave, trying to do something good....*

He felt dizzy and disoriented again. Maybe this was one of those swamps he'd heard about in Boy Scouts where there were swamp gases that could knock you out. Maybe they were doomed no matter what.

"Jonah?" Katherine said beside him. "Are those the right troops?"

She pointed at a cluster of silver helmets in the clearing ahead of them.

Jonah tried to remember the map JB had drawn.

"I think so," he said.

The cluster of helmets, the bright sunshine, the screams from the battlefield—everything was so much more vivid than it had seemed from the crude pencil drawing JB had shown them. It was hard to get oriented.

"I'm going to climb this tree and look," Katherine said, bracing her foot against the trunk of a nearby oak with low-hanging branches.

Jonah remembered the arrows whizzing through the air not that far away.

"No! No—I'll do it," Jonah said, pushing her out of the way.

He pushed a little too hard, and Katherine landed on her backside in the mud.

"Jerk!" she called up to him.

Jonah didn't bother answering, or helping her up. He scrambled up the tree—tree climbing was something else that was made much more complicated by armor. He ended up clinging to the thick central branch, peering out through the leaves.

Hundreds of silver helmets lay before him, worn by hundreds of soldiers fidgeting on the sidelines of the battle.

"Well?" Katherine called from the ground below. "Do you see Chip and Alex?"

"I . . . I don't know," Jonah stammered. He hadn't thought about this being hard too, just finding their friends. Why hadn't he asked JB exactly what kind of armor Chip and Alex would be wearing, exactly where they'd be standing?

Why hadn't he requested a GPS reading, while he was at it?

"Let me see," Katherine demanded.

"No, no—stay where it's safe . . . ," Jonah began.

But Katherine already had a foot on the lowest branch. A second later she was standing beside him, on the other side of the tree trunk. Silently she surveyed the rows and rows of helmets.

"See?" Jonah said. "It's not doing any good to stand up here, we're just putting ourselves in danger. . . ."

Katherine opened her mouth—*To tell me off*, Jonah thought. *To argue.* But she surprised him by throwing her head back and screaming at the top of her lungs, "Chip Winston! Where are you?"

That was really stupid, Jonah fumed. *No one could hear her over the sounds of the battle. Or if they do hear her, it'll be the wrong people, soldiers who'll think we're spies, maybe. . . . They might not even look for us, they'll just, I don't know, set the tree on fire. . . .*

At first nothing happened. And then, slowly, slowly, one of the silver helmets began to turn around.

THIRTY-TWO

"Third row from the back, fourth person in," Katherine said, jumping down from the tree.

She landed hard and rolled forward, practically doing a somersault in her armor. Some of her hair dragged out on the ground, collecting more mud to go with the mud on the chest and backside of her armor. She took off running.

"Wait for me!" Jonah cried.

He jumped too, his armor clanking as he hit the ground. A few of the soldiers in the back row looked around nervously, but Jonah ignored them.

Katherine was darting through the rows of soldiers, dodging bulging packs of arrows and jutting-out bows and swords that the soldiers kept at the ready, pointed out, as if they were sure they'd be called into the action at any moment. Jonah did his best to keep up.

They came upon Alex first, standing quietly and resolutely in the lineup of soldiers. Because of the armor and helmet Jonah could see nothing but Alex's face, which looked surprisingly like the twenty-first-century Alex's, rather than the fifteenth-century Prince Richard's.

Oh, yeah, Jonah thought. *If Chip aged from twelve to fourteen between 1483 and 1485, Alex would have aged from ten to twelve. Not that much different from the thirteen-year-old I knew . . .*

Chip was just beyond Alex, standing a little apart from the other soldiers. Up close it was even weirder to see him two years older, with facial hair and a more defined jawline and a thick, muscular neck. *Did they have steroids in the fifteenth century?* Jonah wondered. But it wasn't really the physical changes that startled Jonah the most—it was the look in Chip's eyes, a wise, worldly look, as though he knew all sorts of things a thirteen-year-old wouldn't have learned yet.

Katherine planted herself exactly between the two boys.

"Chip? Alex?" she called softly.

Neither boy moved a muscle. Both continued staring, as if hypnotized, directly out into the battle.

Jonah began to doubt that it really was Chip who'd turned around when Katherine screamed his name. He stepped back for a moment and counted—Chip was the sixth person in from the edge, not the fourth. The fourth person was an old, whiskery man. They were just lucky that that man had turned around, that he'd been standing so close to Chip and Alex.

Hopelessness began to sweep over Jonah. What if they couldn't even get Chip and Alex to acknowledge their presence?

Jonah stepped forward and tugged on Chip's arm. Not hard—he wasn't trying to get Chip completely away from his tracer. It wasn't time for that yet, and he couldn't do it in front of all the other soldiers. But he wanted Chip—the real Chip, the twenty-first-century Chip—to come out just for an instant, just long enough that Jonah could tell him what was going to happen.

Jonah's fingers seemed to slip right off Chip's arm.

"Let me try," Katherine said.

She pushed at Chip's back just as uselessly. She pushed harder. She tugged, she yanked, she stepped back, got a running start, and tried to tackle him.

"Careful," Jonah said. "This is what made JB pull us out the last time."

"But it's not working!" Katherine muttered through gritted teeth.

Jonah sidled up beside Chip and leaned in close to whisper in his ear.

"Please, Chip," he begged. "Remember who you are. We've got to get you out of here, for your own good. Remember home? Remember cell phones and iPods and TVs and computers and cars and . . . and pizza! Remember pizza?"

Chip turned his head. But it was only to look at Alex, only to say, "Watch Norfolk's men. They're fighting the hardest."

"Hello?" Jonah screamed. But the sound got lost in the cheers and shrieks from the battlefield. Chip continued to look right through Jonah.

"I have an idea," Katherine said.

She shoved past Jonah and put her arm around Chip's shoulder. She had to reach up high and stand on tiptoes; he was that much taller than her now.

"Chip," she said, her lips almost touching his ear, "six boys have asked me to be their girlfriend in the past year."

"Katherine, what are you doing?" Jonah fumed. "Nobody cares about that right now!"

Katherine glared at him for a moment, then went back to whispering to Chip.

"I told them all no, and do you want to know why?" she asked. "Everybody's supposed to have a boyfriend or girlfriend in sixth grade, but I didn't really care about any of those boys—it wouldn't have meant anything to say that Tyler Crawford was my boyfriend, or that Spencer Rajan was my boyfriend."

"Spencer Rajan asked you out?" Jonah asked incredulously. "I didn't know that."

Katherine ignored him.

"But you know what, Chip?" she said, leaning in closer. "If *you'd* asked me to be your girlfriend, I would have said yes. That would have meant something."

Swaying a little on her tiptoes, weighed down by her mud-covered armor, she turned her head and gave him a timid kiss on the cheek.

At first nothing happened. But then there was a small flare of light around Chip's face, the reappearance of his tracer, barely separated from Chip. The tracer continued staring out at the battle, but Chip turned his head to look at Katherine.

"Really?" Chip said softly, his nearly invisible mouth moving while the tracer's mouth stayed firmly shut. "You really like me?"

THIRTY-THREE

"Well, duh," Katherine said. "I came all the way to the fifteenth century for you, didn't I?" She took a step back, as if she was a little stunned that Chip had heard her. She looked him up and down. "And it's not just because I know now that you're going to be really hot by the time you're fifteen."

"I am?" Chip said. "Hot? You think so?"

"Hey, hey—can the romance and hot talk, all right?" Jonah interrupted. Both Chip and Katherine turned toward him, looking annoyed. "Or save it for later," Jonah amended. "We've got a lot of other things to worry about right now."

"Aye, the battle," Chip said. His face started to retract into the older, fifteenth-century version of himself, into his tracer.

"No, no, Chip—wait," Jonah said frantically. "Katherine and I came to get you and Alex out of here. So you don't die in this battle."

Chip's face hovered, barely apart from his tracer's.

"I won't die in battle," he said confidently. "I'm an expert swordsman. Everyone says so."

"That doesn't matter," Jonah said. "All the time experts say you and Alex are going to die if we don't take you away."

Jonah saw a flash of light—it was Chip's arm separating from his tracer's. Chip reached out to grasp Alex's shoulder.

"My brother?" Chip asked. "*He'll* die?"

Jonah got an idea.

"Pull him out of his tracer," Jonah said. "Let him hear what's going to happen." This had worked before, Jonah remembered. Chip had been able to separate Alex from his tracer when Jonah and Katherine failed.

Chip glanced around, his head separating from his tracer's head even more dramatically. None of the soldiers around them were watching Chip and Alex. They all had their eyes glued to the battle. Chip jerked on Alex's shoulder.

Alex's head pitched forward, leaving his tracer's face behind. Dazedly, he peered around, his eyes focusing slowly on Jonah and Katherine.

"Two years," he murmured. "I haven't been able to fully think with this brain for two years."

"We're almost ready to take you back," Jonah said. "You can think with that brain all the time after this."

Alex blinked.

"I—," he began.

Suddenly there was a thundering of hooves, drowning out whatever Alex had planned to say. A man on a white horse sped toward them, leaning forward in the saddle, intent on his goal.

It was King Richard III.

Jonah stiffened. *Our cue!* He wanted to scream at Katherine, "Remember? We can pull them out after Richard sees them!"

But he and Katherine had to step out of the way, because Richard galloped right up in front of Chip and Alex. Both boys had completely rejoined their tracers and were staring up at their uncle. Around them the other soldiers had their hands on their swords, but Jonah couldn't tell if they were prepared to attack Richard or defend him.

Richard slid off his horse. His eyes flicked from Chip to Alex and back again.

"My nephews," he said, sounding stunned, as if he couldn't quite believe the sight before him. "So it is true. . . . You live?"

"Aye," Chip said, a challenge in his voice. "Against your wishes."

He stood bold and strong, his hand tight on the hilt of his sword.

Would he try to kill Richard? Jonah wondered. *Right here? Right now? What could we do about that?*

"And yet, you've been betrayed," Richard said mockingly. "Spies told me you were here."

"Spies told us not all of your subjects are loyal," Alex countered, stepping up beside Chip. "Some of your noblemen refused to fight for you."

Jonah remembered Lord Stanley, refusing to fight for Richard even if it meant his own son's death. Richard grimaced, every bit as pained as if Alex had struck him with a sword. Jonah expected Richard to lash out, maybe grab for his own sword at the insult. Jonah put his arm protectively on Alex's shoulder, ready to snatch him away at the first thrust of a sword. Out of the corner of his eye Jonah saw Katherine do the same thing to Chip.

But Richard didn't reach for his sword. He dropped to his knee and bowed his head before Chip.

"My nephew," Richard murmured. "I have sinned before God and man, but I have been granted a second chance. When the battle is over . . . when we have vanquished Henry Tudor . . ." He looked up, his eyes boring into Chip's. "As soon as this battle ends, I will give you back your crown."

THIRTY-FOUR

Jonah's jaw dropped. This was a complication he'd never expected, one he'd never even dreamed was possible.

Why didn't JB warn us about this? Jonah wondered. Maybe it was just Jonah, but it seemed like it would have made a lot more sense for JB to tell him and Katherine they could yank Chip and Alex out of time "after Richard offers the crown back," rather than "after Richard sees them."

Before Chip could answer, an overwhelming wave of cheers and screams and gasps flew through the crowd, seeming to drown out all other sound. *How could all those people have heard what Richard said?* Jonah wondered. But they weren't reacting to Richard's proclamation. They were reacting to something that had happened out on the battlefield.

"That's Norfolk. . . ."

"Norfolk is down. . . ."

"Norfolk is dead. . . ."

The news flew through the crowd, one update instantaneously replaced by the next.

Jonah remembered how it was Norfolk's men that Richard had said he could count on; it was Norfolk's men that Chip had said were fighting the hardest.

Richard looked stricken.

He scrambled up from his bent knee and back onto his horse. High above the crowd, he could probably see straight out to the battlefield now.

"My friend Norfolk, fallen," he murmured, a quiver in his voice. "But now his son will take charge. . . ."

Even Jonah, who knew nothing about medieval battle tactics, could see that Norfolk's men were disorganized and scattered, unable to forge on without their original leader. A group of soldiers behind yellow banners swept against them, pushing Norfolk's army back and back and back.

Richard looked down at Chip.

"I must defend the crown I would give you," he said. "This will be my last act as king. . . ." He spun his horse around and galloped off.

For a long moment Jonah lost sight of Richard in the chaos. Then the king reappeared in the center of the battle. He was leading a charge all the way across the field, through the thick of the fighting. It was easy to follow his progress because he'd crammed his crown on top of his helmet, and it gleamed in the sunlight. He was the only man on the battlefield wearing a crown.

Richard passed the yellow-bannered troops that had swept away Norfolk's men; he passed deep into the heart of Henry Tudor's men. It was an amazing breakaway—no one seemed able to touch him.

And then Richard reached the man carrying Henry Tudor's dragon banner. The dragon banner plummeted to the ground.

"He killed Henry's standard-bearer?" Chip murmured in amazement. "He's that close to killing Henry?"

But a second later it was Richard tumbling to the ground. *No, wait*, Jonah thought. *It's not Richard who's hurt. It's his horse.* The horse's white coat seemed to have turned red. He lay on the ground, unmoving. But Richard was up on his feet, fighting back as Henry Tudor's men surrounded him.

"That's the line I remember from the Shakespeare play!" Alex said suddenly. "He's supposed to say, 'A horse! A horse! My kingdom for a horse!'"

"Then what happens in Shakespeare?" Jonah asked.

Alex frowned, a contrast to the hopeful face of his tracer.

"Don't know," Alex said, but he was distracted, watching the battle.

Richard really did need a horse. He was fighting valiantly, but more and more of his enemies surrounded him, and he couldn't escape. After a few moments Jonah could no longer see Richard's helmet or crown or sword because of all the other helmets and swords flashing around him. And then a circlet of gold rolled out of the center of the fighting. Men just stepped back and let it roll.

It was Richard's crown.

Richard was dead.

THIRTY-FIVE

An eerie silence hung over the battlefield, as if everyone was holding his breath. Then Jonah realized it was only his mind that had blanked out the noise temporarily. Swordsmen were still waving their swords; archers were still launching their arrows. In the thick of the fight they couldn't see what had happened to the king.

But Chip had.

"My crown!" he screamed. "That's my crown!"

He dashed forward, dragging Katherine along with him.

"My brother!" Alex yelled behind him, and took off running as well.

"No, stop!" Jonah shrieked. "We've got to get you out of here!"

Nobody seemed to hear Jonah, because all of the soldiers around them were surging forward alongside Chip and Alex, battle cries ringing from their throats. Jonah wasn't sure if the soldiers really wanted to help Chip regain the Crown, or if they were just tired of standing around. But they were all rushing into battle, toward Henry Tudor's men.

How soon will Chip reach his first opponent? Jonah wondered. JB's words "You have a very narrow window of opportunity" echoed in Jonah's mind. Chip and Alex had already been seen by Richard. Richard had had time to ride off into the battle and die. How much time did Chip and Alex have left?

Alex, running, tried to shake Jonah's arm off his shoulder, the action momentarily separating him from his tracer. Stubbornly Jonah leaped forward, wrapping his arms tighter around Alex's neck.

"You can talk to him," Jonah whispered in Alex's ear. "*You* can tell him he has to leave."

"I'll do what my brother wants me to do," Alex said, and Jonah couldn't tell which version of Alex was speaking. Jonah saw no flash of tracer light, but his eyes didn't seem to be working properly as he jolted along, arrows whizzing past him, swords flying around him. Jonah didn't think Alex could have progressed very far, weighed down by Jonah on his back; evidently the battle had come to them.

"Chip!" Jonah screamed. "Katherine!"

This was his worst nightmare: He'd lost sight of both his sister and his friend.

What am I going to tell Mom and Dad? he wondered.

Sunlight flashed off a sword several yards ahead of him, blinding him temporarily. The sword slashed the air—and crashed into a sword held by Chip.

"Go help your brother!" Jonah screamed in Alex's ear.

Alex raced forward, as if he'd had the same thought. The old, whiskery soldier whose turning head had first led to Chip and Alex raced alongside them, like a guardian fending off attacks. Jonah wondered if the man was a particular friend of theirs—a relative, a servant?—but there wasn't time to ask.

Chip was fighting furiously now, whipping his sword this way and that, countering his opponent's every blow. Katherine stood behind him, ducking when he ducked, dodging every parry and thrust.

"Look out!" she shrieked. "On your right!"

But Chip was already reacting, pulling his sword back to block another opponent's swing of a battle-ax.

"That one's mine!" the whiskery soldier shouted, spinning his sword forward so Chip could go back to focusing on the first opponent.

It would be impossible to capture Chip's attention while he was engaged in battle. Jonah took a risk: He leaped off Alex's back and landed on top of the swordsman who was attacking Chip. This worked better than Jonah had hoped, as the swordsman crumpled to the ground.

Bafflement spread over Chip's face; it seemed to be a mixture of the tracer not understanding why his opponent had suddenly fallen down, and Chip not understanding how Jonah had appeared out of nowhere.

"Jonah?" Chip whispered.

"We've—got—to—leave—now!" Jonah screamed.

The swordsman was squirming out from underneath him. Any minute now he'd spring back into action.

"I'm king again," Chip said. "I'm getting my crown back."

"It's not going to work that way," Jonah argued. "If you don't leave, you're going to die!"

Chip's face seemed to bubble back and forth, tragic medieval king one moment, uncertain twenty-first-century teen the next. It was like Chip was having trouble making up his mind. And then his face hardened with the strong jawline, the mustache, the wise-beyond-his-years eyes. He was the medieval king.

"Sometimes you have to fight for what you want," Chip said, his expression set. "Sometimes the fight is all you get."

"Is this really what you want?" Jonah asked. "Death on a battlefield?"

The swordsman sprang up from behind Jonah, swinging his weapon at Chip. Jonah ducked down out of the way; Chip's sword rang out against his opponent's.

"My crown!" Chip cried. "My throne! My glory!"

Jonah jumped up, too angry now for caution.

"You're just like your father," he snarled. "Back home. Remember? Remember how selfish he was, how he never thought about anyone but himself? Katherine just told you she wanted you to be her boyfriend, and you don't even care. You don't care that we came all the way back here, risking our own lives to save you. When you die— for so-called *glory*, but for no reason really, accomplishing absolutely *nothing*—when that happens, Katherine's going to spend the next five hundred years crying over you."

Chip stopped in the middle of a sword thrust, though his tracer's arms continued forward. At the last possible second the whiskery soldier blocked Chip's opponent, swinging for him again.

Chip turned to face Katherine, his body twisted almost completely backward from his tracer's. Jonah saw Chip's opponent blink in astonishment, a burst of tracer light in his face—as far as Jonah could tell, the opponent probably thought Chip had disappeared entirely.

"Would you really cry for five hundred years if I die?" Chip asked Katherine.

Katherine peered up at him.

"I'd rather not," she said. "I'd rather save your life instead."

Chip looked around wonderingly, as if he were only now really seeing the battle around him, only now hearing the clash of swords and the zing of arrows and the cries of dying men. Fear and awe battled in his face.

"Let's get out of here, then," he whispered.

"Get Alex!" Jonah screamed.

Chip stepped back toward his brother, and Jonah thought it would be good for him to get completely away from his tracer. But the tracer was striding back toward Alex too, practically running.

Alex was in danger: A soldier stood over him, a battle-ax raised high.

"Get him *now!*" Katherine screamed.

Chip scooped up Alex's shoulders and yanked him backward. As soon as he was away from his tracer, Alex turned invisible again, like Chip and Jonah and Katherine.

Behind them, Chip's and Alex's tracers gleamed with a ghostly light. The soldier with the battle-ax hesitated, confused, separating from a tracer of his own.

"JB!" Jonah hollered. "We're ready!"

"I've got you covered," the whiskery soldier said, taking something that resembled a plain, flat rock out of his pocket and pushing a button on its surface.

He has an Elucidator, Jonah thought. *He's on our side. He's from the future too. How come he's allowed to have an Elucidator and we're not?*

And then Jonah and the others were spinning through time, away from the fifteenth century.

The last thing Jonah saw, before everything disappeared, was a ghostly tracer battle-ax slamming down on two ghostly tracer boys.

THIRTY-SIX

They landed on their backs on solid rock, with a view of a solid rock ceiling arcing above them.

They were back in the cave.

Jonah could hear screaming and wailing, and for a moment he thought they'd brought the battle with them. But these screams were high pitched, like at a middle school pep rally: the voices of teenage girls and boys who could still sing in the treble clef if they needed to.

Dizzily Jonah sat up. He checked to see that Katherine and Chip and Alex—and the whiskery soldier—were all on the floor beside him. Then he faced forward, looking for the source of all those screams. A group of kids were clustered nearby: all the other kids who were missing children plucked from history. He recognized Andrea Crowell, with her long braids; Ming Reynolds, though she was missing her name tag; Emily Quinn, who'd been so calm before (and in fact, she was one of the few kids not screaming now). And behind them, Anthony Solbers and Sarah Puchini and Josh Hart and Denton Price . . .

A statuesque African-American woman rushed forward—it was their friend Angela, the only adult from the twenty-first century who knew about time travel.

"Are you all right?" she demanded.

Jonah realized she was peering only at him and Katherine. Chip and Alex, incredibly enough, were wearing the same clothes they'd had on in the beginning: the Ohio State sweatshirt and jeans and Nikes for Chip; the Einstein T-shirt and jeans for Alex. They looked clean and tidy, perfectly normal.

Jonah and Katherine, on the other hand, were still wearing dented, battered, muddy armor, which, strangely, now also seemed a bit rusty.

"We're fine," Jonah said. "We just look awful."

"Speak for yourself," Katherine corrected him. Then she looked down at the clumps of mud clinging to her hair, the leather straps on her armor that seemed to be worn almost all the way through. "Oh, well," she said. "Sometimes you can't help getting a little messy."

Jonah was glad that at least the whiskery soldier looked

muddy and battered too. The soldier stood up, creakily, and stuck out his hand to Angela.

"Hadley Correo, ma'am," he said politely. "I'm very glad to meet you."

"You too," Angela said, equally politely. "Angela DuPre. I take it you're a friend of JB's?"

Jonah didn't have the patience for stupid grown-up chitchat.

"Where's JB?" he demanded. "Did everything work out? Chip and Alex are safe, but what happened to history?"

JB stepped out from behind the screaming kids, who were finally beginning to settle down a little. Jonah wasn't sure if he'd been there all along, or if he'd just arrived from some foreign time as well.

"We have an expression in this business," JB said. "Time will tell. It will take a while to be sure of the outcomes—"

"Oh, come on," Jonah said, annoyed again. "I know how time travel works now. You probably zoomed up to the future before coming back here—you probably already spent years studying how the changes rippled through history!"

JB laughed, unoffended.

"It's true that I could have," he admitted. "But I didn't. My first priority was making sure all of you were all right."

Jonah watched JB's eyes and decided he was telling the truth. Maybe JB wasn't concerned solely about time after all.

"These kids are troopers," Hadley Correo said, patting Jonah and Katherine on the back. "I'd put them up against some of the best time agents I've ever worked with."

"Thanks a lot!" JB said, rolling his eyes. "Remind me of that the next time I nearly kill myself getting recertified! I still won't be as good as thirteen-year-old amateurs!"

Despite his words, he didn't seem truly offended. Jonah guessed that Hadley and JB had probably worked together before.

"Why didn't you tell us somebody else was there on the battlefield to help us?" Katherine demanded.

"All our projections showed that wouldn't work," JB said. "You had to feel responsible. And . . . you were. Hadley wouldn't have known to talk about Chip's dad. He wouldn't have known to talk about Katherine's variety of boyfriend choices."

Jonah noticed that Katherine was blushing under her coating of mud.

"Um," Emily said hesitantly now that the other kids had stopped screaming. "I don't get it. Those kids were only gone an instant. How'd they get so beat up? Why are you talking about battlefields and boyfriends and time agents, like a lot of stuff happened while they were away?"

"An instant?" Chip asked. "Are you crazy? We were gone for two years!" His voice shot up an octave and squeaked on the word "years," and he looked stunned and embarrassed. "Two years," he tried again, only marginally deeper. He clamped his mouth shut, his face turning as red as Katherine's.

Oh, yeah, Jonah thought. *Chip probably got used to being fourteen and a half, almost fifteen—his voice probably never squeaked then. It must be pretty grim to have to go back to being thirteen all over again.*

"See," Alex explained to Emily, "with time travel you can be away for years—decades, even, if you need to—and then come back to your original time so quickly that no one would even notice that you were gone."

"Oh," Emily said. "I get it."

"Is that what's going to happen to the rest of us?" Andrea Crowell asked in a small voice. "You're going to send us away, and then we're going to come back looking that . . . weathered?"

Weathered? Jonah thought. *What kind of a kid uses a word like that?* He sort of liked it, though. It was better than being described as "battered" or "beat up."

"I don't know about the 'weathered' part," JB said, "but yes, you're all going back in time."

Andrea gulped.

"Now?" she asked.

"No," Jonah said.

JB and Hadley turned to him in surprise.

"Well, actually, I thought—," JB began.

"No," Jonah said again. "You're going to give us a chance to go home and get used to the idea that we're missing kids from history. You're going to let us eat our favorite foods and hug our parents good-bye if we want to."

JB frowned; Jonah could tell he wasn't convinced.

"Look," Jonah said. "It's not like we can tell anybody about this, because nobody would believe it anyway. So . . . just give us some time to adjust."

Several of the other kids were nodding. Even one of the scariest-looking kids, who had a skull on the back of his sweatshirt, muttered, "He's right, dude."

Angela stepped forward.

"I think you should listen to Jonah," she said. "He knows what he's talking about."

Me? Jonah wanted to say. *Somebody's acting like I'm the expert?*

JB and Hadley exchanged glances. Jonah couldn't be sure, but he thought maybe the two men's images flickered for a second, as if they'd time-traveled out of the cave to have a long discussion about the pros and cons of Jonah's suggestion and then returned to give their final decision.

"All right," JB said reluctantly. "If Jonah thinks that's for the best, that's what we'll do."

"What about us—me and Alex?" Chip asked. "Now that we've been to the past and back, aren't you going to erase our memories or something, so it doesn't mess up our lives now? Like in the *Men in Black* movies?"

JB looked puzzled.

"Chip, we can't do that. It's not possible. Or desirable," JB said. He appealed to Angela. "Don't people in your time know the difference between science and science fiction?"

Angela shrugged. "From my perspective a lot of it looks the same," she said dryly.

"No, listen," Chip said, a panicky edge to his voice. "I was the king of England, then the prince hiding in exile. I know Latin now. I can sword-fight. I know diplomacy. I can recite *The Dictes and Sayings of the Philosophers* almost word for word, by memory. I can't go back to being who I used to be!"

Hadley looked down at him sympathetically.

"None of us can, kid," he said. "That's the point. You get what you get. Life changes you. Time travel or no, you always have to build on what you live through."

Chip still looked a little upset, but he shut his mouth firmly.

Is that what diplomacy looks like? Jonah wondered. He wasn't sure he'd ever be capable of it himself.

"So we're going home?" he asked eagerly.

"Yes," JB said. "You're going home."

Katherine started to stand up, and the leather strap on her armor gave way, one huge metal boot crashing to the ground.

"Oh," she said, "do we at least get our regular clothes back? That was one of my favorite shirts."

"Oops," JB said. "It's all in the back of the cave. I stashed it there when . . . well, never mind, it'd take a long time to explain, and it doesn't really matter. You can take turns changing. And when you're done, just leave the armor back there. I don't want anyone asking why kids at an adoption conference were playing with priceless antiques."

Things happened quickly after that. Jonah and Katherine changed back into modern clothes (blue jeans never felt so good), JB returned the cave to the twenty-first century, and all the kids hiked back to the high school, where their parents were meeting to talk about "identity issues for teen adoptees."

It was strange to see Mom and Dad again, when Mom and Dad thought they'd only been apart for a matter of hours, and Jonah and Katherine knew they'd traveled half a millennium away and back. It was actually rather hard for Jonah not to run up to his parents and throw his arms around both of them and cry out, "I thought I'd never see you again!"

"Hey," Jonah grunted in the crowded high school lobby as soon as he spotted Mom's familiar tan raincoat, Dad's familiar bald spot.

Mom and Dad rushed toward Jonah and Katherine and Chip, as other kids and parents reunited all around them.

"How was it?" Mom asked cautiously. "Do you feel like you learned a lot?"

"Yeah," Chip said. "Actually, we did."

Jonah knew that it would take Mom only a moment to notice that he and Katherine had mud in their hair. He wanted to talk about something that was a lot more important first.

"It was okay, but they didn't feed us nearly enough," he said. "Could we please, please, please pick up some pizza on the way home?"

Mom laughed.

"Jonah, I swear, nobody could ever feed you enough. You can't go five minutes without eating, can you?"

"You'd be surprised," Jonah said. "You'd really be surprised."

EPILOGUE

Jonah, Katherine, Chip, and Alex were playing basketball in the Skidmores' driveway. A week had passed since the so-called adoption conference, and they were proud that they'd managed to convince their parents to let their "new friend," Alex, come over, even though he lived half an hour away. The basketball game was mostly just a ruse, though, since they were all much more interested in talking about their trip through time.

"I've been doing research on medieval history all week, and it's disgusting—nobody knows much of anything about me and Chip," Alex complained, bouncing the ball halfheartedly.

"Just about everybody thinks we died in the Tower of London," Chip agreed. "Just because some Tudor historian told a bunch of lies, just because they found some unidentified bones in the Tower in the 1600s . . . didn't anybody who saw us at the Battle of Bosworth say anything? It's *much* more honorable to die in battle than to be a silly youth murdered in his own bed."

Jonah and Katherine exchanged glances, and Chip grimaced.

"I'm talking medieval again, aren't I?" he asked.

This had been a recurring problem for Chip all week. He'd used the word "doth" in language arts class, and everyone had laughed at him; he'd explained to a bully on the school bus exactly how it was possible to carve out a man's innards with a sword or battle-ax.

On the bright side, this had made the bully stop bothering anyone on the bus.

"Are you having problems with that, Alex?" Chip asked wistfully. "Forgetting that you're not an English prince in the 1480s anymore?"

"Some," Alex said. "But people always thought I was weird anyway, so nobody really cares. I'm just telling Mom it's all her fault because she's always quoting Shakespeare at me. I told her it's finally happened—she's completely rotted my brain." He caught the basketball on its next bounce. "Look, this is starting to hurt my hand. I can see the point of archery and swordsmanship—men needed to know how to do that in the fifteenth century to protect themselves and their families and their lords. But basketball—why?"

"We don't have to play," Jonah said, though he wondered if Alex had always disliked basketball, or if this was another way the fifteenth century had changed him. "Here."

He motioned for Alex to bounce the ball his way, and he dropped it on the concrete. Then he flopped down in the grass by the driveway, and all the other kids followed his lead. For a second Jonah got a flashback to weeks earlier, when he and Chip had been playing basketball and then flopped down in the exact same spot, carefree and laughing, only moments before Jonah got the first hint that there was something very odd about his life.

At least Chip and Alex know who they really are, and where they came from, Jonah thought. *Even if they have trouble remembering to speak modern American English, at least they have their mysteries solved.*

In the cave, after returning from the Battle of Bosworth, Jonah had been so eager to return to normal life—to see his parents, to eat pizza, to be a typical twenty-first-century kid again—that he hadn't asked about his own original identity. This was what bothered him now, more than any lingering questions about the fifteenth century. Sometimes when he was alone in his room, late at night, Jonah would whisper, "JB? JB, can you hear me? Are you watching? Is it my turn in history yet?" But then he felt foolish, talking to no one. And scared. Chip and Alex had come so close to dying tragically in their moment in time. What if Jonah's original identity was even more dangerous?

"But did you read anything about the Shakespeare play?" Katherine was asking indignantly. She shook her ponytail for emphasis. "His Richard the Third is pure evil. And a deformed monster, when, really, he looked perfectly normal."

"Shakespeare changed all sorts of things in his history plays, to make his stories better," Alex said. "And when Queen Elizabeth, a Tudor, was on the throne, it was definitely to his advantage to make the Tudors' old enemy seem like the devil incarnate." He clapped his hands over his mouth. "Oops," he said, wincing. "I think I'm quoting my mother *exactly*. Ugh!"

Jonah had gotten a good look at Alex's mother when she dropped him off. She was not exactly what he'd expected: She had bright-red-framed eyeglasses and dark blond hair that was even curlier than Chip's and Alex's— practically an Afro—and she was wearing a T-shirt that said something Jonah thought maybe would be obscene, except that it was in Shakespearean English.

"But people should know that Richard wasn't that

bad," Katherine said. "They should know what he did at the very end. Do you think . . . do you think he really was forgiven?"

"*I* forgive him," Chip said softly. "I . . . I know what it's like to be willing to kill for the throne."

Jonah had a flash of remembering the murderous look in Chip's eye as he charged out onto the battlefield, crying, "My crown! That's my crown!"

No wonder Chip looked so haunted by his past. No wonder he'd wanted JB to erase his memory.

"Isn't it different, being willing to kill someone on a battlefield?" Jonah asked. "Instead of wanting to kill innocent kids in their beds at night?"

"*You* said death on the battlefield was pointless," Chip reminded him. "You said if I died there, it would mean absolutely nothing."

"I didn't know you were supposed to die trying to save your brother's life," Jonah said.

He'd surveyed the others—he was the only one who'd caught that last glimpse of the tracers, the glowing ghostly versions of Chip and Alex under the battle-ax. He was actually glad none of the others had had to see it.

But he was also glad he knew how the story had ended. It made him think better of Chip.

Jonah saw Katherine reach out hesitantly and squeeze

Chip's hand. To Jonah's relief, neither one of them had made a big deal about the whole boyfriend/girlfriend thing. Chip squeezed back, and then they both let go.

Jonah peered off into the distance—a distance defined by two-story houses and faux wrought-iron streetlamps and neatly trimmed suburban oaks and maples. Even after the brief time he'd spent in the Middle Ages, it was still a bit of a jolt to see so much . . . civilization. *It must be much, much stranger for Chip and Alex,* he thought. *What's a "doth" here and there if they can still manage to act somewhat normal?*

Far down the sidewalk a man was coming toward them, walking a large English sheepdog. Beside Jonah, Katherine suddenly stiffened.

"Oh, no," she muttered. She jumped up and began running toward the man.

Jonah squinted, and understood.

The man was JB.

"No!" Katherine yelled at him. "I know what you're here for—you *can't* take Jonah away. I won't let you! I've been thinking about this all week, and I'm going to scream and yell and say you're a kidnapper, and—"

"I'm not here to take Jonah back to his time period," JB said. "I didn't come to force anyone to go anywhere they don't want to go."

Katherine still stood firm, blocking the sidewalk—a

five-foot-tall, eighty-five-pound barrier. The sheepdog probably could have knocked her over with one paw. But Jonah was a little touched that she was trying.

"I promise," JB said, drawing closer. "Look—I've learned a new expression from your time period." He raised his right hand. "Scout's honor."

Jonah exchanged glances with Chip and Alex. He wondered which of them would have to tell JB that no grown man should do that, unless he was a Scout leader—dealing with really, really little kids.

Both of the other boys just shrugged.

"Well, then . . . ," Katherine sputtered a little, shifting gears. "Tell us this: When are you ever going to release the ripple? Is everything okay with time?"

JB seemed to be trying hard to hide a smile at Katherine's using a time-travel term like "release the ripple." JB had explained this to them back when they'd first learned about being missing children from history. JB and his fellow agents had frozen the impact of the kids' being stolen; the whole point of returning them was to allow time to follow its natural courses again.

"We already did release the ripple," JB said. "Everything's fine."

"But . . . but . . . unless it changed in the last ten minutes, none of the Web sites have the right information about what really happened to Chip and Alex and Richard the Third," Katherine objected.

JB stopped a few steps away from her.

"Did you expect history to say that Richard got religious advice from time travelers the night before he died?" JB asked. "Did you want it on Wikipedia that Chip and Alex were saved at the last minute and carried off to the twenty-first century?"

"No." Katherine shook her head stubbornly. "But people should know that Richard wasn't all bad. He repented at the end. He wanted to give his crown back."

"Sit," JB told the sheepdog. The dog eased his hindquarters down onto the sidewalk. Then he lay all the way down and put his head on his front paws, as if he expected this to take a while.

"Time needed Richard to be a villain," JB explained carefully. "The year 1483 was something of a turning point in history. Before that, killing for political gain was . . . expected. Ordinary. But the way the princes disappeared from the Tower, the way everyone thought they knew what had happened, the way people were so horrified at Richard killing kids . . . that changed history. Killing children became something you usually couldn't do and still be considered a decent human being. It became part of the change in how people viewed children, how they viewed humanity. Richard was held up forever after that as an example of what leaders shouldn't do. In some ways this was almost as important as the Magna Carta."

JB sounded as earnest as a college professor trying to explain why history mattered. Jonah couldn't quite remember what the Magna Carta was, but everything else kind of made sense.

Of course Katherine wasn't satisfied.

"But that's not fair to Richard," she complained. "He doesn't deserve his bad reputation."

"Do you think that matters to Richard?" JB asked. "He died five minutes after offering Chip the Crown."

"But did he go to heaven?" Katherine persisted.

"That's between him and God, not him and history," JB said.

Alex started, jerking so spastically that he kicked the basketball, and would have sent it spinning out into the street if Chip hadn't caught it. Amazingly, Chip still seemed to have a swordsman's quick reflexes.

"*You* believe in God?" Alex asked JB incredulously. "But you know how to travel through time. You're a scientist." He hesitated. "Aren't you?"

JB rolled his eyes.

"It amazes me how people of your time set up such a false dichotomy between science and religion. Fortunately, that only lasts for another . . . well, I can't tell you that," he said, stopping himself just in time. "But I assure you, the more I travel through time, the more I witness, the more I realize that there are things that are both strange and wonderful, far beyond human comprehension." He turned to Jonah and Katherine. "Like how a couple of untrained kids could save time, when expert professionals would have failed every time."

Katherine tossed her head as if she was ready to launch into a victory dance: *So there! We showed you!*

"You helped us some," Jonah said modestly. "With Hadley signaling us there by Chip and Alex on the battlefield so we'd find them in time. And with how you let us use invisibility."

JB shook his head.

"But you did everything wrong," he said. "We're still cataloging how many sacred rules of time travel you broke. No certified time traveler would have dared to speak directly to Richard—and you did it twice!"

"Why didn't you yank us out of time when we were breaking all those rules?" Jonah asked.

"We, uh, couldn't," JB said sheepishly. "We kept being blocked by the impact of your actions. And then . . . we kept discovering that everything you did worked."

"But . . ." Alex shifted uncomfortably. "We didn't stay

with our tracers exactly. Chip and Jonah and Katherine and me . . . we did change history. Why doesn't anyone know that?"

"Well," JB said. "There was the matter of a certain Shakespeare quote being widely used more than a hundred years ahead of time. . . ."

"Oops," Alex said.

JB shrugged.

"In the scheme of things that was *nothing*," he said. "Otherwise . . . everyone who heard Richard offer Chip the throne died on that battlefield. So did everyone who saw you separate from your tracers, saw the princes vanish into thin air. The way everything worked, it almost seemed . . . preordained."

He seemed embarrassed saying the word, which seemed out of place on this sunny autumn day, in twenty-first-century America.

"Still," Alex said. He looked around, as if suddenly scared. "You can't tell me nobody else thought of this. I'm not ruining anything talking about this—"

"What?" Katherine demanded. "Would you just spit it out?"

Alex looked down, biting his lip. Then he peered back up at JB.

"Chip and me, we still don't belong in the twenty-first

century," Alex said. "Okay, so it didn't mess up the fifteenth century to have Jonah and Katherine rescuing us—that's great. Whatever. But anything we do here, now, aren't we changing *this* time period? Should we plan never to come up with any brilliant scientific discoveries, never to have a job, never to get married and have kids, never to have an impact at all?" He looked over at Chip, whose jaw had dropped. "Sorry. I had to say it."

JB stepped forward and crouched down before both boys.

"Alex, I can see where you would think that," he said gently. "But you're proceeding from a flawed hypothesis. Or . . . incomplete information. You don't have to worry about trying to stay invisible in this time. Live. Use your brain to make all the discoveries you want, scientific or otherwise. Fall in love, marry, have children—well, years from now, I mean. Have an impact. There are time experts who would have agreed with your assessment, before. But we're all seeing things a little differently now. This time period is much more in flux than we thought. It's starting to seem like . . . well, like maybe the time crash was supposed to happen. Like maybe it's supposed to be part of history." He chuckled. "We're not even worried anymore that Angela DuPre is never going to marry that plumber we thought she was supposed to marry. Which would be a relief for Hadley . . ." He muttered this almost to himself, then looked back up at the kids. "All sorts of things are changing. And that's okay."

If Jonah were making any bets about which of them was most likely to make the scientific discoveries of the future, he'd put his money on Alex. Even Katherine always did better in science at school than Jonah ever did. But Jonah had a thought about time travel that nobody else seemed to have figured out.

What if all those changes are because of us too? he wondered. *What if we had an even bigger impact than we'll ever know?*

"Speaking of changes . . . ," JB began, putting his knee down and turning slightly so he could look at all of the kids at once. "I really didn't come here just to talk."

Katherine put her hands on her hips.

"I knew it!" she said. "You're still going to try to get Jonah to take his turn now, aren't you? I told you, I am not going to let that happen!" She whirled toward the house as if she was about to let out a huge bellow: *Mom! Mom! Come quick! Call 911! Someone's trying to kidnap Jonah!*

"Will you just let me explain?" JB interrupted. "Before you start panicking?"

Katherine looked confused for a moment, then let the air fizzle out of her lungs.

"Explain fast," she muttered.

"We are ready to send the next kid back in time—but it's not Jonah," JB added quickly. "It's Andrea Crowell. Remember her?"

"Oh, yeah," Jonah said. "The really quiet girl with the braids?"

"That's right," JB said. He began toying with a twig that had landed on the driveway. He pushed it one way, then the other. He looked back up, directly at Jonah. "We've run all sorts of projections, like we always do. And we keep finding unbelievable odds against success. Unless . . ."

"Unless what?" Katherine said suspiciously, glaring down at JB.

"Unless she has help from people who aren't time travel experts," JB said.

"Us?" Alex gasped.

JB nodded.

"Partially. It's Jonah, Katherine, and . . ." He grimaced, as if he found what he was about to say preposterous. "This dog." He lifted the leash toward Katherine's hand. "Don't ask me why that combination works. I don't know. I don't even know why the analyst thought to include the dog in the projection. But . . . sending the two of you and the dog with Andrea gives us our best chance of success."

Katherine pointedly did not take the leash from JB's hand. She looked like she was in shock.

"You want us to go back in time again," Jonah said numbly. "And not even to my own time. To help someone else."

"I thought we were done." Katherine spoke as if she was in a trance, staring off past the basketball hoop, past the neighbor's chrysanthemums. "I thought all I had to do was make sure you didn't take Jonah away. . . . Do you know I have nightmares about the fifteenth century? Every night I'm back there on the battlefield. Every night I'm invisible, and I can't get Chip and Alex to listen to me, to hear what they have to do. . . ."

"Are you refusing?" JB asked.

"Oh, I didn't say that . . . ," Katherine mumbled dazedly.

JB didn't pressure them. He didn't say, "You do realize that all of history is depending on you, don't you?" He didn't say, "You don't really have a choice." Jonah almost wished he would pressure them and try to boss them around—because then it would be easier to say no. Then it would be all about standing up for himself, about defending his rights. Defending his life.

This was something else. This was leaving him free to imagine another kid, Andrea, going back in time all by herself, having no one at all to help her through. This was forcing him to be all mature and self-sacrificing and responsible—and choosing it for himself.

He sighed.

"I'll do it," he said.

"Really?" Katherine stared at him. "Well, that's just great. It's horrible having you for a big brother, always trying to set a good example. Because now I have to do it too!" Despite her words, there was a note of excitement in her voice now. "*Please*, can't Chip and Alex come too?"

"No," JB said. "Sorry. After their experiences they'd be just a little bit too trigger happy. Er—arrow happy."

Another time period with bows and arrows? Jonah thought. *Great. I bet they won't have decent food then, either.*

"Katherine," Chip said. "Please . . ."

Katherine glanced at him, and it was almost like watching Mom and Dad communicate silently. It was like she was telling Chip, *Don't get all mushy or macho-boy protective on me now. Don't make this harder than it already is.*

"To you it'll be like they're just gone an instant," JB assured Chip.

"But I'll know," Chip retorted. "I'll know that they'll really be gone much, much longer. They'll be so far away. . . ."

He was gazing toward Katherine, but Katherine dived down toward the dog's head, burying her face in the fur.

"So if the dog's coming with us, we need to know his name," Katherine said, speaking almost directly into the fur.

"It's Dare," JB said softly. "The dog's name is Dare."

Jonah knew he should be asking about the exact time period they were going to, and Andrea Crowell's other identity, and his own identity and time period as well. But for a moment he just sat there in the grass peering around his neighborhood: at the peaked roofs of his neighbors' houses, at the wide street where he'd ridden his bike so many times, at the mailboxes and garage doors and sewer drains. . . . If he didn't stop himself, he'd start blubbering about how much he was going to miss the fire hydrant across the street.

It's incredible how precious everything looks when you know you're about to lose it, Jonah thought. He wondered if Richard III had felt that way in his last moments on the battlefield at Bosworth; he wondered if Chip and Alex had felt that way leaving their tracers behind, leaving their fifteenth-century lives forever. Someday he'd have to ask them. Someday after he'd met his own tracer. But for now . . .

"So, we're going with Andrea Crowell, huh?" Jonah said, trying to sound cocksure and confident, like going back in time again was no big deal. "Does *she* know what we're all getting into?"

"No," JB said. "Nobody does, really. To quote a famous philosopher revered in my time, 'But this is no different from regular life. When have you ever known what's going to happen in the future?'"

Wait a minute, Jonah thought. *I said that. Back at Westminster, with Katherine. Does that mean I'm going to be a famous philosopher in the future? Does that mean I'm going to be revered?*

There wasn't time to ask.

AUTHOR'S NOTE

People have been trying to figure out what really happened to Edward V and his brother Richard ever since the fifteenth century. Here are the facts that everyone seems to agree on:

Edward IV, the king of England, died on April 9, 1483, and his twelve-year-old son, Edward, was named as his successor. Edward V's coronation was scheduled but never held. Instead, after accusations about the boy's parents, his uncle was proclaimed king and crowned on July 6, 1483.

Edward and his younger brother were known to be in the Tower of London during the summer of 1483. Then they vanished.

And already, writing that last sentence—"Then they vanished"—I have to resort to extreme vagueness to avoid adding qualifiers like "and most people think that . . ." or "at some point within the next year or two . . ." Most people seem to think that the boys were murdered—but were they? If they were, who did it? When? How? Why?

I did my best in this book not to fudge or change any facts that are irrefutable. Chip's description of what happened to Edward V during the spring of 1483 is as historically accurate as I could make it. (So are his and Alex's descriptions of Edward IV's eating habits—and I bet you thought bulimia was only a modern problem!) Fortunately for my job as a fiction writer, the historical record regarding Edward and Richard is full of gaps and disputed details, so that left me lots of room to fill in with my own imagination.

Historians studying an event like the disappearance of Edward and Richard look for accounts written by people living at the same time, who were close enough to the action to know what they were talking about, but not so close that they were overly biased and might be lying. In this case, the perfect account just doesn't exist—or hasn't been found. When I was researching this book, I had to laugh at the many, many times I would read, *"The Croyland Chronicle* was surely right about this detail, but probably wrong about . . . ," or, "Though Sir Thomas More was accurate about this part of the story, he must have been confused about . . ." And then I'd put down that research book, pick up another one, and discover that the author of the second book totally reversed which details of which versions were surely or probably right or wrong.

For centuries Richard III was painted as the villain of the story. One notable account says that, years later, a man who'd worked for Richard III confessed to killing the boys on Richard's orders. But that account rather conveniently came out during the reign of Henry VII—a.k.a., Henry Tudor, the man who defeated Richard and took the Crown at the Battle of Bosworth. And Henry had every reason to want to discredit Richard as much as possible to make his own claim to the throne look stronger. (By then Henry was also married to Edward V's sister—yes, this is a very tangled tale—and so it also helped him to make sure everyone believed Edward V had deserved to be king but was very certainly dead.) Almost a century later William Shakespeare—writing when Henry's granddaughter Elizabeth I was on the throne—based his play about Richard III on the earlier account. In Shakespeare's version Richard III is a complete monster, the kind of villain audiences love to hate.

More than three hundred years later a group of Richard supporters began trying fervently to change Richard's reputation. The Richard III Society, founded in 1924, now claims nearly 3,500 members worldwide. Richard's defenders offer very different views of history. Some blame Richard's onetime friend the Duke of Buckingham or even Henry VII for killing Edward V and his brother. Others give credence to accounts that say the boys survived, in hiding or in exile in another country. In the 1490s a man showed up in England claiming to be the younger brother, Richard, seeking the throne for himself. His claim was convincing enough (or useful enough) that other European rulers supported him, and he raised a rebel army to fight Henry. His efforts failed, though, and he was eventually hanged for plotting against the king.

One piece of evidence that is almost always cited in this story is the fact that workmen renovating the Tower of London in 1674 found skeletons in a spot that could fit a description of where the boys' bodies were once buried. (However, the same account that describes that burial place also says a priest later dug them up and moved them.) The skeletons were assumed to be Edward's and Richard's; they were moved to Westminster Abbey. In 1933 scientists got permission to unearth the skeletons again to study them closely. Even though the scientists couldn't actually be sure if the bones belonged to males or females, they concluded that the bones were the right size and age to belong to Edward and Richard if they had been killed in 1483. Everything I read about that study made me wonder what the scientists would have concluded if they hadn't known ahead of time whose skeletons they were supposedly looking at. And I wonder what scientists now would be able to discover examining the same bones with more-modern techniques—especially DNA testing. (So far, no one's been allowed to do such tests.) But even if scientists could prove conclusively that those skeletons were Edward's and Richard's, we still wouldn't know how they died.

That pretty much leaves time travel as the only way to completely solve the mystery. And if we could travel back in time to begin solving all the mysteries of history, how could we resist wanting to save all the victims?

After helping Chip and Alex survive fifteenth-century London, Jonah and Katherine are ready for another challenge. Andrea is really Virginia Dare from the Lost Colony of Roanoke, and Jonah and Katherine have to help bring her back to her proper time and fix history. But their mission goes horribly wrong from the outset. They've landed in the wrong time period. Andrea doesn't seem all that interested in leaving the past. And even worse, it appears that someone has deliberately sabotaged their mission. . . .

Jonah fidgeted in his seat, and his chair fidgeted right along with him. In another mood, Jonah would have been fascinated by this—how was the chair programmed? Did it have a computer chip making it squirm? But right now Jonah was too distracted. He was sitting in a sterile, nearly empty room, waiting to travel back in time to an unknown era and unknown dangers. So all he could do was fidget.

You'd think, with time travel, there wouldn't have to be any waiting, he thought grumpily.

Beside him, his eleven-year-old sister, Katherine, bounced in her chair—making the chair bounce too—and chattered away to Andrea, the third kid who would be going to the past with them. Indeed, Andrea was the most important time traveler that day. She was the reason they were all going.

"Don't worry," Katherine told Andrea. "You don't have to hold your breath or anything to travel through time. It's easy."

"That's good," Andrea said softly. She sat perfectly still, and so did her chair. She had her eyes focused on the blank wall across from her and barely seemed to be paying attention to Katherine. Normally Jonah would have approved of that—he tried to ignore his younger sister as much as possible too. But unlike Katherine and Jonah, Andrea had never traveled to the past before. She didn't know what time period she was going to, or what she'd have to do there. Shouldn't she be asking questions? Shouldn't she at least act like she cared?

"Only, if you get time sick, that's no fun," Katherine rambled on, flipping her blond ponytail over her shoulder. "When we went back to 1483 with Chip and Alex, I thought I was going to throw up for sure. And I felt really dizzy, and—"

"Katherine!" Jonah interrupted, because he could put up with Katherine's babbling for only so long. "Andrea won't get time sick like you did. Remember? She's going back to her proper time. Where she belongs. So she'll feel good."

At that, Andrea's whole face brightened.

Wow, Jonah thought. *She's really pretty*. He honestly

hadn't noticed before. Of course, he barely knew Andrea. The first time he'd met her, there'd been thirty-four other kids around, and four grown-ups fighting about what was going to happen to the kids, and people being Tasered and tied up and zapped back in time . . . Jonah had had a good excuse for not looking closely. All he remembered from that first meeting was that Andrea had worn her long brown hair in two braids, and she hadn't screamed and panicked like a lot of the other kids. And he guessed he knew that—like him and the other kids the grown-ups were fighting over—Andrea was thirteen years old, and she was a missing child from history, one who had been stolen from her proper time and place by baby smugglers. One who had to go back, to save history.

Suddenly Jonah really wanted to remind Andrea that he and Katherine had already proved that they could save history *and* save missing kids, all at once, even when the time experts thought it was impossible. They'd managed to save Chip and Alex from the 1480s, hadn't they? Jonah started to smile back at Andrea and was working up what he wanted to say to her: something suave but casual and not too conceited-sounding . . . . Did, *Don't be scared. I'll take care of you* sound stupid?

Katherine began talking again before Jonah had a chance to say anything.

"Andrea can too get time sick," Katherine argued. "Not the kind from being in the wrong time period, but the kind just from traveling through time. Remember JB thought I had both kinds? And that's why I felt so awful? And . . ."

Katherine broke off because the door opened just then and JB, the very person she'd been talking about, stepped through.

JB was a time traveler from the future, and the main person who was trying to fix time by returning all the stolen kids to history. Tall, with gleaming chestnut-brown hair, JB was so good-looking that Katherine had nicknamed him cute janitor boy before any of them had found out what he really did for a living. For some reason, JB's appearance really annoyed Jonah right now. Depending on how you looked at it, Jonah had known JB for only a few weeks—or for more than five hundred years. (Or, actually, more than a thousand, if you counted the fact that Jonah, Katherine, Chip, and Alex had traveled between the fifteenth and twenty-first centuries in *both* directions.) Regardless, it had taken Jonah a while to figure out whether to trust JB or not. JB had helped Jonah and Katherine and their friends, but Jonah still wasn't sure: If JB had to choose between saving kids and saving history, which would he pick?

I have to make sure that isn't the choice, Jonah told himself grimly. He gazed over at Andrea again, with her clear pale skin and her gray eyes that somehow looked sad again—haunted, even. *I will* protect *you,* he thought, even though he figured he'd really sound foolish if he said that now. He kicked his foot against the ground, and his chair kicked too.

"Careful," JB warned. "Those are calibrated to a very sensitive level." He seemed to notice Katherine's bouncing for the first time. "They're not really meant for kids."

Katherine stopped mid-bounce. Her chair rose up and caught her.

"Sorry," Katherine said. "Can we go now? There's no chance that we'll hurt your precious chairs if you just send us to the past."

She sounded offended. Jonah wondered if he should warn JB that it wasn't a good idea to offend Katherine.

"Not yet," JB said. "You need to be debriefed first."

Katherine leaned forward in her chair, and her chair leaned with her.

"Really?" she breathed, seeming to forget any hurt feelings. "You'll tell us where we're going this time—before we get there?"

JB laughed.

"You didn't give me much of a chance the last time," he reminded her.

"That wasn't our fault," Jonah argued hotly. "If you

hadn't sent Chip and Alex back without telling them anything, and if you hadn't cheated when I gave you the Elucidator, and if—"

JB held up his hand, cutting Jonah off.

"Hey, hey," JB said. "Calm down. I'm sorry, okay? That's over and done with. Water under the bridge. Haven't you ever heard the expression, 'No need to relive the past'?"

Katherine and Jonah both stared at him blankly.

"Um, isn't it kind of, uh, contradictory, for a time traveler to say that?" Katherine asked.

"Yep." JB beamed at them. "You caught the irony. Time-traveler humor—gotta love it."

He turned toward Andrea, who was still sitting quietly, unaffected.

"As far as I'm concerned, we're all on the same team this time around," JB said. "From the very beginning. No keeping secrets unnecessarily. Deal?" He held out his hand to Andrea.

"Of course," Andrea said calmly. She shook JB's hand, before he moved on to shake Jonah's and Katherine's in turn. Maybe if Jonah hadn't been paying such close attention to Andrea now, he wouldn't have noticed that Andrea hesitated slightly before speaking, before taking JB's hand.

She is scared, Jonah thought. *She really does need me to take care of her.*

"So you'll tell Andrea who she really is?" Katherine asked eagerly.

And me? Jonah almost asked, forgetting that he was supposed to be all about protecting Andrea at the moment. Jonah had seen his two friends Chip and Alex learn their original identities in history. And he knew that, ultimately, he would have to return to his original time period, at least briefly—just like all the other missing kids from history. But, as much as he wanted to know his own identity and his own time period . . . maybe he wasn't quite ready to know right now?

The moment when he could have asked was past. JB was answering Katherine.

"I thought I'd just show her," he said.

JB flipped a switch on the wall behind Jonah's chair, and the wall opposite them instantly turned into what appeared to be an incredibly high-definition TV screen. Waves crashed against a sandy beach, and Jonah had no doubt that, if he looked carefully enough, he'd be able to make out each individual grain of sand.

"Just skip to the part she's going to be interested in," JB said.

Jonah wasn't sure if JB was talking directly to the TV screen (or whatever futuristic invention it actually was) or if there was someone in a control room somewhere who was monitoring their entire conversation. Sometimes Jonah just didn't want to think too much about the whole time-travel mess. He knew that JB had already pulled them out of the twenty-first century, and the waiting room they were in was a "time hollow," a place where time didn't really exist. He knew that JB was probably about to show them some scene from Andrea's "real" life, before she'd been kidnapped by unethical time travelers, and before she'd crash-landed (with all the other missing kids) at the very end of the twentieth century. But it made Jonah feel better if he told himself he was just watching a TV with really, really good reception.

The scene before him shifted, seeming to fly across the water to a marshy coastline and then inland a bit to a primitive-looking cluster of houses. Some of the houses were encircled by a wooden fence that was maybe eight or nine feet tall. Both the houses and the fence looked a bit ramshackle, with holes in several spots.

The view shifted again, focusing on a woman rushing out of one of the nicer houses. The woman was wearing what Jonah thought of as old-fashioned clothes: a long skirt, long sleeves, and a funny-looking hat covering her head. The skirt wasn't quite as sweeping as the ones he'd seen in the fifteenth century, but Jonah wasn't sure if that meant that he was looking at a different time period now, or if he was just watching different people. Poorer ones. Not royalty anymore.

"Mistress Dare's baby has arrived!" the woman called, joy overtaking the exhaustion in her face. "A wee girl child, strong and fair!"

Other people began rushing out of the other houses, cheering and calling out, "Huzzah, huzzah!" But Jonah got only a brief glimpse of them before the camera—or whatever perspective he was watching—zoomed in tighter. Through the door, across a clay floor, up to a bed . . . On the bed a woman hugged a tiny baby against her chest.

"My dearest girl," the woman whispered, her face glowing with love, even in the dim candlelight. "My little Virginia."

"NO!" someone screamed.

It took Jonah a moment to realize that the screaming hadn't come from the scene before him. He peered around, annoyed that Katherine would interrupt like that. But Katherine, beside him, was gazing around in befuddlement too.

It was Andrea—quiet, calm, unperturbed Andrea—who had her mouth open, who was even now jumping to her feet, eyes blazing with fury.

"NO!" she screamed again. "That's not me! That's not my mother!"

THE MISSING

"Fans of Haddix's Shadow Children books will want to jump on this time travel adventure. . . . An exciting trip through history."—*Kirkus Reviews*

New York Times BESTSELLING AUTHOR

MARGARET PETERSON HADDIX

FOUND   SENT   SABOTAGED

FROM SIMON & SCHUSTER
BOOKS FOR YOUNG READERS

Mac is the coolest kid in town. . . .

He just doesn't know it yet.

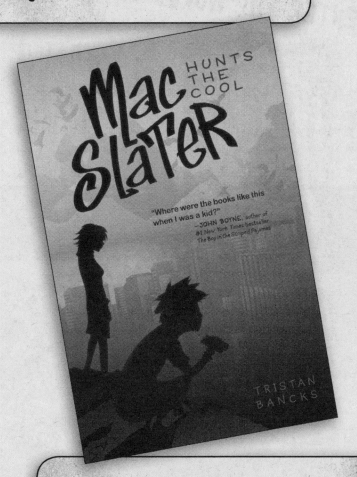

Look for *Mac Slater vs. New York* coming Spring 2011!

MYSTERY. ADVENTURE. HOMEWORK

ENTER THE WORLD OF DAN GUTMAN.

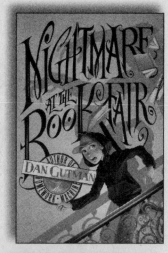

PUBLISHED BY SIMON & SCHUSTER BOOKS FOR YOUNG READERS
KIDS.SIMONANDSCHUSTER.COM

WHAT HAPPENS
WHEN A SEVENTEENTH-
CENTURY BAD GUY HAS
TWENTY-FIRST-CENTURY
TECHNOLOGY?

THE GIDEON
❖⊷ TRILOGY ⊷❖

"For kids who love Harry Potter."
—*Entertainment Weekly*

From Simon & Schuster Books for Young Readers
KIDS.SimonandSchuster.com